AFTER
DARK

OTHER TITLES BY MINKA KENT

AFTER DARK

A THRILLER

MINKA KENT

THOMAS & MERCER

Published by Thomas & Mercer, Seattle

www.apub.com

Amazon, the Amazon logo, and Thomas & Mercer are trademarks of Amazon.com, Inc., or its affiliates.

ISBN-13: 9781662511424 (paperback)
ISBN-13: 9781662511417 (digital)

Cover design by Jarrod Taylor
Cover image: © Aleah Ford / Arcangel; © hanibacom / Shutterstock

Printed in the United States of America

This one's for J

PROLOGUE

December 23, 2003

"What have you done?" My mother's shrill cry slams me into the present moment. With horror in her copper eyes and a single trembling hand clinched over her mouth, she lets her heavy leather purse fall to the floor with a lifeless thump.

Mom gags, turning her back to the gruesome scene.

A metallic odor lingers in the air as dampness soaks through my jeans and clings to my skin. Between my fingers is a thick, sticky liquid.

I'm covered in blood.

Not only that, but there's a gore-stained butcher knife in my left hand. I release it as if its wooden handle is fire-poker hot. It lands next to my white Converse, which are also sullied and mottled with crimson.

It's then that I notice him—the dead man on our living room sofa.

He's slumped over, his neck in an unnatural position.

His white button-down shirt is marred with deep red blotches that start high and fade into half-dried drips before they reach his khakis and finish with a handful of splatters on his pristine dress socks.

"Afton," my mother says my name, rushing to his side but keeping a careful distance at the same time. Mom reaches toward him before retracting *her hands and holding them tight against her chest. Her face is pinched in horror, as if she doesn't want to look at him, and yet she can't help it. She's never had the stomach for blood. In my younger years, she could hardly bandage my scraped knees or pull a loose tooth without retching. "I . . . I don't . . . why would you . . . what did you . . ."*

Tears slide down her rosy cheeks as she struggles to find her words, but her questions are pointless because I wouldn't begin to know how to answer any of them.

I don't know what happened.

The last thing I remember is being with my best friend, Sydney. We were kicking off the first day of Christmas break with takeout pizza and a movie marathon in her basement. I was supposed to stay the night, but by the end of the third movie, I wasn't feeling well, so her boyfriend drove me home.

Now I'm here.

Covered in blood.

Sydney's father's blood.

"I . . . I think I blacked out," I say.

My mother huffs as if she doesn't believe me. I haven't blacked out in years thanks to the medications I've been taking, but I don't know how else to explain this.

I may not know what happened, but I'm not a murderer.

I wouldn't . . .

I couldn't . . .

I hiccup, my mouth filling with the sour tang of the vodka and sugary sodas we'd been drinking all afternoon. The thought of admitting that to my mother somehow feels dangerous, not because she would care about the underage drinking, but because it would ruin any chance of her believing my innocence.

"Well, don't stand there—call 9-1-1." She throws her hands in the air, pacing our small living room, still wearing her oversized puffy winter coat that swallows her petite frame whole. Ripping off her pilled wool gloves, she tosses them on the coffee table and runs her fingers through her messy blonde curls.

"I can't," I manage to say, lifting up my blood-stained hands. I need to wash them, but my body is anchored, paralyzed.

I couldn't move if I tried.

"My God, Afton." She scans the room for her purse, which is still lying on the floor where she left it a minute ago. Crouching and scrambling, she digs into its bottomless pit, pulls out her cell, and makes the call.

Everything around me fades into the background, and her voice is distant and jumbled, like background noise in a movie. She might as well be speaking a foreign language from a thousand miles away.

Squeezing my eyes shut, I attempt to remember something—anything—only my mind is blank.

Everything that happened after Drew and I left Sydney's is . . . gone.

"I . . . I swear I must have blacked out," I say when she finishes the call. "It's the only thing that makes sense. I must have had an episode."

"An episode? Really? Little convenient, don't you think?" She rolls her eyes. She's already decided I'm guilty, and while I don't blame her, it steals the air from my lungs like a sucker punch. "I'm sorry, but you must take me for an idiot if you think I'm going to buy that—no, if you think anyone's going to buy that."

"I didn't do this." I place as much conviction in my words as possible, though it does nothing to remove the incredulous glare from my mother's face; one that's laced with utter hatred. We've had our differences like any other mother and daughter, but we've always had each other's backs.

This feels different.

Mom's lips press flat and her fists ball at her sides. She's never struck me a day in my life, but there's a first time for everything.

I brace myself for a blow that may or may not come.

"Please." My voice is fragmented as hot tears cloud my vision. "You have to believe me."

I heard once that the more you use words like "honestly" or "I swear to God" or "I'm telling the truth," the more likely people are to assume the opposite. It doesn't stop me from screaming those very words so loud on the inside my head throbs.

The unmistakable wail of emergency sirens in the distance becomes deafening with every second that settles between us.

"Stay here. Don't move. And don't touch anything." Mom zips her coat, flicks the hood over her messy hair, and steps out onto the front porch. The door slams behind her, rattling every window in the front of the house.

The furnace kicks on, blowing warm air through a floor vent beside me and ruffling the curtains above, but it does nothing to take the chill out of my bones. I can't stop shaking—and I can't stop staring at Mr. Carson's limp, lifeless, blood-soaked body.

Last month, when I first learned Mom was having an affair with Sydney's dad, I waged an all-out war with her that started with a screaming match, continued with a barrage of hateful, accusatory, and threat-filled text messages, and ended with a silent treatment that's been going on three weeks now.

I called her every name I could think of.

I told her what a pathetic mother, friend, and human being she was.

I told her I'd be better off without her.

I told her if she didn't end it immediately, she'd be sorry . . .

I was only trying to get a reaction out of her so she could see the error of her ways and come to her senses. But who would believe me now?

Lowering my gaze to the floor, I focus on a melting clump of snow Mom must have tracked in on her boots.

Mr. Carson's body is wilting, waiting.

I think of his wife—my mother's second cousin, lifelong best friend, and a woman I've always considered a second mom. Cynthia remembers my birthday more than my own mom does. Eight years ago, she started the tradition of making me double-fudge walnut brownies every year. And she always makes sure to hang a stocking for me on their mantel each Christmas, filling it with candy and other random trinkets. Three summers ago, she let me name their new yellow Lab puppy when they couldn't decide between Poppy and Penny. I've stayed at their house more times than I could attempt to count, and Sydney and I have been inseparable since we were in diapers.

What Mom and Mr. Carson did makes me sick, but it doesn't mean I'd kill because of it.

My mother returns from outside, letting in an arctic blast of Missouri winter air along with a team of paramedics and two uniformed police officers. I search her face for something, anything that tells me she might have my back in this, but she refuses to so much as look in my direction.

"Are you Afton?" One of the cops, a younger man with bronze hair cropped short and fresh razor burn on his chin, approaches me with slow, relaxed steps. He reaches into his left breast pocket to retrieve a small notebook, maintaining eye contact with me all the while.

I nod, swallowing the hard lump in my throat. My mouth is dry, my throat burns, my chest aches like it's about to explode, and speaking more than a handful of words is going to be difficult, but I'll try.

Someone has left the front door ajar, letting in frigid gusts of snowy wind, but no one seems to care or notice. They're all huddled around the dead man, speaking in low voices.

I try to watch, try to listen, but the cop angles his body to block my view.

"I'm Officer Pendleton," he says to me. The radio on his shoulder squawks, which startles me, and he wastes no time adjusting the volume. "Sorry about that."

His last name is familiar, and now that I give it more thought, his face is, too. I'm pretty sure there's a picture of him at school in a track uniform with a medal around his neck. He's slim and not the tallest, which means he probably didn't play football . . . which means maybe he won't be as gutted when he realizes that the dead man on the sofa is none other than Shelter Rock's beloved longtime high school football coach.

"Why don't we move over here?" He motions to the dining room across the way—the one we never use because Mom works weird hours at the Midtown Diner and picks up double shifts all the time. These days it's a place to pile unsorted laundry, delivery packages, and stacks of mail that tend to topple over before we have a chance to go through them. "I need to get a statement, if that's all right with you."

He has beautifully kind eyes: olive green with a ring of gold in the middle, and thick auburn lashes that paint shadows on his cheeks.

"I didn't do this," I say before he has a chance to ask his first question. Hugging my arm against my side, I attempt to still the little tremors running under my skin, but it's no use. They only grow more intense by the second, working all the way up to my jaw, which shudders so hard I bite the inside of my cheek. The salt of my own blood fills my mouth until I swallow it down.

Officer Pendleton notices my quivers. Turning and motioning to the other officer to come near, he asks her to get me a blanket and a water.

"The shaking is normal," he says. "It's a trauma response. It'll stop eventually."

I nod, unable to speak because of how clenched my teeth are.

The other officer returns from outside a minute later, a water and a tinfoil-looking blanket in hand. She shuts the door behind her this time.

"Why don't you have a seat." He pulls out one of the dining chairs and gives me a warm smile. Maybe that's what he's supposed to do—shower me with kindness and compassion so I'll trust him and tell him everything.

I would if I could.

I wrap the blanket around my shoulders and take a seat.

Twenty minutes later, after he's asked me several variations of the same questions, my story remains the same: I was at Sydney's, I didn't feel well, Drew took me home—then my mom got off work and found me covered in Mr. Carson's blood.

I debate telling him about the vodka, but by the time we're done, the compassion has left his voice and the hopeful light that was in his eyes at the start of this has all but extinguished. He's already building a case against me, I can tell.

"Stay here for now, Afton," Pendleton tells me. "We'll bring you and your mom in to the station for more questions in a bit . . . standard procedure."

He adds a stiff smile, as if he senses my apprehension, but it does nothing to make any of this easier to swallow.

If kindhearted Officer Pendleton doesn't believe me, if my own mother doesn't believe me . . . who will?

While I stand by my innocence, I wouldn't be lying if I said the tiniest part of me doesn't believe me either.

CHAPTER 1

AFTON

Her eyes follow me—Millicent's. It's what I've named the sour-faced lady in the Victorian-era oil painting across from the hotel check-in desk. Most nights it's nothing but the two of us, the hourly chimes of the antique grandfather clock, and the occasional guest tromping off the elevator in their pajamas to tell me the ice machine on the second floor is screeching again.

I pace from one side of my desk to the other, tracking old Millie's beady gaze as she tracks me back.

Working nights does this to a person. I'm always finding novel ways to entertain myself during these quiet, never-ending hours when the rest of the world is asleep. Sometimes it's crossword puzzles and sudoku. Other times it's library books and laughably horrible attempts at sketching. We're allowed to do anything that doesn't involve being on our phones—understandably. While this isn't the classiest hotel in the area, it's the oldest and best preserved. We can't tarnish our reputation with a night clerk who can't be bothered to look up from her dead-eyed Reddit scrolling to properly greet a guest.

Outside, the wind howls, creating whiteout sheets of snow that obscure my view of the parking lot. The forecast is calling for seven to nine inches tonight, which means we'll likely get half of that, but hey—at least the grocery stores will get to clear out their old milk and bread inventory.

It never fails . . . some people grow up with these kinds of winters their whole lives, but one day of higher-than-usual snowfall and the next thing you know, every store shelf in a thirty-mile radius is empty and there are lines twenty cars deep at every corner gas station.

Sometimes I think people enjoy panicking. It's exciting. Not exciting-good, but exciting in a way that it gives them something new and novel to worry about; a break from their usual first-world problems.

Watching the snow pile up by the minute, I make a mental note to shovel the front walk when I get home later this morning, and I smile when I think about how excited Gram's going to be to wake up to this. Despite my grandmother having spent the last two decades indoors, nothing brings her more joy than a crisp blanket of alabaster snow. She'll stare out the window for hours, just watching it in a trancelike state.

I like to think it brings her peace . . . or maybe it reminds her of happier times.

Sometimes I imagine Gram as a little girl, laughing and making snow angels with her friends, unencumbered by life's complexities and blissfully unaware of the cards she'll be dealt one day in the distant future.

The speakers in the ceiling play a cliché Frank Sinatra song that's been covered to death by every crooner wannabe who's ever lived. The hotel owner insists we play "classic" music 24-7, and while it gets old not being able to choose the songs that haunt my every working minute, at least it's better than hanging out alone in silence.

The Grantwell Hotel has been a mainstay in Shelter Rock since the beginning of time—or at least 1904, when it was built across from the courthouse on the square. A few people have died here over the years—natural causes, but locals like to claim it's haunted. Years back, some TV network came and did an overnight show here. They brought all kinds of gadgets with them as well as a psychic medium. I refused to watch the episode when it aired. I've never given much credence to the whole haunted hotel legend. If there's one thing Shelter Rock folks are skilled at, it's spreading lies and believing rumors.

The grandfather clock next to Millicent reads 3:14 AM. I'm less than halfway through my shift, but this is the time of night I start to get a little stir-crazy. Making a move for the bottom desk drawer, I make a sly effort to check my phone for any texts. The bartender I've been seeing should be getting off work by now, though Thursday nights tend to be busier for him, requiring extra cleanup. Sometimes he messages me on his way home, sometimes not. Since we're taking things slow, we've yet to establish those kinds of expectations. I hold my breath, tell myself not to get my hopes up, and exhale my disappointment.

There's no text waiting for me.

No social media push notifications.

Not even a spam email.

It's only when I'm placing my phone back in my bag that my fingers graze a crumpled piece of white paper slightly thicker than a store receipt. Peeling off the spearmint gum stuck to the back, I unfold the Missouri Lottery ticket I forgot I'd purchased last week.

The other day, I overheard one of our guests claiming the jackpot winner purchased their ticket at the Qwik Star on Newmont Road here in town—coincidentally the same place I purchased mine. The gas station happened to be all out of my go-to crossword scratchers when I stopped to fill up my tank that night. It was payday. I was feeling unusually lucky. And I didn't want to leave the cash register empty-handed.

I shake the mouse on my computer, pull up an incognito Chrome browser, and search up the winning numbers.

36-16-47-54-7

And lastly . . .

21

Comparing the numbers on the screen to the numbers on my wrinkled ticket, I choke on my spit when I realize they're a perfect match.

There's no way . . .

I double-check them again, this time reading them out loud, slowly and carefully.

"Thirty-six . . . sixteen . . . forty-seven . . . fifty-four . . . seven." I swallow. "Twenty-one."

Once again, the numbers are a dead match.

My skin flushes, hot then electric, as I check the numbers a third time.

Then a fourth.

This can't be real.

These kinds of things don't happen to people like me.

"Hello?" A woman with heavy-lidded bloodshot eyes smacks her hand on the counter bell in front of me. Yanking off her snow-covered cap, she shakes the thick flakes onto the glossy marble floor, where they melt the instant they hit.

Shoving my bag out of sight, I draw a startled breath.

I hadn't heard her come in.

"I was worried you were asleep for a second," she says with a sideways glance. "Need to check in. Reservation's under Mortimer . . . Sherryl Mortimer. Sherryl with an S, two Rs, and a Y. S-H-E-R-R-Y-L. Mortimer is spelled how it sounds."

I close out of my incognito browser and pull up our main system, which is asking me to sign in again. Despite being on the clock for hours, I haven't checked anyone in since well before midnight. That's the best thing about working the night shift at a boutique hotel: it requires minimal face-to-face exchanges. It isn't that I'm lazy; it's that most people around here prefer not to have to interact with me.

Can't say the feeling isn't mutual.

My name and likeness are notorious in Shelter Rock. Everyone knows what happened twenty years ago—or rather, everyone *thinks* they know. Regardless, their minds are made up. I'm a pariah. An outcast. A girl who "went crazy and killed her mother's boyfriend in a blackout fit of rage."

In the end, they couldn't prove my innocence beyond a reasonable doubt. I was found guilty of voluntary manslaughter and willful injury, but my public defender managed to put together a convincing self-defense storyline. We even found a psychiatrist willing to state that in her educated opinion, she believes that I suffered from a dissociative episode and that I wasn't aware of what I was doing nor did I have memory of it. That combined with a well-documented history of psychiatric care, rage-fueled blackouts, and my tender age of seventeen at the time, and the judge took pity on me, giving me a deferred twenty-five-year sentence barring successful completion of five years of supervised probation.

Shelter Rock locals were outraged at my perceived "slap on the wrist."

If it weren't for my grandma Bea, I'd have left this town years ago, much like my mother did the second her name was dragged through the mud. She left us in the dust, going as far as to blame *me* for ruining *her* life.

She'll come back from time to time, usually when she needs money and only because she knows Gram will give it to her out of pity. That gravy train isn't going to last forever, though. I suspect one day, when Gram is gone for good, Mom will stop coming around.

Her woeful lies and manipulations might work on her own mother, but she knows they won't work on me. That, and I owe her nothing. She abandoned me in my time of need. In my eyes, the mother I knew and loved died right along with Mr. Carson that day.

"Sorry. Give me one second here." My fingers tremble as I type her last name into the booking system, only to come up with nothing. "Hmm. Would it be under another name?"

I'm here, but I'm not. The vibration of my voice hums against my throat and my tongue and my lips, but it's as if someone else is speaking.

My mind is locked on that lottery ticket.

"It's the only one I've got, so no." Resting her plump elbow against the counter ledge, the guest gives me an incredulous sigh. Peeling her purse off her shoulder, she plops it down with a careless thud. A tube of cherry ChapStick, a used tissue, and an empty water bottle topple out. She doesn't attempt to retrieve them—only digs farther into the bottomless abyss of her trashed-out purse and produces a shiny new iPhone. Her thick fingers tap in a six-digit passcode before she all but shoves the thing in my face. "I booked this place less than an hour ago over the phone. See here? I called them fifty-eight minutes ago. Maybe your system hasn't updated?"

The blue-white headlights of an idling SUV outside shine aggressively into the double front doors, the bulbs casting an electric haze far too intense for three o'clock in the morning.

"I called the main 800 number on your website. Spoke to someone with an accent. Sounded like they were in a call center or something? They could hardly understand me." She rolls her eyes then pauses, as if she's waiting for me to commiserate on the frustrations of overseas call centers.

No comment.

"We usually receive our reservations in real time." I type her last name into the system once more, verifying the spelling. Chewing the inner corner of my lip, I add, "I'm so sorry, but I'm still not seeing anything."

"I don't believe you, but okay," she says with a puff of breath.

I'm not a liar, would never lie about something like this, and being accused of lying has been a trigger for me my entire adult life. Not to mention, what would it benefit me to tell her she's not in my system?

My blood runs hot, but I force a smile that implies *I'm on your side, Sherryl with an S, two Rs, and a Y* . . .

"Okay, well, do your job and give us a room then." She shoves the spilled contents back into her bag along with her phone, which she chucks carelessly into the mishmash of miscellany. "Two queen beds and a pullout sofa or rollaway."

My jaw clenches as she speaks to me as if I'm less than.

I get enough of this kind of treatment from the locals, I don't need to get it from Sherryl.

My fingertips tremble as I tap the keys, but not because I'm scared. I'm furious.

A lifetime ago, something like this would have put me into a reactional tailspin or even a blackout. Fortunately for Sherryl, I'm on enough medications to take the edge off and prevent me from doing something I might regret.

Still, my vision flashes red and the lobby feels twenty degrees warmer than before, and it's not because the heat kicked on again.

The sensation running through me is uncomfortable and unsettling, but I push through it.

No one wins when I get reactional.

"Of course. Let me see what I can find here." I inject my voice with a customer-service-worthy tone, force another stiff smile, and steal a glimpse at the wrinkled paper beside me, desperate for a chance to check the numbers again. Disbelief invades my thoughts, though my excitement is still live-wire hot. Between this and Sherryl, it's almost too much to process. Nevertheless, I persevere. "Unfortunately the only rooms I have available tonight are standard king rooms. And all our rollaway beds are spoken for. All I have left are two infant cribs."

Sherryl chuffs before straightening her slumped posture. "We have *five* people, none of whom are babies. That's not going to work."

"I can put you in two separate king rooms?" I bite my tongue to keep from reminding her we're not the Hilton. At this point, she's lucky we have anything. "How does that sound?"

"Are they adjoining?" she asks. I catch a whiff of her stale breath from across the counter—old coffee and Fritos, if I had to guess.

"Unfortunately not." I debate telling her there's a leadership conference in town this weekend, hence the reason we are almost at capacity, but something tells me she wouldn't care. "Again, I'm so sorry."

If there's anything I've learned in my years of hotel clerking, it's to always apologize for everything, even if it's not my fault. Ironically that's been one of the main themes of my life—apologizing for things I had nothing to do with. At this point, it's second nature to me.

"Oh, for the love of Pete." Her arms fall like dead weights. "We've been on the road ten straight hours. Is there anyone who hasn't checked in yet? Maybe we could have their room?"

Seeing how it's three o'clock in the morning, everyone with standing reservations has already arrived and checked in. Even if I wanted to, I couldn't bump a reservation that's been secured with a credit card. The system won't let me override those. Even if the rooms are empty, they're technically paid for, so I can't double-book them.

My patience is growing paper thin by the second, and my fists rest clenched beside my keyboard.

A shock of pain shoots through my head—an invisible bullet of tension, anger, and frustration.

This woman needs to piss or get off the pot.

"I'm sorry, but at this time, the only option is to place your group in two separate, nonadjoining rooms." I maintain eye contact and my professional disposition, though it's unbearably difficult to do when she's standing here shooting daggers my way.

"No. No, that's unacceptable. That's not going to work for us." She clucks her tongue and points her shaky glare on my computer screen, hunching over the counter to see for herself, once again implying that I'm a liar. "You're going to have to come up with a different option."

There's an unspoken "or else" lingering in the silence between us, all but broadcasting across her forehead.

"There's another hotel across town. The Staybridge. You could try them?" They're our biggest competitor in Shelter Rock and I wouldn't normally send them business, but Sherryl needs to be their problem tonight or else I might have a problem . . .

She sniffs, shaking her head. "I'm not driving clear across town."

"It's only a few miles from here. Straight shot down Grove Avenue, then right off First Street, past the fire station and on the left. Can't miss it." Grabbing a pen and paper, I write down the name and address, sliding it toward her. "Safe travels."

She refuses the handwritten directions, her head cocked sideways as if she's wondering if I'm being cordial, condescending, or both.

"Let me get this straight. *You* messed up *my* reservation, and now you expect me to get back in my car and drive somewhere else?" she asks. "What kind of bullshit backward customer service is this?"

Like a junkyard dog with a bone, Sherryl isn't going to go down without a fight.

I draw in a long, slow breath, lips sealed to keep from reminding her *I* didn't mess up her reservation—among other things.

"This is absolutely absurd. Is there a night manager I can speak to?" She rises on her toes, making a show of peering over my shoulder and into the dark office behind me.

"You're looking at her." It isn't true. Not technically. But I'm the closest she's going to get this time of night. "Again, safe travels, Ms. Mortimer."

I slide the paper even closer to her, attempting to tamp down any hint of smugness that's surely radiating off me in waves at this point.

Sherryl's bloviating confidence deflates as she swipes her overflowing leather bag off the counter ledge, knocking over a rack of brochures in the process—a mess she doesn't inconvenience herself with picking up.

The sheets float to the floor, landing in a puddle of melted brown snow.

15

"I'll be emailing corporate as soon as I'm back home." She rubs her baggy eyes, leaving smudges of black eyeliner in the process. "They need to know how *unhelpful* the management is here."

I remain composed as she grabs her overstuffed suitcase, storms outside, and peels out of the parking lot.

Screw that woman.

And screw her for not believing me.

The molten sensation flooding me the past few minutes dissipates, taking the tension in my head and jaw along with it.

I return to my wrinkled ticket.

Pulling the winning numbers up on the computer again, I compare them side by side, pressing the pad of my finger against each number on the paper before matching it to its corresponding number on the screen.

36.

16.

47.

54.

7.

And lastly, 21.

Clamping my hand across my mouth, I exhale through my fingers and accept the fact that this is real.

I won.

I've never won a single thing in my life, and now the universe is dumping $33 million in my lap.

Chuckling at my stupid luck, I bring up another incognito browser to search for a lottery winnings calculator. I'm seconds from finding out how much I'd get after taxes when a pair of blinding headlights careens into a thirty-minute parking spot outside. Through the blinding snow, it appears to be a dark SUV, much like the one Sherryl was driving, and it's parked at a slight angle, like the driver was either careless, drunk, or in a hurry.

If it's a Shelter Rock local, it's likely all three.

The headlights flash dark and the driver's-side door swings open before slamming shut, but between the sheets of snow clouding the view, I can't determine who it is. All I can do is cross my fingers that Sherryl with an S, two Rs, and a Y isn't back for round two.

When the lobby doors slide open a few seconds later, it isn't Sherryl at all.

It isn't even a woman.

A man in gray joggers, white sneakers, a black wool peacoat, and a navy-blue Yankees cap strolls in. He jangles a set of keys in his hand before twirling them around one finger and shoving them in his pocket. Whistling, he makes his way to the elevator, keeping his head down and avoiding eye contact. The knit scarf around his neck obscures the lower half of his head, but there's something familiar about him, something I can't place.

It isn't until he steps on board and turns around that I catch a glimpse of his eyes.

Our gazes catch in the seconds before the silver door wipes him from view.

"Drew?" I call out, trotting out from behind the front desk.

But it's too late.

The display above the elevator shows him getting off on the fourth floor.

Returning to my station, I pull up a listing of all the reservations for that level—and none of them are under Drew Westfeldt's name. In fact, I don't recognize a single person on that registry.

If he had a fight with Sydney and she kicked him out of the house, the room would at least be registered to one of them.

Pulling up the security system software, I click on the hall cameras for the fourth floor and catch him knocking on room 437's door. As soon as it opens, Drew disappears inside. Returning to the main software system, I search up that room and see that it's registered to a guest by the name of Vanessa DeOliveira.

Never heard of her.

According to this, she checked in at nine PM—before my shift started, and she's checking out later today.

I click back to the security camera footage, rewinding that clip and watching him walk down that hallway, knock on her door, and disappear inside all over again.

It's amazing what some people will do after dark, when they think no one's watching.

Gram says that's when my mother would always get herself into trouble, though if you ask me, she did a fine job of getting herself into trouble during daylight, too.

Taking a seat, I lean back and wrap my head around what I saw. I've never been a fan of Drew. Even when we were teenagers, I knew Sydney was too good for him. But I could never tell her that. And I still can't.

Things between us are . . . *delicate*.

Even if they weren't, I don't think she'd believe me.

No one wants to believe that the person they trust most in this world, the person they promised to love and cherish until their dying day, is capable of the ultimate betrayal.

I spend the next hour stewing and intermittently checking the cameras, waiting for Drew to come out so I can give him a proper greeting on his way to the parking lot. But four turns into five and five turns into six, and by the time the morning clerk arrives, I'm forced to go home without the privilege of calling Drew on the proverbial carpet.

Sydney doesn't deserve this.

And Drew doesn't deserve her.

Now I'm stuck between a rock and a hard place.

Do I tell her? I'd want someone to tell me if it were the other way around . . .

Or do I let it play out and indefinitely ignore the heavy drag on my conscience every time I'm around them?

I drive in silence to the avocado-green bungalow on Wainwright Street where I've lived with my grandmother for the past twenty years. Knuckles white against the steering wheel, I ruminate on Drew's audacity to cheat on Sydney. By the time I arrive, I'm so worked up from having fictional, one-sided conversations with the bastard in my head that I don't even think about the lottery ticket until I'm pulling into the driveway.

My God—how could I forget?

They say money can't buy happiness.

But I imagine it's pretty good at making problems go away.

CHAPTER 2

SYDNEY

"You look cute like that," I say to my husband as I lean against the kitchen counter, nursing a hot cup of blonde roast coffee before work. After picking up a night shift at the ER, I need all the caffeine I can get before I head to my med spa. Drew always jokes that I'm some kind of Super Nurse, saving lives at night and fighting wrinkles during the day. He's always been good at spinning stressful situations into a positive light.

Drew yanks his knit cap off, ruffling his messy brown waves. His naturally tan cheeks are flushed cherry pink from snow-blowing the driveway for the past half hour, but it gives him an air of youth. If I squint, he looks like he did when we first met a lifetime ago at Clarence Wilson Elementary.

Who'd have thought my second-grade boyfriend would one day be the man I'd marry?

Who'd have guessed that the mischievous little boy with the missing front teeth and the yellow Batman lunch box would be the future father of my children?

"Like what?" he asks, clueless as always.

"All bright-eyed and bushy-tailed. Like you were building a snow fort or something," I tease. "I don't know. There's something different about you today. You're . . . refreshed or something. There's a light in your eyes."

"Twenty degree temps will do that to you." He tugs off his thick black gloves, sets them aside, and pours his own cup of coffee. I'd have done it for him, but I was too distracted by his snow-kissed charm.

"When are you going in?" He glances at the clock on the microwave.

"First appointment's at eight thirty," I say, "but she's always early. I should probably leave soon."

How I long for the days when we were younger: before we had three busy kids and a mortgage and real jobs, before we started scaling the debt-ridden mountain to reach the elusive American dream at the top, before we thought each of us opening our own businesses and working for ourselves would make life *easier*.

The joke was on us on that last one.

The hours are longer and the workload is heavier, and, sure, you can flex your schedule, but you still have to make up for those lost hours somehow.

Cozying up to Drew, I breathe in the scent of his aftershave, its bergamot middle notes sharper than usual thanks to the cold air. His jacket is still cold from the outside, but I wrap my arms around him anyway.

"I wish we could call in sick," I say. With the kids already gone and off to school for the day, it'd be easy to sneak away to our room for a bit like we used to. And lord knows, we're overdue for some alone time. But alas, Kate Conover's masseter Botox isn't going to inject itself, and if the past is any indication of the future, she'll ask for a little touch-up between her brows and at her crow's-feet, too. "Like the old days."

Drew sniffs a laugh. "Why can't we?"

I playfully pat his chest. He knows the answer to that.

Paid time off and sick leave isn't a thing when you're your own head honcho.

"Think about what you want for dinner tonight," I say as I kiss him goodbye and begin to gather my things: travel coffee mug, keys from the bowl, phone off the charger, lunch from the fridge . . . "Text me and let me know, will you?"

As busy as I am, the last thing I want to have to think about when I come home from work is what to make for supper.

A few years ago, I pivoted from ER nursing to nurse injecting and opened a med spa out of a salon suite on the square. For the first couple of years, business was booming. It helped that platforms like Instagram were in their heyday and beauty filters and the Kardashians were giving everyone a perfection complex. But lately I'm booking a fraction of the number of clients I was seeing even six months ago, and it's only getting worse. With the looming recession in the news every day and rumors of layoffs at some of the largest employers in Shelter Rock, no one wants to drop a cool six hundred on lip filler or a grand on a laser facial without giving it a little more consideration now.

As a result of my half-empty schedule, I've been picking up night shifts at the hospital—desperate for some reliable income to cover our basic expenses.

Drew's income from his insurance sales business is steady and consistent, at least, but it's not enough to support all five of us. Maybe if we lived in a bigger city we could each scale up, but living in a middle-of-nowhere town of fifteen thousand makes that a bit of a challenge.

I'd like to think that someday things won't be so tight, but then I'm quickly reminded we still have three kids to put through college in the next ten years . . .

"Love you," Drew says as he kisses me by the door. "Wait. You forgot something."

He hands me my lunch bag—baked lemon pepper chicken, quinoa, and broccoli. I must have set it down when I was putting on my shoes a second ago.

"What would I do without you?" We've been meal prepping lately. It's not the most exciting thing in the world to eat the exact same foods five times a week, but it's helping with our grocery budget and bonus points if I shed a few pounds in the process. I've been getting soft lately—a direct result of taking care of everyone else but myself. There's nothing more depressing than having to suck myself into every pair of pants I own.

Drew hasn't said anything—and he wouldn't.

He's not that kind of guy.

Speaking of men, they have it easy in the aging department. The older they get, the better they look. Meanwhile, I feel like a vintage, high-maintenance Mercedes. The more miles I rack up, the more I fall apart and require expensive fixes to stay operable.

Hormones.

Talk therapy.

Vitamins.

Collagen supplements.

Special diets.

Facials.

Injectables—even at cost, those things add up.

My husband could easily trade me in for a younger model if he wanted to. I've seen the way other women look at him when we're out together. He's naturally charming. An innocent flirt. And with his dimpled grin, wavy chocolate hair still as lush as it was twenty years ago, and ability to weaken knees with his incandescent half smile, it's no wonder he gets so much attention.

Not to mention at thirty-eight, he's yet to come close to having a "dad bod." The day he noticed the first sprouts of salt-and-pepper hair at his temples, he screamed so loud with excitement from the next room that I lost my grip on the basket of laundry I was hauling downstairs.

I'm halfway to work a few minutes later when a text from my mother pops up on my phone.

Today is Afton's birthday, she writes, followed by, **Call her—even if you don't want to.**

CHAPTER 3

SYDNEY

August 17, 2003

"Sweetheart, I need you to pick Afton up for school this morning." My mom peeks into the hall bathroom as I flat iron my hair.

"I don't have time," I say, eyeing my own reflection as I talk to her. "I'm already running late."

Not to mention it's the first day of my senior year and Drew and I are meeting early in the parking lot to walk in together.

"I know, but Vangie's car is in the shop and she took Afton's to work. Afton has no other way." Mom's tone is apologetic, but is she sorry?

"Why can't you just take her?"

"I have a patient coming in at eight o'clock," she says. "Or else I would. Plus you're already going there."

I flat iron my sideswept bangs, which aren't laying right for some reason today.

Mom steps into the bathroom, placing her hand on the small of my back and meeting my gaze in the mirror. Her Opium perfume fills the small space, giving me a nostalgic burst of comfort. It's the fragrance she's worn my entire life. When I was younger and starting grade school, she'd spray the tiniest amount on the inside of my wrist so I'd always have a part of her with me.

"You look absolutely beautiful," she says. "I hope you have a lovely first day of school. Now, don't forget to swing by for Afton on your way."

With that, she's gone.

Grabbing my things, I give myself a final once-over in the mirror by the front door, and then I'm out.

Ten minutes later, I pull into Afton's driveway and lay on the horn. She scrambles out the front door of the little white ranch that the sun has turned yellow over the years. Wriggling her heavy backpack over one shoulder, she trots down the front walk with a giant smile on her face.

Squinting from behind my sunglasses, I analyze her outfit—black gaucho pants, a navy-blue Juicy Couture T-shirt, and glittery gold flip-flops.

This is definitely not what I helped her pick the other week . . .

She's always struggled in the fashion department, not that I personally care—I just hate to see people judge her for it. And because we're best friends and distant cousins, her problems become mine. Last year Sam Conover called her a "greasy-haired skank," and I shoved them in a locker for it. I got a detention, but it was worth it.

"Hey," she says, climbing in. She places her bulging backpack on the floorboards between her feet. "Thanks for the ride. I had no idea my mom was going to steal my car today . . ."

"Of course," I say, pretending like I didn't grumble to my mom when she asked me to pick Afton up this morning. I was annoyed at the time, but I'm over it now. I just hope Drew is still waiting in the parking lot for me when we get there.

"Crazy in Love" plays from the speakers. I dial the radio volume higher and crack the window a few inches. This song is overplayed, but it always makes me think of Drew and me.

Tapping my fingers on the steering wheel and bobbing my head, I quietly sing along.

"I swear I've heard this song three times this morning already," Afton says over the music. "She needs to come out with something new."

"It's a popular song." I shrug.

"I'm surprised you're not listening to the classic rock station," she says, taking a subtle dig at Drew since that's all he listens to. Or maybe her dig is directed at me. The other day she made a comment about how Drew and I were melting into the same person, taking on each other's likes and personality traits and mannerisms.

I told her that's what happens when you spend a lot of time with someone, and it's not a bad thing as long as you never forget who you are.

Afton then made a comment about how her mom does the same thing—adopts a new personality based on whoever she's dating at the time.

I didn't hesitate to remind her I'm nothing like Vangie.

When I was a little girl, though, I used to think Vangie was the coolest person I'd ever met. She wore cropped T-shirts and cutoff jeans, hair sprayed her permed hair to the heavens, and even had a Tasmanian Devil tattoo on her ankle.

I don't see her as much anymore.

Neither does Afton.

Mom says the older Afton gets, the less she needs Vangie, and since Vangie had Afton as a teenager, she missed out on having a real teenage experience. Mom says it explains why Vangie is the way she is now—irresponsible, living in the moment, making reckless decisions, seeking validation from men.

I don't pretend to understand half of it, I just know that Mom has picked up Vangie's slack over the years.

We all have.

It's weird how Mom and Vangie used to be best friends. They're night and day. Mom is intellectual, conscientious, trustworthy. She does everything with a purpose. Vangie's living for the moment and living for herself—at least that's what Mom says.

Mom is always psychoanalyzing people. I get that she does it for a living, but she's never off the clock. She finds everyone fascinating, and she's the least judgmental person I've ever met.

I hope to be just like her someday.

Brilliant, family oriented, and kind to a fault.

"You nervous or excited for our last year?" I ask Afton as we pull into the high school parking lot. I spot Drew's Firebird and my heart trills when I see him leaning against it, waiting for me.

I knew he would.

"Neither," Afton says. "It's weird that this is our last year. Kind of sad, honestly."

"Why? You want to stay in high school forever or something?" I chuckle as I pull into a parking spot. I'm slightly crooked, but backing out and straightening it up would be embarrassing.

"I've had a lot of fun, that's all. You and Drew are probably going to Tech next year, and I still haven't decided what I'm going to do," Afton says as she climbs out.

We trek toward Drew, whose face lights up like the Fourth of July when he notices me.

"Just come to Tech with us," I say.

She might be clingy and annoying, like a desperate kid sister (and I already have one of those), but she's also my best friend. As much as I complain about her, it would be weird if she wasn't around.

"You have plenty of time to figure it out, okay?" I tell her as we walk. "Things are only going to get better from here . . . promise."

CHAPTER 4

AFTON

I place my lottery ticket in the fireproof safe under my bed, alongside my Social Security Card, birth certificate, and a handful of miscellaneous jewelry that isn't worth much but is sentimentally priceless to me. The lock is busted, and I've been meaning to get a new safe altogether, but for now I slide the little metal box inside an old pillowcase and cover it with a blanket before hiding it all beneath a crumpled-up wad of pajama pants and shoving it all under my bed.

The only person who enters this house on any given day is Gram's home health nurse, Izzie, and she never goes into my room. Gram avoids my room out of respect, something that I appreciate given the fact that my mom never did that.

Growing up, Mom was always snooping, though I never caught her in the act. I only knew because my room would smell distinctly like her Calvin Klein perfume when I'd come home after school. Occasionally I'd have a sweater or pair of boots go missing and I'd find them in her closet. Other times my diary would be resting at a different angle than normal.

Every once in a great while, Mom stops by to bug Gram when she needs money, but Gram swears she won't let her set foot upstairs. I believe her. The main level always reeks of my mother after those visits, but the upstairs is always unspoiled by her cheap fragrance and riffling hands.

Plopping on my bed, I reach for one of the pill bottles in my night-stand drawer and pop two of the round blue ones that are meant for anxiety attacks but help me fall asleep after working nights. These aren't intended for long-term use, but I learned years ago that I had two choices: I could rely on pills to help me fall asleep, or I could simply not sleep.

Working a normal nine-to-five would be the solution to my little problem, but even if I wanted to, no one would hire me around here.

Once I cash this ticket, though, I won't have to worry about any of that stuff.

I lie back, a smile spreading across my face as I stare at the ceiling and think of all the things I could do with this money. My first instinct is to buy a house for Gram and myself far away from here. Maybe someplace warm with an ocean view. Florida or California. Or maybe Colorado. A cabin in the mountains. Gram used to go to Denver all the time to visit her sister—before the agoraphobia took hold of her.

She won't even leave to see the doctor.

Fortunately I've found a physician in town who does home visits, and they set us up with a home health aide who stops by twice a week to help Gram with miscellaneous tasks, medication management, and medical equipment cleaning. Years ago, I offered to be Gram's full-time caregiver, but she refused. And since her Social Security income barely covers her property taxes, utilities, and medications, we still needed an extra income to get by.

Drawing in a long breath, I close my eyes and wait for my pills to take ahold of me. I usually feel it in my eyelids first, a heaviness. Then my muscles grow slack, melting and making my bed feel more like a pillow of clouds than a lumpy old mattress on a metal frame. Next, my mind begins to quiet and when that happens, I'm mere minutes away from being out cold.

Only today I'm tossing and turning.

I can't get comfortable.

There's no heaviness, no melting, and definitely no quiet mind.

The tension taking hold of my body makes it impossible to unwind, and there's enough adrenaline coursing through me that I could easily lace up my sneakers and go for a run.

Every time I close my eyes, I see Drew walking to the elevator, going inside that woman's room . . .

After a solid hour of tossing and turning, I sit up when I remember my lottery ticket. That's what I need to focus on—the good that came out of this day.

My life is never going to be the same in all the best ways after I claim my millions, and that's more than Drew Westfeldt can say.

Grabbing my phone, I do a Google search for tax attorneys. From what I understand, I can claim my winnings in a lump sum or as an annual annuity, and I need someone to explain my options as well as the tax consequences. Also, I want to ensure I can claim the winnings anonymously.

The first listing I find is the Bradford and DeOrr law firm on the square uptown. I tap the call button and lift my phone to my ear. I'll need to be quiet in case Gram is sleeping. Most nights she stays up until two or three watching TV and sleeps in until noon, and she's always been a light sleeper.

"Bradford and DeOrr, this is Tonya, how may I help you?" a woman answers.

"Hi, Tonya, I need to make an appointment with one of your attorneys," I say.

"Sure thing. Can I ask what the appointment is regarding?"

I open my mouth, but nothing comes out. Speaking the words "I won the lottery" is going to sound insane coming from anyone's lips, but most people here already think I'm crazy.

Clearing my throat, I sit up a little straighter and I say, "I'm, um, coming into some money soon. A significant amount. I need some advice on how to proceed. Taxwise and such."

"And your name?" she asks. There's no congratulations. No excitement. No fanfare. I know it's not her job to be my personal cheerleader, but a little bit of a reaction would've been nice. Then again, working for a tax attorney, I'm sure she deals with situations like this all the time. Inheritances and settlements and whatnot.

"Afton," I say.

"Last name?" she asks.

I brace myself. "Teachout."

The line goes silent. I check the screen to make sure we're still connected. We are.

"Hello?" I ask.

"Yes, I'm sorry. Writing this down," she says. Her voice has taken a different tone. It's a little less "chipper receptionist" and a little more "skeptical Shelter Rock resident."

"This information will remain private, right?" I ask. The last thing I need is the whole town knowing about this. If people think justice wasn't served twenty years ago, they'll be outraged when they learn I'm set for life.

I'll never forget the barrage of hate mail that arrived almost daily the first few years. They came from all over the world, but the majority were from right here in town. People would tell me to kill myself, that I didn't deserve to live, that I was scum, that I was psychotic, that karma would one day catch up with me.

I burned the letters in the fireplace in batches every night. It was therapeutic in a way. I only wish I could have burned their cruel words from my memory, too.

The letters, however, didn't come close to the verbal accosting I received the first several years. I couldn't go to the bank or grocery store without someone saying something awful to my face.

One man spit on my shoes.

Another keyed the words "psycho bitch" into the driver's-side door of my car while I was inside a gas station buying milk.

Then there was the woman who refused to cut my hair because it *went against her religious beliefs.*

Oh, and the teenagers who egged my front door every week for a year.

If only I could incinerate those memories like I did those letters.

"Of course," Tonya says, though I'm not sure if attorney-client privilege applies to receptionists at legal firms.

"Thank you. You're the only one who knows this," I say as an added insurance policy. If this gets out, it's on Tonya.

"When were you wanting to come in? Looks like the next available appointment I have is in four weeks from today with David DeOrr. Nine AM. Will that work for you?"

"Sure." I grab a pen and notepad off my nightstand and jot it down—which reminds me, I should turn in my notice at the hotel. "Thank you."

As soon as the call is finished, I grab my laptop and type up a quick and unemotional resignation letter. I don't get sentimental or make it some sort of profound experience. It's bittersweet at best. They'll replace me in a heartbeat and a few years from now, it'll be some one-liner people say when they're bored and drinking at the bar on the square: *Did you know that psycho killer girl used to work at that creepy hotel across the street?*

My index finger hovers over the send button.

I've been there fifteen years and assumed I'd be there until I retired—or at least until after Gram passes away so I can finally move out of this godforsaken town. I've always had a plan, and this was never part of it, though I don't suppose a person can plan winning the lottery.

I think of my ticket, reminding myself I checked the numbers over and over and over.

I *won*.

I'm a *winner*.

I'm set for life—there's no reason for me to work the night shift at the hotel anymore.

I'll never have to deal with another Sherryl Mortimer again.

I'm not sure how long it takes to claim the winnings, if they write you a check on the spot or if it has to go through some tedious process, but I have a little south of ninety grand sitting in my savings account. It's a nest egg I've managed to accumulate over the years by living with Gram, driving reliable used cars, and not blowing my money on trendy shoes or spendy vacations.

Still, the thought of leaving the hotel forever is nothing short of terrifying. Editing my email, I change my two weeks' notice to a thirty days' notice—it's the least I can do given how accommodating and compassionate my boss has been over the years.

"Do it," I whisper to myself. "Hit send."

Closing my eyes, I bite my lip and press the key.

My computer makes a whooshing sound effect.

I've officially resigned.

My heart hammers a little harder than before, but there's a lightness basking over me; one I don't think I've ever experienced in my adult life. If I could see it, it would be shimmering, warm, and cashmere soft: *freedom. Hope. A second chance.*

Maybe I can finally clear my name. I could start by hiring a private investigator—the best one money can buy. There's some renowned forensic hypnotherapist in Kansas City who claims she can retrieve repressed memories. She isn't cheap, but if money isn't an object . . .

I lie back down on my bed, hoping maybe now I can finally relax after taking care of the resignation. Only another half hour passes. And another. This happens from time to time—usually when I've had too much caffeine or something that counteracts the medication's ability to make me sleepy. But I didn't have a single drop overnight. Nothing but tap water with crunchy pellets of ice from the hotel ice maker.

Maybe I grabbed the wrong prescription bottle? Wouldn't be the first time I've taken an upper instead of a downer—though I'm usually careful about that.

Sitting up, I yank my nightstand drawer open. Everything rattles as the half dozen or so plastic bottles roll around and bump into one another. One by one, I place them on top of the little table.

Cefapramine for wakefulness (as needed).

Predsalformax for depression and generalized anxiety.

Somatapine for anxiety and insomnia.

Iomotine to stabilize my moods.

Vinperidol for back muscle spasms (as needed).

Arizepam for anxiety attacks (as needed).

Predivudine—the antipsychotic I was placed on by a court-ordered psychiatrist after Mr. Carson's death.

Once-daily women's multivitamins with extra iron.

Magnesium citrate capsules.

Advil PM caplets.

Removing the childproof cap on the somatapine, I peek inside. Sure enough, they match the blue round tablets I'd swallowed earlier. The label shows it's a ninety-day supply that was filled two months ago, so they're not even close to being expired.

It's got to be the excitement.

There must be a gallon of adrenaline coursing through my veins by now.

I mean, it makes sense—someone doesn't win the lottery and go home and go to sleep like it's any other day.

Throwing in the towel on getting some shut-eye, I make my way downstairs to do some light housekeeping and put a load of laundry in. I'm halfway to the kitchen when my phone chimes with a text.

SYDNEY: Happy birthday, Afton! Dinner and drinks soon? ☺

With the events of the past six hours, I'd completely forgotten what day it is.

With some quick mental math, I realize I'm thirty-seven years old today.

Passing a mirror in the hall, I stop and take a look at the older version of myself, the one who is thirty-seven on paper—but on the inside she still feels like a lost, confused, and stuck seventeen-year-old who's never fully gotten over what happened.

Cynthia says trauma can "live" in the body.

As part of my probation after Rick's death, I was ordered to attend therapy and assigned to a mousy-looking woman named Fern Somerfield who claimed she wasn't afraid of me, but her pen-holding hand was always tremoring during our sessions.

My true therapy came in the form of late-night talks with Cynthia—talks which were only made possible because Cynthia contested the no-contact stipulation of my sentence. Championing mercy and forgiveness from day one, she delivered a heartfelt speech about the importance of understanding and compassion, stressing how this would be the best route to healing for all involved, emphasizing that she'd always considered me one of her own, and that she knew my heart as a mother would know her daughter's.

My mom was livid—mostly because she was portrayed as a jezebel during the trial while Cynthia was depicted as a saintly victim. Mom swore it was all an act, though she couldn't tell me what Cynthia stood to gain and I couldn't figure it out either. As far as I knew, Cynthia was always a private person. She was never starved for attention or accolades.

That and on some level, she suspects my mother was the one responsible for Rick's murder.

Cynthia's theory is that he wouldn't leave her for my mother, so my mother hired someone to kill him. When the murder was pinned on me, my mom saw it as an opportunity to ditch town.

Cynthia says an innocent person wouldn't do that, nor would most people.

But Vangie Teachout has never been like most people.

Still, there was no denying that I was the main suspect, I was the one standing trial, and all of the evidence pointed to me, not my mother. Those were all facts no amount of Cynthia's forgiveness or compassion or gut feelings could change.

I tuck a strand of jet-black hair behind my left ear, run my fingertip along a brow in desperate need of plucking, and tip my chin up to see if anything has fallen or settled since the last time I took a lingering gander at myself.

Aging is such a strange process. It happens every day, right in front of your own eyes, but you don't see it unless you're looking for it. And once you notice it, it's nothing short of jarring—like looking at a photo of a stranger and trying to convince your mind it's you.

I decide I look firmly in my midthirties—for now.

Sydney's always been amazed that my crow's-feet are barely visible, that the faint lines on my forehead aren't deeper than they are, but working nights and avoiding the sun for fifteen years has that effect, I suppose. Plus, I don't have the pressure of raising kids in today's world. All things considered, I have less stress in my life than the average person. That, and my medications keep me numb and even-keeled.

Perhaps I've accidentally discovered the fountain of youth.

ME: Thanks, Syd. Are you free tomorrow night by chance?

The thing about Sydney is she doesn't know how to sit still. She's constantly on the go—always for other people's benefit. If she isn't carpooling her three kids to every activity under the sun, she's doing administrative work for her med spa, and when she's not doing that, she's picking up night shifts at the hospital. She hasn't said it, but I think they're struggling financially. I can't think of any other reason she'd be working two jobs.

And then there's Drew with his cushy nine-to-five. As his own boss, he works from home most days—half the time he doesn't bother changing out of his sweats and house slippers. I've never understood why Sydney always seems overwhelmed while Drew hardly breaks a sweat. I won't pretend to know what it's like to be married or to raise kids, but things in the Westfeldt household have always seemed . . . disproportionate.

I don't need dinner and drinks for my birthday, but I imagine Sydney could use a break from her busy schedule.

ME: Been craving margaritas and tacos lately . . .

I tempt her with her two favorite things in the world.

SYDNEY: Seven o'clock tomorrow at El Guapo's?

ME: See you then.

It's a miracle the two of us have remained friends considering what happened, but it wasn't always this way. For the first several years, Sydney wouldn't speak to me. While I was devastated at the loss of my closest and most cherished friendship, I couldn't blame her. Her father died in my house and I was the one holding the knife.

I'd have believed everyone else, too.

It wasn't until her mom urged us to talk again in our early twenties that Sydney reached out to me. As a clinical therapist, Cynthia suggested we pursue acceptance and forgiveness with the goal of closing that traumatic chapter rather than let it follow us around the rest of our lives.

Cynthia's support has meant the world to me these last twenty years. She and Gram were the only ones who had my back from the beginning, and my public defender, John Gregory. Even if he was just doing his job, he always gave me the benefit of the doubt.

In many ways, I owe all three of them my life—or at least a lifetime of gratitude.

The day that lottery money hits my bank account, I'm making it up to each of them.

I head to the kitchen, quietly unloading the dishwasher so Gram can continue to sleep in peace. The house is eerily quiet save for a few creaks and moans. Peering out the window above the sink, I scan the neighbor's yard. The single mom next door has three kids whom Gram jokingly refers to as The Ferals. They appear to be five, six, and nine if I had to guess. Home alone more often than they should be. And despite always having milk mustaches and Kool-Aid–stained lips, all three are skinny little bags of bones. They're cute, though, dirty clothes, messy hair, and all.

I'm surprised they're not outside playing in the snow—until I remember it's a Friday and they're probably at school. Fifteen years of working nights makes it hard to keep days and dates straight sometimes.

I load the dirty dishes from the sink into the dishwasher next, pour in some powdered soap, shut the door with a quiet click, and start the load.

Gram's medications are sitting out next to the fridge. Two of the bottles are empty, which is surprising because Izzie's always been on top of managing refills.

I'll have to say something next time I see her.

No, on second thought, I should call the refills in myself.

I dial the pharmacy and use the automated system to refill her salipril and arilmaprazole.

Heading to the basement next, I throw a load of laundry in the washer, then fold a load of Gram's clean muumuus and housecoats as well as another load of towels that smell like they were left to sit in the washer for days before someone (Izzie, probably) dried them. I toss them back into the dirty clothes hamper for a rewash. A cup of vinegar should help remove the mildew stench.

By the time I'm hauling everything upstairs, I'm still bursting with energy. I place Gram's clean laundry next to her door. This time, the faint sound of *The Price is Right* plays from the other side.

"Gram?" I knock a couple of times.

She doesn't answer, but this isn't uncommon. Sometimes she wakes midmorning, turns on the TV, and falls back asleep for another couple of hours. Gram says the sound of daytime television always makes her sleepy and relaxed, like thunderstorms or white noise.

In the living room, I stretch out on the saggy sofa—one that's definitely getting replaced as soon as I have my money. I drape a fuzzy blanket over my lap, reach for one of Gram's paperback Harlan Coben books on the coffee table, and read a few pages in an attempt to make my eyes tired.

Three chapters in and all I am is restless and unfocused.

Reaching for my phone, I pull up Google and type in "Vanessa DeOliveira"—the girl who Drew snuck out to see last night. Is it technically sneaking, though, if your wife was at work? It's not like she was lying in bed at home, passed out. And granted, the kids are old enough to be left home alone, but what if something had happened? A house fire or a burglary? Was he thinking of that when he was hooking up with some random woman?

Doubtful.

The search results are less than promising.

Over the past several years, it seems like people have become jaded with social media. It used to be fun to look people up, to peek into their haphazardly curated internet lives, and get a small sample of their real-life personality. Their profiles were open books. It wouldn't be uncommon to be able to feast upon hundreds of photos, learn where someone worked, if they were in a complicated relationship, where they lived, where they went to school. Those were the social media glory days, and anyone who feels otherwise is lying.

Now every profile is buttoned up tight.

Some people have even removed the ability to friend request them.

The worst is when someone's profile picture is a random landscape from some old vacation—a photograph of mountains or a cactus covered in Christmas lights. I've never understood that—or when people use a photo of their dead grandparent as their profile pic.

Why?

It's like everyone took their balls and went home and now no one can play the game of innocent cyberstalking.

Sighing, I click on the first LinkedIn result at the top of the page, not holding my breath. Those are usually hit or miss. But as the page loads, I'm met with a photo of a fresh-faced, raven-haired beauty with a blinding white smile and dimples so deep you could hide pennies in them.

Vanessa DeOliveira
Dental Hygienist, Brian Knoll, DDS & Associates
Shelter Rock, Missouri
June 2022–present
AAS, Dental Hygiene—Camelot Community College—May 2022
Shelter Rock High School—May 2020

She's young, twenty or twenty-one at most maybe? No denying she's gorgeous.

Does she know she's sleeping with a married man old enough to be her father?

More importantly, does she care?

"Homewrecker," I whisper to myself. The fact that they went to a hotel in the middle of the night during a snowstorm to hook up is disgustingly desperate. Again, Sydney deserves better. And if Vanessa is compliant in this affair, she's getting exactly who she deserves.

Returning to my fruitless search, I click a few other links and articles—none of which are referencing the same Vanessa.

Grabbing my car keys and jacket, I hop in my Accord and go for a drive around Shelter Rock, stopping first at the little coffee shop on the corner by the Lutheran church. I order a decaf mocha.

There's something about driving on snowy streets with a warm drink in your hand that takes the edge off an unsettling mood. Back when I was active in therapy, my counselor was always teaching me ways to funnel my energy into better, more productive channels, and simple enjoyment was one of them. Doing things that bring you joy is an act of self-care, she told me. And she wasn't wrong. It's a motto I plan to take with me even after I officially become a multimillionaire.

Sipping my mocha, I turn the radio on low and cruise the familiar, emptied-out streets of my hometown. Everyone's either at work or school or holed up in their warm homes, refusing to drive in the snow unless they have to. Except for a handful of random cars and a quad-cab Ford, it's like I have the whole town to myself.

I turn off on Dayton Avenue, the miles-long stretch of street we used to cruise in Drew's red Firebird for hours back in high school when there was nothing to do. Drew, Sydney, and I were an inseparable threesome—or maybe that's what I told myself. Looking back, I was a bona fide third wheel, and Sydney was struggling to equally divide her time between her best friend and her favorite guy. It was easier if we did everything together.

Every once in a while they'd try to set me up with one of Drew's friends so we could double-date. I dated his basketball friend, Ian, for eight months my sophomore year (which is forever in teen years). I'd never seen Sydney so excited, rambling on about how we were going to get married to them and raise our kids together and how our kids would be best friends like us and our moms. When Ian dumped me for another girl, I'd never been so devastated, but Sydney propped me up with one of her motivational speeches and a pint of banana peanut butter chip Häagen-Dazs, and my heart didn't hurt as bad after that.

I always envied Sydney's ability to see the world through rose-colored glasses.

Twenty years later, nothing has changed.

She still acts like Drew hung the moon, still loves her job as a nurse, still wholeheartedly believes she has the most amazing kids in the entire world (in my objective opinion they're pretty average), and she and her mother are closer than they've ever been. If anything, the unspeakable tragedy that took place December 23, 2003, only made Sydney more resilient, more forgiving, and more determined than ever to live her best life, circumstances be damned.

I wish I could say Rick's death had the same profound effect on Sydney's brother and sister, but last I knew, Stacia was battling a wicked opioid addiction and Max is currently serving time for his third DUI and driving while barred.

Rick would be heartbroken to see what became of his youngest two.

I'd like to think that had Rick never died, Max would have followed his father's footsteps into public education. He was a hell of a math scholar and an even better football player. And Stacia would've been incredible doing something in sales had she decided not to pursue her passion for ballet. She was so outgoing, so effervescent, so persuasive. It's no wonder she turned to partying to deal with the loss of her father, but that partying led her down the dark and narrow road of illegal drugs.

Two years ago, Stacia overdosed at a party. If there hadn't been NARCAN on site, she would have died. Cynthia shipped her off to some expensive rehab facility in California after that, but Stacia was only home a couple of days before she relapsed.

I'm halfway done with my mocha latte when I come to a slow stop at a traffic light. From the corner of my eye, I spot a red-brick office building with white colonial details. The sign out front reads BRIAN KNOLL, DDS & ASSOCIATES.

Vanessa DeOliveira . . .

Running my tongue along the top of my teeth, I try to think of the last time I had a cleaning. Seven, eight months maybe? I tend to go to Kansas City for any and all appointments. I'm more anonymous there (or at least I'd like to believe I am). If it means not getting sideways looks and thousand-yard stares, I'll gladly drive the eighty miles each way.

Pulling into an empty parking lot, I take out my phone and call the number on the dentist's sign.

Five minutes later, I have an appointment for a cleaning with Vanessa Thursday at eight AM—only because she had a last-minute cancellation. Otherwise they're booked out for months, the receptionist told me.

With all this dumb luck I'm having, maybe I should buy another lottery ticket . . .

I chuff, dialing up the volume as an old Billy Joel song plays on the radio, and then I continue on my little drive. Half a mile down the road, I pass Drew's insurance office. It's dark inside and the sign on the door is flipped to CLOSED.

Must be another work-from-home-in-your-pajamas-day . . .

I detour past Drew and Sydney's house on my way home, slowing down on their road like I always do since it's nothing but young families who reproduce like bunnies.

The Westfeldts' cornflower-blue Dutch colonial is still outfitted for Christmas, with its candle wreaths on all the windows and the snow-flake lights adorning its hipped roof. Not surprising that it's late January and Drew's yet to take the Christmas lights down. Never mind the sunny, fifty-degree weather we had two weeks ago. I'm sure he was busy sexting Vanessa or playing fantasy football or whatever he does with his plethora of downtime. Honestly, I wouldn't put it past him to hire someone else to take them down while Syd's at work.

Gram always says the laziest people are the most resourceful.

By the time I get home, the house is exactly the way I left it, and Gram's TV is still playing in her room with the door shut. I don't knock this time in case she's still sleeping. The dryer downstairs buzzes, but I decide to switch the clothes later. I'm yawning, which means I'm finally tired.

I'm cozied up in my bed when my phone dings with an email alert. Rolling to my side, I plan to ignore it—until I remember I quit my job this morning.

It might be my boss . . .

Plucking my phone off the charger, I pull up my email. Sure enough, it's a response from my boss—and judging by the size of the paragraphs in her response, she isn't happy.

Yawning again, I darken my screen.

I'll read it later.

Right now, I need all the rest I can get.

Something tells me these next weeks are going to be insane.

CHAPTER 5

AFTON

September 3, 2003

The Real World: Paris *plays on Sydney's basement big-screen TV, but I've already seen this episode, so I tune it out, picking at a loose hangnail.*

"Ugh. Just remembered I need to unload the dishwasher before my parents get home." Sydney climbs off Drew's lap when a commercial comes on. She fixes her messy ponytail before bending down to give her boyfriend a kiss, then she dashes upstairs. A second later, the beep of the dishwasher is followed by the clinking and clamoring of plates and silverware.

Drew sits up, somehow ending up closer to me than he was before. It's just the two of us on this L-shaped sectional, so I'm not sure why he needs to be on the cushion directly beside mine. Little by little, he adjusts his posture and position, and by the time the show comes back on, the outside of his thigh is flush against the outside of mine.

Keeping my gaze locked on the TV, I ignore it.

Guys can be dumb sometimes, doing things when they don't even realize it. Even Cynthia says men don't always pay attention to detail. Something about how their brains are wired differently from evolution.

C. T. and Ace are arguing about something stupid on the screen, but all I can focus on is the fact that Drew's fingertips are now grazing the top of my thigh.

"What the hell?" I jump back, though I'm already on the edge of the sofa. There's nowhere else for me to go unless I stand up. "A little space, please."

Drew's attention is homed in on me, and there's a wicked little glint in his eye.

I don't like the way he's looking at me.

"Oh, come on," he says, moving his hand on top of my knee.

I hate the way my body responds with goose bumps and a quickened heart because nothing about Drew is remotely attractive to me. Remove his conventional good looks and athleticism and he's nothing but an arrogant idiot.

I've seen the way he flirts with other girls every time Sydney's not around.

I watched him tickle Shayla Greenberg in health class last year when we had to pair up and wear fake pregnancy bellies. The two of them enjoyed that a little more than they should have, in my opinion, but I never breathed a word to Sydney because it would've crushed her.

I push his hand off my knee.

He leans closer, invading my space with his abundance of disgusting Cool Water cologne. The distance between us grows narrower by the second, yet somehow I'm frozen in place. I can't move and this doesn't seem real.

"Just one kiss," he whispers, his lips inches from mine. "I've seen the way you look at me. I know you're curious, too. Syd never has to know . . ."

"Are you insane?!" Without giving it another thought, I spring to life, elbowing him in the crotch. While he's folded over, writhing in pain, I lean down and say, "Touch me again and I'll kill you."

With that, I grab my purse and sprint upstairs.

"Hey," Sydney says as she's sorting silverware. "You leaving already? You just got here."

"Yeah." I wear a fake smile because I don't want to worry her. While nothing happened, something almost did. Despite being the one who stopped it from going further, an unsettling amount of guilt seeps through me. "Just remembered I have an English report due tomorrow."

I'll never be able to look at Drew the same again.

"That sucks." She closes the silverware drawer with her hip. "Good luck."

"Thanks," I say. "See you tomorrow."

I don't understand why Drew would have done that—he knows I hate him.

If he thought he could come on to me, how many other girls has he tried that on? Girls who actually like him?

Driving home, I think about telling Sydney.

It'd be a waste of time and energy, though, because she'd never believe me.

That or she wouldn't want to.

Drew is her world, her everything.

At home, I sort laundry, make myself a box of Kraft macaroni and cheese for dinner, and try to force all of this from my mind, but the more I attempt to ignore it, the louder it begs for attention.

It consumes me the rest of the night.

The next night, too.

And every night for weeks.

I have to tell her.

CHAPTER 6

SYDNEY

"Before I forget." I hand the tray of double-fudge walnut brownies to Afton from across the table. The scent of fried tortilla chips is in the air, and Mexican polka music plays from speakers in the ceiling. "Happy birthday . . . my mom wanted to come tonight, but she was booked back-to-back. She sends her love."

Afton places her palm on her chest, head tilting. "Thank you so much. How is she these days? I haven't talked to her in forever."

"Busy working and dealing with my sister . . . the usual." I try not to overspeak. It's easy to vent about Stacia and her issues, but every time I open my mouth, I feel awful later. I love my sister more than anything, but she's been in a bad place for years now and we can't seem to help her anymore. I feel like I'm watching someone die the slowest of deaths and there isn't a damn thing I can do to stop it. "What flavor marg are you getting tonight?"

I open my menu and flip to the alcohol section on the last page. Besides the occasional glass of wine, I hardly drink anymore. Alcohol ages and dehydrates a person, and I'm in the business of antiaging and helping people look their best. No one wants to get Botox from an injector who looks like the Crypt Keeper—not that there's anything wrong with looking like the Crypt Keeper. It's not ideal in my line of work. On the other hand, no one wants to go to someone who looks flash frozen and smooth as plastic. It's a delicate line to straddle, but I manage.

"I'm thinking lime," Afton says. "On the rocks. Double salt. You?"

It's always lime on the rocks with double salt. She never tries anything new. Even as a kid, she gravitated toward the familiar. She'd eat the same thing for breakfast, lunch, and dinner for weeks on end. And God forbid we ever took an alternate route home from the park. Afton would lose her mind. Mom says her need for routine and control is part of her childhood trauma, but as far as I know her childhood was pretty ordinary save for having a dad who passed away in a motorcycle accident two months before she was born.

"Raspberry," I say. "Going to live dangerously and try a different flavor."

Afton reaches for a tortilla chip, dips the corner in the tiniest bit of salsa, sprinkles on a dash of extra salt, and takes a bite.

"So what's new?" she asks between bites. "I feel like I haven't seen you in forever. It's been, what, at least a couple of months?"

Afton's not the type to guilt-trip people, but her words are a reminder that I've let my social obligations fall to the wayside lately. There's an invisible list in my head of all the people I owe coffees and brunches and get-togethers with, and I swear it gets longer every day.

"Spa staying busy?" she asks a follow-up question before I can answer the first two, and the way she toys with her hair and bounces ever so slightly in her seat makes me wonder if she's nervous or excited. Either way, she's antsy. "Maybe one of these days I'll make my way over there for a facial. What's the one you were telling me about? The hydration one?"

"The HydraFacial," I say. "You'd love it. I'd give it to you at cost, too."

I don't know why I said that—I mean, I'd love to give it to her at cost, but I still owe thousands on that machine and it's not getting much use these days.

"How's the hotel?" I redirect the topic.

"Same." She wrinkles her nose as if she doesn't want to talk about it. Fine by me.

Those customer service horror stories are painful to listen to because there's rarely any justice. It's always some angry person spewing hatred at an innocent worker, and in the end no one walks away a winner. You can root all you want for the poor customer service associate, but where's the comeuppance for the jerk?

"How are the boys?" Afton asks after we order our drinks, a plate of barbacoa tacos, and a bowl of queso blanco. She's going to town on these chips, which is interesting because most of the time she eats like a bird. "Is Cal still doing rugby or did he decide not to this year?"

"He finished his season last month," I say, tilting my head because something's up with Afton. She *never* asks about the boys' sports. "They were six and four."

This stilted small talk is . . . not us.

We're not these people.

We've always deep dived into the topics below the surface, not at or above it.

Her formality and her antsy-ness are throwing me off tonight, especially because she's the one who invited me out to dinner. I figured she had something on her mind, but so far all she's done is make mind-numbing small talk.

"And Quincy?" She moves on to my quiet middle child, the one I'm sure she knows the least about because there are days even I feel like I know next to nothing about him. "Is he still . . ."

"Quincy's doing well," I say as our drinks arrive. I slide mine close. "And so is Alec. Are you still talking to that bartender guy?"

"Keith? Yeah." Her inky brown eyes fill with light as a sheepish smile spreads across her face. "I'm not trying to rush anything, but it's going well, it's . . . we're happy."

"Exclusive?" I ask with a raised brow.

She flicks her gaze at the ceiling, unable to contain the enormous grin on her face. Afton gets like this when she's talking to a guy, though. I imagine much of it has to do with the fact that men are few and far between in her life. It used to be that her intensity was off-putting. Then after my father was killed, it was her name and all the rumors and stories.

At one point, the only men trying to date her were the ones who were betting their friends fifty bucks that they could "screw the psycho killer chick."

"I'd love to meet him . . . finally put a face to the name you've been talking about since last summer." I offer a smile. If the past is any indication of the present, odds are the bartender is nothing to write home about. Afton always scrapes the bottom of the dating barrel.

However, I'm intrigued—if only because I want to know how Afton met a bartender when she works nights and never goes out, and the number of times she drinks in a year she could probably count on one hand.

But stranger things have happened.

"For sure." She takes a sip of her lime margarita, licking a sizable flake of salt from her upper lip. "How's Drew?"

"Okay, wait. What's going on? What are we doing here? Why does this feel like an interview or something?" I keep my voice light, adding a chuckle. "And you're all fidgety. Are you . . . are you feeling okay? You're not yourself tonight."

She squints, as if she's considering my question for the first time.

"What? I'm fine." She swats her hand and takes a longer-than-necessary sip from her cactus-shaped glass. "How's Drew?"

She repeats her question, and I commit to getting through the rest of this dinner without trying to read into every little thing. It's been a long week, my sleep hasn't been the best, and right now a manageable buzz and some salty chips are the only thing I should be focusing on.

If anything's wrong, Afton will tell me.

She always does.

I'm her person—her *only* person.

A few tacos and twenty minutes of idle chat later, our server places the tab between us and says, "I'll take this whenever you're ready."

We both reach for it at the same time, but I get to it first.

"It's your birthday," I say, clutching it against my chest. "I'm not making you pay for your own dinner on your own birthday."

"My birthday was yesterday," she teases.

I won't argue with facts, but I'm still paying.

I slide my debit card out from my wallet and flag down our server.

"You didn't have to do that, but thank you anyway," Afton says.

Two minutes later, the young man returns, his eyes soft with sympathy.

"I'm so sorry, ma'am, but your card didn't go through," he says.

Warmth floods my cheeks. This is the first time in my adult life my card has been declined—and for a forty-two-dollar tab, no less.

"Oh, my gosh. I must have given you the wrong one. I'm so sorry about that." I try to play it off, fishing in my purse for another card, but the only other one I have is over its limit. Turning back to the two of them, I exhale. "This is awkward, but I think one of my kids must have taken my other debit card because it's not in here."

The server looks to Afton, who's already reaching for her wallet. She pulls out three twenties and gives me the kindest smile before mouthing, "It's okay."

I blink away the embarrassment-fueled tears that were forming in my eyes a second ago and reach across the table to squeeze her hand.

If she had any idea how much that meant to me . . .

There's a tightness in my chest, working its way up my throat, and then a fullness behind my eyes. Despite fighting them off, the tears are already coming back.

The levee is close to breaking, and once it does . . .

"Syd, what's wrong?" Afton asks, immediately moving from her side of the booth to mine. She puts her arm around me and rests her cheek against my shoulder like she used to do when we were kids. "Talk to me."

This is the Afton I know and love, not the manic version from earlier tonight. She's always been so attuned to me, genuinely concerned with my needs and moods over her own sometimes. It doesn't surprise me that she didn't have other friends growing up. Her intensity is a lot to take if you don't understand where it's coming from.

While our past is complicated, it's moments like this that make me grateful to have her in my life—and I don't think most people could begin to understand that.

"I got a notice in the mail today," I say. "The bank wants to repossess the van."

"What? That's terrible. I'm so sorry."

"And we're already late on this month's mortgage," I continue. "Which has never happened before. We . . . things have been slow for me at the spa, and Drew lost some major contracts last year, so his income is down . . . even with picking up shifts at the hospital, we're barely making ends meet. It never used to be like this. We used to be comfortable. And now . . . it's like . . . Quincy needs braces and Cal's basketball club costs $1,500. Alec fell in gym class and needed an MRI but our insurance company is refusing to cover it, saying the school needs to, meanwhile, the hospital wants to get paid, so there's another $600 out the door. Our car insurance went up twenty percent for no reason. Market rates or some crap like that. On top of that, we've got basketball shoes to buy and instrument lessons and next year we have to find Alec a car. It's just a lot all at once, you know? It's like all of a sudden, everything got very, *very* expensive. I get physically ill every time I go through the mail. There's always something . . . a notice or a bill."

Afton gives me a side hug, saying nothing, which is her way of saying she's listening, and she's here for me.

She's always been here for me.

She's been a constant in my life since before I could speak.

Even when I look at how different our lives are, how polar opposite we've become as grown women, the thought of breaking off our friendship feels like killing off a piece of myself.

"You're going to be okay," Afton says, giving me a tight squeeze before letting her arm fall from my shoulder. "Everything that's ever happened, you've always come out fine in the end. You always land on your feet."

I dry my eyes with a wrinkled paper napkin and thank her for listening before we head out to the parking lot to leave.

When I get home, the house is in that twilight, cozy-glow state I love so much in the evenings. The boys have all retired to their rooms for the night, and Drew is passed out on the sofa, the remote still clutched tight in one hand as ESPN highlights play on the TV. I noticed three boxes of takeout pizza (that we can't afford) on the kitchen counter on the way in, but tonight I'm choosing my battles.

Grabbing a throw blanket, I curl up beside him, nuzzling against his warm arm. If I have nothing to my name, at least I have him.

With a sharp inhale, Drew stirs awake.

"Oh, hey," he says, slipping his arm around me. "How was dinner?"

"Good," I say, drawing in a breath, "until my card got declined when I went to pay."

I thought about it the entire drive home, debating whether or not I should bring this up to him tonight or wait until we can actually sit down and talk, but it can't wait anymore.

"Drew, we're bleeding," I say, "financially. We have to figure something out. The bills keep piling up and our—"

"Hey, hey, hey." His voice is whisper soft as he captures my hand in his. "I know. I know it's . . . it's rough, I know. But we've always had good years and bad years and we always recover. Sure it's a little stormy, but storms always pass."

"That's really cheesy, by the way." I snicker, feeling slightly better that he isn't as worried as I am. If Drew were worried about anything, it'd be a red flag.

"Yeah, but it made you smile, didn't it?" he asks. "Anyway, we've gotten through plenty of bad years before, we'll get through this one, too."

From Drew's lips to God's ears . . .

CHAPTER 7

AFTON

September 19, 2003

"Sorry your mom couldn't make it tonight," Cynthia says as she's popping popcorn on the stove.

After school, Cynthia took Sydney, Stacia, and me to Family Video so we could rent A Walk to Remember for our girls' movie night. We invited my mom, too, thinking it could be a mothers-and-daughters thing. Mom said yes at first, then an hour ago she called to say she wasn't coming, that something came up.

I have no doubt that "something" was probably a "someone."

"How is your mom these days?" Cynthia asks. "I don't hear from her much anymore."

Rolling my eyes, I say, "She's got a new boyfriend. Ted or Ed. I can't remember."

I stopped keeping track of their names years ago because it was a revolving door of men who all looked the same—unshaven, oil-stained hands, perpetual beer breath, zero interest in playing stepdad to a mouthy teenager. All I know is Mom loves the thrill of being with someone new, and once she's got her sights on them, they become her sun, moon, and stars. She morphs *and adjusts her interests to match theirs, which ultimately makes them fall hard and fast for her. At this point, she has her system down to a science.*

"She's probably on a date tonight," I say.

Cynthia frowns. "I'm sorry. That must be disappointing."

"I'm used to it," I say.

"You shouldn't be." She pours the pan of hot popcorn into a large Tupperware bowl before drizzling melted butter over top. "Here, take this downstairs. I'm popping a second batch and I'll be down soon."

She gives me a warm smile that wordlessly implies "everything's going to be okay, we'll still have fun tonight," and I take the bowl from her hands and head down where Stacia and Sydney are waiting with the movie cued on the big screen.

I still haven't told Sydney about Drew trying to kiss me the other day. With each day that passes, that ship is sailing farther away from the shore. At some point it'll be too late to mention it. That and homecoming is next weekend and I'm slated to go with their group. They pawned me off on the German foreign exchange student.

Or maybe they pawned him off on me . . .

By the time the movie is over two hours later, I help Cynthia carry the empty bowls upstairs while her daughters straighten up the family room.

"What a tearjerker," Cynthia says. Her eyes are damp, but there's nothing sad about her. "It's okay to feel things, you know. It's good to have that release. Keeping it all in can be really toxic on the mind and body."

I nod, listening, silently wishing my mom was always doling out little kernels of wisdom. Sydney acts annoyed by it sometimes, but I find Cynthia's advice to be priceless and never wrong.

"Are you doing okay?" she asks.

"Of course," I say.

"No, really. Are you doing okay? You've seemed a little . . . distant lately."

I can't ignore the weight of her gaze following me around the kitchen as I clean up. It's pretty sad when your own mom doesn't notice you've got something on your mind, but your best friend's mom sniffs it out in a heart-beat and cares enough to ask.

"Does it bother you that Sydney and Drew are always together?" Cynthia asks.

"Not really." They've been together three years now. I'm used to it.

"What about your mom? Does it bother you that she canceled our movie night to go on a date?"

"I'm disappointed, yeah." I dry the bowls with a kitchen towel. "I just wish she could settle down, find someone reliable, someone who treats her the way Mr. Carson treats you."

A warm palm on my shoulder anchors me gently into place.

"One thing you should know," she says, "is you can't control what anyone else does. It's much easier to focus on yourself."

"I know."

"I'm sure it's difficult seeing everyone around you in happy relationships and being the odd one out," she adds. "I promise you, Afton, someday you'll meet someone wonderful and they'll be worth the wait. The key is to find someone you wouldn't mind doing taxes and laundry with the rest of your life."

I chuckle. "Okay . . ."

"I know it sounds silly, but it's true. Trust me. I might know a thing or two about relationships." Cynthia winks, rubbing my shoulder.

Even though we're in their big open kitchen, the space between us feels sacred and intimate. The incident with Drew the other day has been dancing on the tip of my tongue since it happened. If I can't tell Sydney, maybe I could tell Cynthia?

"All done," Stacia announces when she comes up from the basement. "Everything's picked up."

The moment is gone.

Another time, maybe.

CHAPTER 8

AFTON

The salty tang of blood fills my mouth, followed by a forceful spray of water and a silicone suction tube.

Vanessa DeOliveira has her hands in my mouth—the same hands that were all over Drew's body last week, but I try not to focus on that—on my bleeding gums.

She's rough and rushing through my appointment like a woman on a mission, like the faster she cleans my teeth, the less time she has to spend actually working. It's a mindset that speaks to her young age, I'm sure.

"So are you from around here?" she asks while she's typing notes into the computer behind me. The question is delivered without a trace of emotion, like it's some boring line she says to fill the silence eight times a day, five days a week.

"I am," I say. "You?"

"Born and raised," she says with a laugh as fake as her mink-y, inch-long eyelashes. I had an extreme close-up of those (and her caterpillar eyebrows) while she was hovering over me a moment ago. "When did you graduate?"

"2004," I say, leaving out the part where I studied from home my final semester due to the whole murder trial thing. My diploma was mailed to me that summer in a plain yellow envelope. There was no cap and gown, no speech to sit through, no principal on a stage waiting to shake my hand. "You?"

"2020," she says. "You're way older than I thought. You look young for your age."

"Thanks . . ." I think?

"So everything looks good, gums look healthy, and you're doing a great job of flossing so keep it up," she says. "I'll let the doctor know you're ready."

The cleaning is over? I didn't have a chance to ask half of the things I was going to ask.

"Hey, random question for you," I say, thinking on the spot. "By chance, do you babysit?"

She wrinkles her nose. "Not anymore. I used to in high school and college? Why?"

While I'm screaming on the inside, wanting to ask if she ever worked for the Westfeldts, I can't. It'd be suspiciously coincidental.

"Never mind," I say, "I have a friend looking for a sitter, and you seem pretty, well . . . on the younger side. Forget I asked."

She smiles. "Yeah, I get that a lot. I'm actually twenty-two. Anyway, Dr. Knoll will be in soon."

With that Vanessa DeOliveira heads for the door in her carnation-pink scrubs, her sleek ponytail bouncing with each step.

Alec is fifteen now so it's been a few years since Drew and Syd have needed a babysitter, but if she graduated in 2020, that fits the timeline. She could have been their family sitter, and if that's the case, it makes what Drew is doing even more revolting.

My stomach knots.

The more I picture Drew screwing their babysitter, the more nauseous I get.

The second Dr. Knoll completes my exam, I'm out of there, but not before stopping by a little plastic donation box by the checkout. The sign says they're raising money to send Dr. Knoll to Mexico to do free dental work in Guadalajara.

Digging in my purse, I manage to find eighty-seven dollars in cash. I fold it into fourths and force it through the narrow slot. A week ago, it would've been a big deal to part with that kind of bread, but now it's a drop in the bucket compared to the massive tidal wave heading my way.

I'm on my way home when I get the urge to call Drew, and in breaking news, he actually answers on the first ring.

"Afton?" he asks, rather than giving me a simple, "Hello."

"Drew, hi. I know this is out of the blue, but I need to talk to you about Syd. I'm worried." Before he can react, I add, "I was hoping we could meet in person . . . maybe tomorrow over lunch?"

I'm normally sleeping when the nine-to-fivers are taking their midday break, but I figured I'd get less resistance by making this easy for him.

"Uh, yeah." He blows a breath into the phone. I picture him sitting in his home office wearing faded sweats, massaging the back of his neck like he's trying to figure out what this is all about. "I can do tomorrow at noon. The Five and Diner?"

"Perfect," I say. "See you then."

I'll sleep when I'm dead—or after I collect my winnings and free Sydney from her toxic marriage.

Whichever comes first.

CHAPTER 9

SYDNEY

"Yes, I realize you waived the late fee last time, but I'm wondering if it would be possible to do it again?" I cradle my phone on my shoulder while checking my schedule. My next client should be here any minute.

"I'm sorry, ma'am, but it's against our policy. Looks like we've actually waived the late fee three times for you in the last six months. I can transfer you to the financial assistance department if you'd like?" the young-sounding customer service gentleman on the other end says.

I waited on hold for twenty-nine minutes to talk to him—I don't have time to be placed on hold again to talk to someone else in a different department.

Glancing toward the parking lot, I spot my one o'clock, Candace, climbing out of her champagne-bronze Audi coupe. She's a few minutes early, but it's for the best because this one's a talker. Love her to death, but I can't inject her face while her lips are moving, so her appointments tend to run longer than everyone else's.

"Sorry—I'll have to call back later." I hang up before he has a chance to ask me to do a survey at the end of the call or whatever he's forced to say by corporate.

Taking a deep breath, I close my eyes and center myself before putting on my best face for Candace. When I get home tonight, I need to figure out our money situation before it snowballs into an avalanche.

Our biggest expense is our mortgage, and we could always downsize, but with interest rates being so high and house prices not budging, we'd likely end up paying more for something smaller. Besides, our house is where we've raised our family. It's our home. It's where we brought each of our boys home from the hospital. Where they all spoke their first words and took their first steps and experienced the childhood magic of Santa Claus and the Easter Bunny. Years from now, I hope to see their own children running through the front door.

The idea of selling our family home makes me physically ill—the same way I feel every time I check the mailbox, only compounded to the nth degree.

The door to my spa suite swings open and Candace saunters in with a dainty finger wave and a giant smile, wrapped in a cloud of her signature Baccarat Rouge 540 perfume. She places her quilted Chanel bag gently on one of the upholstered guest chairs and shrugs out of her fur-lined Moncler parka.

"Ugh, this weather." She feigns disgust. "Remind me why I live here again? I should be in Florida or Arizona or something. Missouri's for the birds. Give me sunshine or give me death."

"You say that every year and yet you're still here," I tease. "Why don't you have a seat in the big chair. I have you down for filler today, is that still the plan?"

Candace is one of my rare clients who has a seemingly bottomless bank account. That and a husband who doesn't care enough to ask questions—her words, not mine.

By the time her hour is through, I've artfully injected her face with two and a half syringes of filler in various areas plus touched up her Botox because she didn't like that she was still able to move her eyebrows after the last time. She also decided to add on a "lip flip," despite my warnings that it might make drinking through a straw a bit challenging. Candace said she'd adapt.

If only every day could be this profitable . . .

Once she's out the door, I check my phone before my next appointment arrives. The hospital left me a voice mail asking if I could take another twelve tonight. Without hesitation, I call the ER supervisor back and tell her I'll be there. Then I text Drew and tell him he's going to have to figure out dinner for the boys. As soon as I get home, I'm taking a nap then heading in.

His message stays on "delivered" for a bit, and I wait another minute or so to see if it changes to "read." Usually his phone is glued to his side like an extra appendage. I typically get a text back instantaneously, even if it's a simple thumbs-up emoji.

Two minutes pass, then five, then ten.

No response.

By the time my next appointment arrives, he still hasn't responded, but I push it from my mind. I'm too busy to worry about little things like this when I have bigger fish to fry.

CHAPTER 10

AFTON

"I don't know if you're aware, but Syd's not in a good place right now," I say to Drew from the other side of the diner booth. It's been a week since I saw him sneaking into the hotel in the middle of the night, though it's been so heavy on my mind that it feels like yesterday.

He scoffs. "She's fine."

"Is she, though?"

"I think I'd know . . . I live with her," he says. "Do *you* live with her?"

Typical Drew—defensive and sarcastic when he's in the hot seat. It's not like I'm blaming him for anything.

At least not yet.

I'm still warming up.

"Maybe she doesn't want to tell you because she doesn't want to worry you," I say, "but I can see it in her eyes. I hear it in her voice. She's holding it together with a string and a paper clip."

He rakes his palm along his smooth jawline, peering out the window to his left. I want to believe he's contemplating my words, but honestly, he looks like he's displeased that we're even having this conversation. He looks like he'd rather be sitting on a white-sanded beach or swinging a golf club or burying his face between Vanessa's thighs.

Anywhere but here.

"Sydney's fine," he says. "And I'd appreciate you not trying to insert yourself into our relationship. This isn't high school. Pretty sure last time you tried to break us up, it backfired on you."

I refuse to discuss something that happened when we were seventeen because it's neither here nor there.

Lifting my palms, I lean back. "No one said anything about breaking you two up . . ."

The harshness in his expression dampens a bit, maybe he's realizing he jumped the gun.

"It's interesting, though," I say, "that I told you Syd's not doing well and your mind instantly goes to your marriage. I never said anything about that."

"Then what is this about? Why are we here?" The grimace on his face is the same one he probably gives to door-to-door salespeople when they interrupt dinnertime. I'm a nuisance. A bother.

"She's working a lot," I say.

"Well aware."

"And she's stressed about your family's finances."

"In case you didn't know, Afton, things like other people's marriage and finances aren't your concern." The condescension in his tone is laid thick and unapologetic.

"They are when it's my best friend," I counter back. "She cried in my arms the other night, talking about the bills that are piling up and how her van is about to get repo'd. You're her husband—*you* should be taking care of your family. It shouldn't all be falling on her shoulders alone. Syd shouldn't be working herself to an early grave while you . . ."

I let my words fade into nothing because I want to gauge his reaction.

He doesn't know that I know about Vanessa.

"While I *what*?" He folds his arms across his puffed chest, reminding me of one of those wild birds that tries to make themselves look bigger when they're threatened.

"Oh, come on. Don't play dumb." I don't fight the smirk claiming my lips.

"I have no idea what you're talking about," he says. "I work, I take care of things around the house, I run the kids around. What exactly are you implying?"

My mouth remains twisted. "You really want to do this? You want to go there?"

Drew's stare is heavy and unfaltering as his nostrils flare with each exhale.

"I don't understand," he says.

"You sure you want me to get specific?" I scan the packed diner. "Here? Around all these people? The lady in the blue sweater over there has been listening to our conversation since we sat down."

The eavesdropping woman's gaze flicks down to her plate of half-eaten pancakes and she clears her throat.

Drew's tanned complexion turns pale as he fidgets with the expensive watch on his left wrist.

"Be the man she deserves," I say, keeping my voice low, not as a favor to him but to Sydney.

"I am," he speaks through clenched teeth.

"You're not even close."

Drew bristles. "Where's this animosity coming from? I have to admit, I'm a little taken aback here."

"You should be."

He leans closer, swallowing hard, his cold eyes searching mine. I remain silent because I sense there's a confession coming on, only he clears his throat and leans back.

"I don't know what you're getting at, but I swear on my life—on my kids' lives. I *love* my wife. She's the only one for me," he says with a shake in his voice.

My jaw falls loose. I wasn't expecting a full-on confession today but that's the next best thing . . . he's worried I know something.

And what can I say? I do.

Rising, I slip my jacket on and swing my purse over my shoulder.

"So that's it?" he asks. "You just wanted to meet me here so you could tell me what a shitty husband I am?"

"Pretty much." I shrug as I stretch my fingers into my gloves. "That and I've got my eye on you, so I suggest you step it up."

Drew scoffs.

"Are you threatening me?" He scans me from head to toe and back. If he's going for intimidation here, his effort is wasted on me; I'm not afraid of an insecure pencil dick.

"Think of it more as a warning." I fight the smile that begs to form on my face.

Drew rises, his small-town star forward physique towering over me. "You're out of pocket."

"*I'm* out of pocket?" I press a gloved index finger against my chest.

His lips press into a tight line as he forces a hard breath through his nostrils.

"Look, Syd's a saint, and I know I don't deserve her. No one does. But don't go causing trouble where there isn't any. We're happy. Leave us alone with . . . whatever the hell this is."

Last I checked, happy wives didn't cry into their best friend's arms in the middle of Mexican restaurants. Also, pretty sure happy husbands don't cheat on their wives—period.

"Ignorance is bliss—is that your motto?" I ask before adding, "I know what you did. And if you do it again, she'll know, too, because I'll tell her personally."

With that, I leave.

From the parking lot, I watch him slink back into the booth, pure bewilderment on his face.

As I drive away, I think of Keith the bartender, who is the antithesis of Drew: easygoing but hardworking. Forty-two. Never married, no kids. No desire for either of those things. As independent as I am. And he's from some pin-sized town in Vermont, so he doesn't look at me the way the locals here do.

He doesn't care about my baggage.

I pass The Crooked Crowbar on the way home, making a last-minute decision to stop by when I spot his russet-brown Ford F150 in the parking lot.

The front door is unlocked, so I let myself in.

A Twisted Sister song plays from the vintage jukebox in the corner. After letting my eyes adjust to the darkness, I spot Keith wiping down pub tables. He glances my way, sprays the next table, flips his rag to a dry section, and carries on.

"Hi." I give him a wave.

I know he saw me.

"I saw your truck outside," I add over the blare of the music. "Haven't heard from you in a while . . ."

"Been busy," he says without looking up.

"Same." My big news is on the tip of my tongue, but I won't mention my winnings. Not yet. I want him to like me for me, not for my millions. "You want some help?"

"Don't you have to work tonight?" he asks without looking up. "Figured you'd be sleeping this time of day."

He hasn't glanced at me for more than half a second since I walked in a minute ago, and now his back is toward me.

His unexpected coldness stings, especially when I came here for a little pick-me-up after my tense meeting with Drew.

Has Keith met someone else?

So much for my lucky streak . . .

"Yeah, I should get going . . . let you get back to work." I fight the threat of tears with a pasted smile so forced it hurts my face, though he wouldn't notice anyway since he won't look at me. "See you around?"

"Yep."

By the time I'm back in my car, my cheeks are damp and itchy from my tears and the cold air. I swipe them with the back of my gloved hand until they're bone dry, and then I tune to a pop station on the radio, eager for an upbeat distraction from this downbeat moment.

I'm halfway home when Sydney texts me to ask if I could stop by her house and turn on her Crock-Pot because she wasn't able to run home for lunch and Drew isn't answering his phone . . . which is interesting considering the conversation we had less than fifteen minutes ago.

If I know him like I think I do, he's probably calling up Vanessa, frantically trying to cover his tracks.

And who knows—maybe there are other women.

I put *nothing* past him.

I text Syd back when I get to the next stop sign and let her know I'm on my way.

CHAPTER 11

SYDNEY

"Are you satisfied?" Drew asks in bed Saturday night when I'm lying in his arms, coming down from a much-needed release.

It's been a while since we were intimate. At least a week, maybe two. Perhaps that's nothing by some couple's standards, but for us it's an eternity. We've always been healthy in that regard. The attraction has yet to fade—at least for me. And he tells me I'm beautiful all the time, even when I roll out of bed in the morning with wild hair, dragon breath, and faded, holey pajamas.

"Why? Did you think I was faking it?" I laugh, brushing a strand of sweat-dampened hair from my forehead.

"I'm not talking about that. I mean, are you satisfied with us? Our relationship? Our marriage?" His questions are unsettling, if only because he's never had to ask them before.

"Why wouldn't I be?" I study his handsome face in the dark as worry lines spread across his forehead. As far as I know, I've never given him a reason to doubt . . . us. He's been my whole world since the moment I first laid eyes on him.

"You seem overwhelmed lately, that's all. I know you're working a lot, but if there's anything I can do to make things easier for you . . ."

His voice trails. "I want to make sure you know I'm here for you. I don't . . . I don't want to fail you."

I have no idea where this is coming from, but I don't like it.

The thing about planting seeds of doubt in a marriage is that eventually they sprout and grow into bigger problems.

"Don't be ridiculous. You're not failing me," I say with a chuckle, silencing his nonsense with a kiss. The taste of his spearmint toothpaste tingles against my lips. "Although, it'd be amazing if you could take down the Christmas lights. I don't want to be one of those houses that leaves theirs up until Saint Patrick's Day . . ."

"Fair request. I just know how important Christmas is to you. You've seemed a little down lately—thought I'd leave them up a little longer."

God, I love this man.

I kiss him again, harder this time.

When my father was killed two days before Christmas, my mother was determined to not let any future Christmases be marred by our family's tragedy, so she always went all out with decorations, baked treats, holiday lights, and traditions—even more than before.

"I love you for that, I do," I say, "but I don't think the HoA feels the same. Last thing we need is a hundred and fifty dollar fine for leaving Christmas lights up past January 31."

"Noted. I'll do it first thing tomorrow morning." He pulls me close and adds, "Thanks for picking up all those hospital shifts lately. I know it's a lot to put on you."

"You'd do the same if you could."

"I thought about driving for Uber or Lyft on the weekends."

"In a town this size, it wouldn't be worth it. Your time is more valuable at home, with the boys," I say. In a perfect world, I could rely on my mother to help transport the kids from thing to thing every weekend, but between her counseling practice and my sister, her plate is more than full.

Growing up, my father was the head high school varsity football coach and we were always division champions. When he wasn't teaching, he was coaching, which was a second job in and of itself. During those months, my mom did it all and we were lucky if we got to see him at the dinner table each night. Looking back, the time we lost with him became time we could never get back. I've always vowed my kids wouldn't have to experience such a priceless loss.

"Oh. Forgot to tell you, I talked to Afton yesterday," he says in the same casual tone he might use to tell me we're almost out of toilet paper.

I jerk my head, not sure if I heard him right. "Afton? What for?"

He shrugs. "She called me up and asked me to meet her for lunch, only we didn't order anything. She wanted to tell me she didn't think you were happy and it was all my fault."

I sit up, draping the sheets around me. "Afton said that?"

It doesn't sound like her at all. Inserting herself into our relationship is something she hasn't done since we were in high school and she hilariously claimed Drew tried to kiss her.

"She said those exact words?" I ask.

"More or less." My husband rolls his eyes. "She's acting like she has some dirt on me or something . . . to be honest, I have no idea what she's talking about, but I went along with it because people were starting to stare."

"Oh, God. She was making a scene?" I cringe. Everyone in this town knows me and my family and there's never been a shortage of gossip on the subject. The last thing we need is more of it. "That's so embarrassing."

"Right? I left sort of flabbergasted. Meant to tell you sooner but I didn't catch you before you went to work last night. Anyway, thought you should know."

"What kind of dirt do you think she has?" I wrinkle my nose.

He runs his hand through his hair, nonplussed. "Your guess is as good as mine."

Afton is . . . Afton. I stopped trying to make sense of her antics long ago. As a child, she would have these blackout rages and her mother never seemed to know what to do with her. That's where my mother stepped in. She found a child psychiatrist in Kansas City as well as a local adolescent therapist. On top of that, she would even spend extra time with Afton, knowing she needed it since Vangie was a single mom who worked long and sometimes strange hours.

Afton was a typical latchkey kid, though starting in fourth grade she rode home on the bus with me every day. There were nights her mom wouldn't pick her up until seven or eight o'clock.

She wanted so badly to be a Carson.

Mom saw that and fed into it probably more than she should have, but she meant well. She felt sorry for Afton. It wasn't her fault that Vangie was so messed up, always bringing random men home and forgetting to buy groceries, winter boots, and one year even school supplies. Vangie never went to Afton's junior high volleyball games either. It was always my family cheering for her from the stands.

I never understood Mom and Vangie's friendship either.

They were cousins who became friends who eventually acted like sisters until life took them in opposite directions. Mom said it was one of those things where Vangie felt like family, and "you don't abandon family in their time of need."

"Drew?" I whisper. The moonlight pouring in through the window beside him paints streaks of light on his bare chest.

He's sleeping now, out cold.

What I wouldn't give to fall asleep as soon as my head hits the pillow, but it's impossible with the weight of the world on your shoulders.

I let my mind weave and wander, settling on Afton's birthday dinner at El Guapo's the other night. I never would've mentioned our finances had I known she was going to turn around and weaponize that information against Drew.

What is she trying to do here?

What's her end game?

What dirt does she think she has on my husband?

It isn't his fault our incomes took a hit this year.

It isn't anyone's fault—the entire world is in a recession.

Reaching for my phone on the nightstand, I start composing a text to her, only to delete it halfway through.

It's late, and this is a conversation we should have in person.

Soon.

CHAPTER 12

AFTON

September 27, 2003

Beyoncé's "Crazy in Love" blares from my stereo as I fix my hair for the homecoming dance. For some reason, it's not cooperating today. The clips aren't staying put no matter how much hair spray I use. The stupid things slide right out every time.

I should've gone to a salon like everyone else and gotten an updo, but Mom only gave me $100 for this dance and my dress and shoes ate up most of it. I barely have enough to pay for dinner tonight—assuming I'm going Dutch with my date.

I change the radio to a different station. Jack White's iconic whiny croon sings "Seven Nation Army" against a heavy bass line and kick drum—a much better fit for my current mood.

Dipping my fingers into a tiny pot of glittery hair gel I bought from Claire's, I twist small sections of hair away from my face and secure them, once again, with the clips.

I'm running out of time and I still need to get dressed.

Shimmying into my cornflower-blue knee-length dress with little white daisies on the straps, I check my reflection in the mirror on the back of my door. Sydney always calls it the "skinny mirror" because it magically makes everyone look ten pounds slimmer. I don't care about things like that, but she once offered to buy it off me. I told her no, though I'm not quite sure why.

Maybe part of me likes having something she wants for a change?

Next, I clip on a pair of blue butterfly earrings I borrowed from Gram's jewelry collection. They're vintage but beautifully detailed, like tiny works of stained glass.

Lastly, I slip into a pair of white platform strappy heels and toss some lip gloss and cash into my clutch.

Outside a horn beeps twice.

Peering out my window, I spot the stretch limo that we all rented for the night at twenty bucks a person. It looks ridiculously out of place on my street, but I'm excited. I've never been in a limousine before.

Grabbing my date's white rose boutonniere from the fridge, I head outside and meet the group. Syd and Drew climb out first, as well as a few others, and lastly my date, Lukas.

"Let's take some pics real quick," one of the girls in our group says, dragging her leggy boyfriend toward the sprawling oak tree in my neighbor's yard. The way she positions herself makes the background an open field with a setting sun.

Everyone's giddiness and high energy is exciting, and while I'm not big into school dances, I'm actually looking forward to this.

It almost makes me forget about Drew trying to kiss me.

We snap several pictures, and Lukas is a perfect gentleman, keeping his hands so light on my hips I barely feel them.

Inside the limo, we're crammed to the max despite there being twelve of us and this supposedly being a fourteen-passenger vehicle.

Sydney wastes no time crawling onto Drew's lap. It frees up a little bit of space, but it's still pretty cramped.

An LED light along the roof coupled with twinkling stars makes this feel like a spaceship. One of the boys is messing with the radio, tuning it to the local rap and R&B channel. Nelly's "Hot in Herre" comes on and *everyone starts dancing in their seats. I don't want to be the odd one out or the only one sitting like a bump on a log, so I smile and laugh and throw my hands in the air like all the other girls.*

From across the limo, Drew and Sydney are making out, his hands cupping her jaw and her legs straddling his lap.

This is a lot—even for these two.

I think it's because I finally broke down and told Sydney about what happened.

Of course she denied it, saying he would never do something like that and that I was probably getting mixed signals or confused. After that, she changed the subject, confirming what I already knew—she didn't want to believe me and she wasn't going to.

I can't help but wonder if, deep down, she thinks about it, questions if it did happen, because lately their PDA has been on overload. It's almost like she's trying to prove a point to me—or herself—that she's Drew's number one.

As frustrating as it is, at least she didn't accuse me of being jealous, of secretly wanting Drew for myself or being the one who tried to make the move.

Our conversation could have been friendship-ending, and I went into it knowing that. I only told her because I couldn't take it anymore. I wasn't eating or sleeping and it was killing me seeing how happy she was with someone who was nothing but a big fat liar who didn't deserve the good thing he had.

We pull up in front of the next house to pick up another couple. I'm not sure how we're going to squeeze two more people into this thing, but I refuse to sit on anyone's lap.

"Okay, let's do more pictures, guys," one of the girls calls.

We all shove and climb our way out of the limo and match up with our dates in front of someone's front porch. A handful of parents are watching, smiling, snapping pictures.

By the time we pile back into the car, Drew heads in first. Somehow I'm behind him, and it isn't until I spot him staring at my legs that I realize my hem has ridden up, exposing my panties.

I shoot him a dirty look, tugging it down, and his gaze flicks away so fast it makes me question if I imagined the whole thing.

We're headed to dinner when Sydney climbs onto Drew's lap again, smothering him with kisses. I do everything I can not to look in their direction, but the one time I do, I realize he's looking at me.

Sydney's lips are on him.

His eyes are on me.

There's a wicked glint in them, too, like he's trying to say "screw you" or "I won."

I hate him.

But more than that, I hate that he's right.

Sydney will always take Drew's side, even when she shouldn't.

CHAPTER 13

AFTON

Drew Westfeldt is still a liar and a cheater.

My blood turns boiling hot when I find Vanessa DeOliveira's name on the reservation list for later this week—a Thursday night once again.

Ballsy.

Or perhaps strategic.

It's hard to say with Drew.

At times, I've suspected him of being below average intelligence-wise, yet other times he's as cunning as a fox.

Fortunately for Drew (and unfortunately for me), I'm off this Thursday.

I glance up at Millicent, whose expression is especially sour and whose eyes are remarkably beady tonight.

It's almost like looking in a mirror.

The hotel is quiet except for the Dean Martin song playing overhead. I've been here a couple of hours, checked in an elderly couple, a single man dressed in an expensive suit, and most recently a bickering married duo who requested a room with two double beds instead of the king suite they'd originally reserved.

If Drew thinks he can call my bluff, he doesn't know me at all.

Given that I have less than two weeks left at the hotel and the lobby is dead, I thwart the no-phone rule and pull mine out to compose a message to Drew.

ME: I wasn't bluffing.

It's late, and I don't expect him to reply . . . and yet he does.

Instantly.

DREW: ???

ME: Did our conversation mean nothing to you?

DREW: I don't know what your deal is but you have to stop this. It's disturbing.

ME: Don't insult me with your lame attempt at gaslighting. Play dumb with someone else.

DREW: Sydney's not too happy about your thinly veiled threats, by the way.

I'm not surprised that he ran home and "told on me." I'm sure he wanted to get ahead of the impending storm, make me look like the crazy one, and control the narrative before the narrative controls him.

DREW: Do Sydney and me both a favor and kindly stay out of our marriage.

ME: Kindly? Wow. So polite. Who knew cheaters could have manners?

DREW: You think I cheated on my wife?!

He all but confessed at the diner . . . I imagine he's only playing dumb in case Syd sees his text messages. She's not the type to snoop, but who the hell knows what goes on behind closed doors.

ME: I don't think, I know. And I have proof you're going to do it again.

As soon as I send that message, I regret showing my hand, but maybe it'll stop him from hooking up with Vanessa this time. Part of me wonders if he wanted to get caught.

Why else would he use the hotel where I work the front desk?

Maybe on a subconscious level he's intentionally sabotaging his marriage because he knows he's not worthy.

Then again, he's arrogant enough to believe he won't get caught and lucky enough to know she'd never believe me in a million years.

I ball my fist and press it against my forehead.

I shouldn't have texted him; I should have let it play out so I could get pictures—physical evidence.

DREW: You need help. Please . . . get help.

I close out of my messages.

That's enough verbal jujitsu for one night.

Tapping on the camera icon, I pull up the photos I took the afternoon I stopped at their house to turn on the Crock-Pot for Syd. While I was in their kitchen, I couldn't help but notice a stack of opened bills on the counter, all of which were past due or included late notices printed on aggressively bold-colored paper—marigold and neon orange mostly.

Ordinarily I'd have looked the other way, but after my conversation with Sydney the other night and the fact that I'm coming into more money than one person needs in their lifetime, I snapped a few pictures of her bills with the intention of paying them off anonymously. She's done so much for me over the years . . . what kind of person would I be if I had the means to help her and chose to turn a blind eye instead?

Over the hour that follows, I call the 800 numbers listed on her bills and use the automated systems to pay them off.

$34,887.56 pays off the bank note on her Chrysler Town & Country.

$4,882.01 covers the statement balance on her Mastercard.

$12,976.83 brings her Visa to $0.

$9,876.22 wipes out her Discover.

I drop another $2,500 on miscellaneous medical bills and $5,000 on this month and next month's mortgage payments.

By the time I'm done, my nest egg is $70,000 lighter, but in a matter of weeks that won't matter. According to my calculations, this saves her almost $2,300 a month. It isn't much, but maybe she won't have to work two jobs anymore?

Satisfaction seeps deep into my marrow when I'm done. Sydney would never expect in a hundred million years that it was me, but even if she did, I'd never fess up.

I didn't do this for the accolades or karma—I did it because it was the right thing to do.

If things were the other way around, I know she'd do the same.

CHAPTER 14

SYDNEY

"Christmas lights are officially down," Drew says Sunday morning.

The clock on the fireplace mantel reads a quarter past eleven. I haven't slept in this late since I can't remember when, but I appreciate that my husband managed to get out of bed and take down the lights without disturbing my much-needed slumber.

"Even had Cal on the ladder, too." He ruffles our youngest son's coffee-brown hair, eliciting a dimpled smile in the process.

I love how they look like twins.

"Good job, Cal," I say. Of the three, he's always been the most helpful. Alec would balk at being asked to work outside in the cold instead of hole up in his room playing Xbox, and Quincy would mutter some excuse about having homework. But not our sweet Cal.

"Thought I'd make some lunch," Drew says. "You hungry at all?"

Drew *never* cooks.

He attempted to make spaghetti once and when I walked into the kitchen to see what was taking so long, I found he'd filled a stockpot all the way to the top with water and had the burner set to medium. He couldn't figure out why it was taking so long to boil the water.

God love him for trying, though.

"You don't have to do that." I get up from my chair, only to have him place his palm out.

"No, no. Stay there. I've got this," he says with a proud smile before vanishing into the kitchen.

The sound of dishes and pans clinking and clamoring follows, and I hear him playing music on our kitchen Alexa—Dave Matthews Band, it sounds like.

He only listens to Dave when he's in an upbeat mood . . .

. . . which makes this entire thing all the more concerning . . .

. . . because sometime in the middle of the night, I woke up from a dead sleep to find him texting someone.

At first I thought I was dreaming, and when I realized I wasn't, I was too speechless to say anything. With Drew's questions last night regarding my satisfaction with him and our marriage, our lackluster sex life lately, and him not answering my texts immediately like usual, I'm beginning to worry about us.

If he were stepping out on me, I don't know what I'd do.

Correction . . .

I know exactly what I'd do—and it terrifies me.

CHAPTER 15

AFTON

"The $33 million Missouri Lottery jackpot winner from earlier this month has yet to come forward and claim their winnings," the perky blonde news anchor says on the TV. "State lottery officials say the ticket was purchased at a Qwik Star in Shelter Rock . . ."

"I bet whoever bought it accidentally threw it away," Gram says, rocking in her sage-green La-Z-Boy as she knits a yellow baby blanket. For as long as I can remember, Gram's been knitting these blankets for the pediatric unit at the county hospital. It gives her a sense of purpose and keeps her busy. "What a shame."

"Maybe they're waiting," I say from my spot on the sofa. It's noon and I should be sleeping, but once again, my medication's not working. I don't tell Gram, though. She'll only worry or ask questions I'm not prepared to answer.

"For what? Hell to freeze over?" She laughs, though it turns into the raspy cough of a former two-packs-a-day smoker.

I turn my attention her way, resting my chin on top of my hand. "What would you do with thirty-three million?"

She loops a piece of yarn around her knitting needle and shoots me a sideways peek.

"I don't even want to waste my time wishing and praying about stuff like that," she says. "No sense in getting your hopes up for no reason at all. Plenty of better things to do with that time."

"Yeah, but what if?"

Gram rolls her eyes, her toes pressing against the floor as she rocks and knits, rocks and knits. She's in the same pink-and-blue muumuu as yesterday, but her hair is wrapped tight in plastic curlers. I've always wondered why she bothers doing her hair when she never goes anywhere or sees anyone besides me, her home health aide twice a week, and occasionally my mother when she rolls into town once every other full moon.

"I don't know." Her head cocks as she contemplates my question. "Most people go broke within five years of winning anyway. It's a proven fact. They've done studies on it."

"You're not most people."

Not by a mile.

"What would you do?" I ask. "I'm curious. I want to know."

I've yet to bring up my ticket, and I don't plan to until after I claim my money. She's got a weak heart and getting her worked up might, literally, be the death of her. Upgrading our lifestyle is going to have to be a gradual process, like acclimating to frigid lake water one body part at a time so you don't shock your whole system.

"Hmm. Well, I imagine I'd invest part of it. Save the rest for a rainy day." She reaches for a ball of white yarn and starts a new row as the news anchor yammers on over some school district drama in Overland Park, which may as well be a world away from us.

"That's no fun."

"And what would you do?" She peers my way over her wire-framed bifocals. "Thirty-three million's a lot of money for a single gal like yourself."

Gram has never understood why I have no desire to "settle down and start a family like everyone else."

"Oh, before I forget," she interjects. "You left the back door wide open last night."

"No I didn't." I always come and go through the front door and we always leave the back door locked since we don't use it.

"It was banging in the wind this morning. Woke me up." She rests the unfinished baby blanket in her lap before placing it aside completely. "Made a heck of a lot of ruckus, that's for sure. Kitchen was freezing, too. Let out all that heat."

"Maybe the latch busted? I'll go check." Bolting up from the couch, I head for the back door, which Gram has since secured closed.

The latch is older than time and rusty as hell, but it's fine.

The lock works.

Weird . . .

Did someone break in overnight when I was at work? It's an old door with hinges that are starting to show their age. Someone with a decent amount of muscle could easily pry it open with enough force.

Drew?

I run upstairs next, checking the safe under my bed and exhaling a tightly held breath when I discover it's still there, right where I left it. Despite no one knowing this exists, the peace of mind I get from knowing it's still there is priceless.

Next I check my nightstand drawer, counting all my prescription bottles and giving them each a couple of shakes to make sure they weren't emptied out.

All good.

Making my way around the rest of the house, I check every corner, every window, every jewelry box, every electronic gadget. We don't have much, Gram and me, but whoever opened that door didn't appear to take anything.

The sound of kids laughing steers my attention to the window above the kitchen sink. Outside, The Ferals are playing in the snow. It's barely thirty-five degrees and they're out there in jackets, soggy gloves, and old tennis shoes. No hats. No boots. No scarves.

I throw my boots and coat on and trot outside, carefully trekking across the icy strip of grass that separates their driveway from ours.

"Hey," I say, drawing my arms close around my sides as my breath forms clouds in the air. "What are you guys doing?"

The youngest one, a little girl with a spray of freckles across her upturned nose, hides behind the oldest, peeking out from behind him with wide, pale eyes the color of an icy winter sky. A shiny glob of pale yellow snot drips from her left nostril to the top of her lip. Her hair is matted with greasy tangles, like it hasn't been washed or brushed in a while.

"Is your mom home?" I ask, though I already suspect the answer. "I wanted to ask her a question."

Tina, their mother, works odd hours much like my mom did. There's a chance she might have been coming or going when someone was breaking into our house overnight, and I'd like to ask if she noticed anything strange.

The middle child, another girl, shakes her head no.

The boy elbows her, as if she wasn't supposed to answer me.

"It's okay," I say.

"Do you have anything to eat?" the youngest one asks, sniffing her red, button-sized nose.

"*Nevaeh*," the boy says, scolding her with a curt tone reserved for someone much older than him.

"Are you hungry?" I ask.

The littlest girl nods, followed by her older sister. The boy swallows, as if his mouth is salivating at the mere mention of food.

"Where's your mom?" I ask.

The three of them stare at me with dead eyes, giving me nothing but silence.

Fair enough.

Maybe she's given them strict instructions not to tell people they're home alone?

"What are your names?" They've lived here six months and we've yet to formally meet, but I've seen them outside so much I feel like I know them. "I'm Afton. I live here with my grandma. Her name is Bea."

I point to my house and offer a smile, attempting to show them the same kindness Cynthia Carson showed me all those years ago when I was a latchkey kid.

"Do you like pizza?" I ask. The oldest girl nods. "What's your favorite kind? Cheese? Pepperoni?"

"Cheese," they all say at the same time.

"If I ordered you some pizza, would you eat it?" It's a dumb question, but I don't want to assume. "Okay. I'll have them deliver it to my house and I'll bring it over for you, okay?"

They nod in unison.

"Why don't you guys go wait inside? It's a little too cold to be playing outside without boots and hats."

The boy rounds up the little girls and the three of them disappear inside their screened-in front porch. I head in and order them a family-sized feast complete with a two-liter of Sprite, cheesy garlic bread, two extra-large cheese pizzas, and a brownie pie for dessert—a Sunday supper special from the pizza place on the square. It should be enough to get them through three, maybe four meals if they don't go to town on it in one sitting.

When the food arrives forty minutes later, I carry it next door. The warm cardboard is cozy against my arms and the piping-fresh feast smells divine. The little boy opens the door and the stench of cat urine, stale garbage, and general household filth wafts out. His royal blue eyes are soulful, better suited for a grown adult and not a child who should be more concerned with video games than raising his sisters.

"Thanks," he says.

He takes each box one by one, placing it in a stack on the floor as it's too much for him to handle at once.

"You're welcome. When your mom gets home, send her my way, okay? And if you ever need anything—anything at all—I'm next door," I remind him before leaving with a smile and a wave and head home.

Once back home, I take a 10mg melatonin gummy plus two Advil PMs to try to get a few hours of sleep. With my blue pills no longer working, this is my best chance at getting any rest. Normally it wouldn't matter since Sundays are my night off, but I switched with a coworker so I can be there when Vanessa and Drew have their little tryst.

I wouldn't miss that for the world.

An hour later, I'm almost out cold when my phone rings.

The caller ID shows "restricted."

I press ignore and shut my eyes.

It's probably nothing.

CHAPTER 16

SYDNEY

October 9, 2003

I'm woken in the middle of the night by the sound of the front door shutting. Squinting at my alarm clock, the glaring red letters read 1:08 AM. It's Thursday; no one should be up and about this time of night. At least not in our house.

Picking the sleep from my eyes, I sit up and peek out my blinds, spotting a car in the driveway. I can't tell because of the tree branches blocking it, but I think it might be Vangie.

Did something happen?

Is Afton okay?

What if it's not Vangie? What if it's one of mom's patients? It wouldn't be the first time one of them showed up at our house, threatening to harm themselves.

Flinging off my covers, I tiptoe to the top of the stairs, take a seat on the top step, and listen to the whispers coming from the living room.

The smell of spiced pumpkin is in the air and the house is stuffy, too cold outside to run the AC, not cold enough to need the furnace.

I can't make out what they're saying, so I scoot down a few more steps. From here, I can almost see the corner of the living room. Leaning forward, I crane my neck until I spot my mother, father, and Vangie standing in a circle.

Mom has her arm around Vangie's shoulders and Vangie's holding a bag of frozen peas over half of her face.

My stomach drops.

Dad looks furious.

"You need to file a report this time," Mom tells Vangie in her softest yet sternest tone. "This can't happen again. Don't let him do this to you."

Vangie is sniffling, sobbing. She says something, but I can't hear what it is.

"Someone like that isn't going to stop unless someone makes them stop. What if he hurts Afton?" Mom asks. "You would never forgive yourself."

I'm not sure if that's true, but it sounds nice.

"Rick, can you take her to the station to file a report?" Mom asks.

"Of course," he says without hesitation. He walks off, maybe to get his keys. I freeze as if that could help obscure me, but he isn't looking at the stairs anyway.

Returning quietly to my room, I shut the door so slowly it doesn't make a sound, then I watch from my window as Dad and Vangie leave. As soon as they're gone, my bedroom door swings open a few inches.

"I thought I heard you up here." Mom takes a seat on my bed, patting the space beside her. She must have supersonic hearing because I was quieter than a mouse.

"Do you have any questions for me?" she asks, her hands clasped neatly on her lap.

"What happened?"

"Vangie's got into a fight with her boyfriend," Mom says with a frustrated sigh. "He hurt her."

"Is she going to be okay?"

"She's got a black eye, some bruising on her face, but she'll be fine. I just hope she stays away from him. People like him, people who hurt people when they're angry, they don't tend to change. Your dad took her to file a police report, so hopefully he'll have consequences and think twice before putting his hands on someone again."

"Do you think he'll hurt Afton? I heard you say that."

"I think people like him are very unpredictable."

I slide my legs back under my covers and fix my pillow behind me. I'm exhausted, but also wired, imagining the horror Vangie must have gone through as well as picturing someone hurting Afton.

"Promise me something, Sydney," Mom says as she straightens my covers. "Never let a man lay his hands on you."

"I would never."

"A lot of women say that, and they think that, they think it won't happen to them . . ." Her words trail into nothing.

"Drew would never hurt me, Mom."

With a tenderhearted smile, she sweeps the hair from my face, saying nothing.

"He's a good guy," I add.

"I'm sure Vangie thought Eddie was a good guy, too, when she first met him."

"We've been together three years." It's practically a lifetime in high school years. "I know him better than anyone, and he wouldn't hurt a fly. He'd never hurt me."

"I like him very much," she says. "But people change all the time, especially as they get older. You just never know."

She's not wrong. In fact, she's almost always right about everything. But she doesn't know Drew like I do.

"Promise me you'll never stay with someone who doesn't treat you the way you deserve to be treated," she says. "I know you know that, but as your mother, I need to say it, too. You need to hear it. Sometimes I think had

Vangie's mom had that talk with her, maybe things would've turned out a little differently for her."

"I'm nothing like Vangie. You don't have to worry about me."

My mother kisses my forehead and pulls my covers to my shoulders. "Thank goodness for that."

CHAPTER 17

SYDNEY

"I'm showing there's no payment due at this time," the Mastercard representative tells me over the phone Monday.

"Are you sure? I'm looking at the most recent statement . . ."

"I'm showing a balance of zero dollars. Looks like it was paid in full over the weekend, using our automated system."

I attempt to speak, but nothing comes out.

Is that what Drew was doing the other night when he was on the phone?

There's no way he suddenly came up with $4,800 and didn't mention it to me.

And why would he pay the entire balance when we have a million other bills to cover this month?

"Are you sure it wasn't a mistake?" I ask.

"All I can tell you is what my computer is showing me," she says.

"O-okay. And you're sure nothing's due at this time?" I realize the idiocy of asking a question she's already answered multiple times, but something seems wrong here.

It has to be a glitch or something.

"Yes, ma'am," she says. "Is there anything else I can help you with today?"

"No, thank you. That's all." I end the call and flip to the next bill in the stack.

An hour later, after a series of similar conversations, I'm dumbfounded.

Every single bill has been paid—to the tune of $70,000. The bank told me our vehicle title will be released this week and mailed to us. The mortgage company mentioned next month's payment was already paid.

I don't understand.

Earlier today I was looking up bankruptcy attorneys . . .

I'd decided there was no way we could dig ourselves out of this hole. While the thought of our names being printed in the *Shelter Rock Herald* and the idea of people gossiping about our financial woes makes me sick to my stomach, what choice did we have?

Until now . . .

It had to have been Drew. He's the only one with access to these accounts, but I can't imagine him suddenly coming into money and not telling me. And it's not like he could have borrowed against his 401(k) without my signature.

His parents don't have that kind of money.

And he wouldn't have asked my mom after everything she's spent on my sister's rehab the last few years.

How did Drew pull this off?

And more importantly, what else is he doing behind my back?

CHAPTER 18

AFTON

I'm eating dinner with Gram Tuesday night when another restricted call comes in.

It's the fifth one since yesterday.

Not a single voice mail.

"Someone was knocking at the door earlier when you were upstairs sleeping," Gram says, pushing the baked ziti around on her plate. "I didn't answer."

She never answers the door.

It could be the Pope and she'd still hide behind a curtain, pretend she's not home, and hold her breath until he's gone.

"It might have been the mom next door," I say. "The other day I asked the kids to send her over."

"The Ferals? Why?"

I steel my fork in my hand. "Gram, please don't call them The Ferals. We've talked about this before—it's hurtful. Anyway, I wanted to see if she heard or saw anything the other day when the back door was open."

"At first I thought maybe it'd be your mom. Haven't seen her in a while. Figured she's due to come knocking with her hand out." Gram shakes her head, reaching for her water. "But it looked like a guy today. The shadow. It was masculine. I don't think it was a woman. He was tall. Besides, your mom just walks right in like she owns the place. She wouldn't have knocked."

"We should get some security cameras."

"That's a little overkill, don't you think?" The ice cubes in her glass rattle.

The first few years I lived here, Gram refused to lock the door at night, saying Shelter Rock was the kind of town where people don't need to do that sort of thing. It wasn't until someone opened our door late one night and threw in a bag of dog shit with an angry letter addressed to me that she changed her mind.

"Not if there are people coming around the house." Er, *a person*. I suspect Drew, but I won't know for sure without proof. It wouldn't be unusual for one of my mother's . . . dalliances . . . to come looking for her around here, but with everything going on, Drew makes more sense.

"Aren't they expensive?"

"I don't think so?" I chew my bite. "Pretty sure they come at all different price points. I'll order some online when I'm at work tonight."

"If you insist." She lifts a palm in the air before returning her attention to her meal. "I just don't like the idea of being watched 24-7."

"Someone's been coming around the house—I want to know who it is," I say. "And the cameras won't be watching you, they'll be outside, so we can see who's opening doors or whatever."

"Did you make an enemy at the hotel?" Gram chuckles, obscuring her mouth with her hand. If she only knew how close she was to hitting the nail on the head. "You're always telling me about those crazy guests who make all kinds of demands like they're staying at a Four Seasons."

"No." I wipe my mouth on my napkin and crumple it over my empty plate. "I should hit the shower."

Carrying my dish to the kitchen, I give it a rinse and place it in the dirty side of the ancient double sink. Renovating this kitchen and finally getting a stove that doesn't take an hour to preheat and maybe one of those refrigerators with water and ice in the door will finally be feasible once I get my money.

On second thought, Gram would hate having strangers in the house ripping her kitchen apart.

I'd be better off buying us a whole new house—which I will—some place far from Shelter Rock.

◆　◆　◆

I'm getting ready for work later when I can't stop thinking about the unlocked back door, the man knocking, and the restricted calls. That coupled with Drew's pathetic attempt to gaslight me and suddenly a vivid picture is being painted.

Putting my hair dryer down, I snatch my phone off the bathroom counter and tap out a text to the man of the house.

ME: Stop.

I don't have to wait more than a few seconds for his response.

DREW: Stop what??

He didn't show up at the hotel the other night. Vanessa ended up canceling the reservation before I got to work. While I want to believe he had a change of heart due to our little conversation, my gut says they likely relocated their rendezvous.

Drew's too prideful to let me be right.

And he's too arrogant to be put in his place by the town pariah; the one they uninventively call "psycho killer bitch."

ME: You know.

I don't spell it out, I don't get specific. If I had hard evidence, it would be different, but for now ambiguity seems to be the most effective approach with him.

The less he knows *what* I know—the more he'll assume I know everything.

Three dots fill the screen as Drew types his response, only they disappear completely after a few seconds.

I wait another minute or two for a text that never comes.

Whatever he was going to say, he changed his mind.

That's all right, though.

I'll gladly have the last word.

CHAPTER 19

SYDNEY

October 16, 2003

"You're home late. Everything okay?" Dad asks my mom when she comes home. We're already eating dinner. Dad ordered Chinese takeout because he's not allowed to cook unsupervised. His rule. He claims it's because he can't cook, he can only burn things.

Mom places her keys and purse on the counter before slipping out of her leather flats.

"Afton had another blackout episode today," she says.

My ears perk.

"Vangie called me in tears. I had to cancel my last two appointments of the day and meet her at the hospital. She said she came home from school and Afton had destroyed her bedroom—ripped all the posters off the walls and the curtains from the windows. Her mattress was hanging off the frame. Smashed her mirror, too." Mom exhales as she locates a bottle of wine from the rack on the kitchen wall.

Dad hands her a corkscrew.

"She needed stitches in her hand—ten of them," Mom continues. "And they're keeping her overnight. Dr. Kleiner can't get there until tomorrow

morning, and personally, I don't trust the new hospitalist they have in the psych unit. Her case is delicate and she needs a doctor who knows her entire history."

"So they're just observing her for the night?"

Mom uncorks her pinot and Dad hands her two glasses—one for each of them.

The number of times I've seen my mother stress-drink, I can count on one hand.

"The poor thing has absolutely no recollection of destroying her room," Mom continues. "Vangie said when she got home, Afton was just sitting there in a daze, no expression on her face, calm as can be."

"Poor thing," Dad says. "Did something trigger this? Maybe seeing her mom with a black eye?"

My mother shrugs and takes a sip from her wineglass, the deep burgundy wine staining her pale pink lips.

"Syd, has anyone been bullying Afton at school? Has anything been bothering her lately? Has she said anything to you?" Mom asks.

I rack my brain.

A couple of days before homecoming Afton pulled me aside and told me Drew tried to kiss her in my basement. My initial reaction was to laugh. Her story was insane. I was upstairs doing dishes. Why would he try to make out with her in my basement with me mere steps away? Not to mention, she's not his type. Not even close. If he cheated on me with anyone—which he wouldn't—she'd be the last one on his list.

Deep down I suspect she's jealous of all the time Drew and I have been spending together lately. Three years and we're going stronger than ever, growing more inseparable with each passing day.

After I brushed off her allegation, I changed the subject and she seemed fine.

Never brought it up again.

I thought maybe homecoming might be awkward, but she was in great spirits, laughing and dancing and having the time of her life.

"I can't think of anything, no," I tell my mom. "Is she okay? Should I call her?"

"I'm sure she'd love to hear from you if you called her hospital room," Mom says. "This is all just so strange. She hasn't had a blackout episode in years . . . not since middle school."

Ah yes.

Those were a bleak couple of years that I'm sure we'd all love to forget if we could.

Seemed like every other week, Afton was blacking out or having some sort of emotional rage-fueled meltdown. As Mom and Vangie brought her from doctor to doctor and specialist to specialist, everyone had a different answer.

It's hormones . . .

It's the stress of junior high . . .

It's bullying . . .

It's deep-seated trauma from not having a father . . .

She's a highly sensitive kid . . .

Vangie used to call her "my little thunderstorm," which I thought was adorable, but Mom claimed it did more harm than help.

After a while, she was placed in regular talk therapy and prescribed medication under the supervision of one of the best adolescent psychiatrists in the area.

"Vangie's beside herself, blaming her work schedule and not being around enough to notice anything was off with Afton," Mom tells Dad.

"Does she really blame herself, or did she just say that because a nurse or doctor was standing there?" I interject.

Mom shoots me a knowing look.

"Anyway, please don't breathe a word of this to anyone at school. You know how kids like to talk . . ." she says.

I zip my fingers across my lips.

If there's one thing I'm good at, it's keeping secrets.

CHAPTER 20

SYDNEY

I wait until Drew's passed out Wednesday night before quietly removing his phone from the charger on his nightstand. Pressing the screen against my stomach so it doesn't light up the room, I tiptoe downstairs.

Never in my life have I done something like this, and I hate that this is what it's come down to, but things aren't adding up.

Desperate times and all of that . . .

Once downstairs, I pad to the laundry room, softly shut the door behind me, and tap his phone screen. The cramped dark space that perpetually smells like Tide and teenage boy body odor fills with bright blue light that sends a sting to my eyes. Squinting, I wait for my vision to adjust before tapping in his phone password: 073105.

Our wedding anniversary.

The iPhone vibrates and tells me to swipe up to use the Face ID feature, which is obviously not an option.

Slinking against the door, I exhale and fight the tears brimming in my eyes.

Drew has never kept anything from me his entire life, not even a password.

Taking my phone from my pocket, I pull up a web browser and attempt to log in to his old Hotmail email—the same one he's had since the beginning of the internet dawn. It's a miracle it has lasted this long, but he's diligent with unsubscribing and he signed up for some special junk mail filter.

That's the thing about Drew—he's a creature of habit. Not to Afton-level extremes, but he's always gravitated toward the familiar. If something's working fine, he doesn't see a need to fix it. On top of that, he's loyal. He's loyal to his sports teams, his favorite sneaker brand, even his breakfast cereal—he'd rather go without than "cheat" on it with a store-brand alternative.

Pins and needles fill my insides, alternating with waves of nausea so intense they rival the extreme morning sickness I experienced with my second pregnancy. Sickness that almost landed me in the hospital at one point. Drew took a week off work back then to take care of me as well as Alec, who was a busy, temperamental toddler. He had his hands full, but he did it all without breaking a sweat or laying an ounce of guilt on me.

With unsteady hands, I type in Drew's email address and password.

The screen turns white.

A second later, his inbox loads.

I'm in.

My shoulders relax, but my neck is stiff with tension that coils up my jaw and settles at my temples.

Thirty minutes later, I've examined everything from his main folder, to his spam, to his trash and sent files.

Nothing appears unusual or out of the ordinary—which is both relieving and disappointing.

I wanted answers.

And yet I didn't want them.

Ignorance is bliss.

But not knowing is agonizing.

Logging out, I pull up our Verizon account next and go through the latest activity connected to his number. Most of the numbers I recognize—his sister in Saint Louis; his grandma in Idaho; his best friend, Judd; his virtual assistant, Margaret; the kids' schools . . . but one of these things is not like the other.

Listed in the text message section of our account activity are a handful of entries that show he and *Afton* have been texting back and forth recently. I can't see what they wrote to each other, only the time stamps—some of which were in the middle of the night.

My stomach burns, and I push myself up to standing, hovering over the laundry sink in case tonight's dinner works its way up.

What are they doing?

What the hell is going on?

A rogue sob escapes my mouth. I hold my breath to keep it from happening again, clamping a trembling hand over my lips.

Five of Drew's work shirts hang from hangers—washed, starched, and ironed the way he likes them. I yank them all, tossing them on the floor. The hangers rattle against one another. I stare at the mess for a moment before deciding it did nothing to help me feel better.

I need . . . more.

A bigger release.

The last time I wanted to both cry and punch something at the same time was the day my father was killed. Pressing my hand over my chest, I wait until I feel my heart beating, then I close my eyes and do box breath after box breath until I've calmed down.

While I'd much rather scream until I'm blue in the face, I don't want to wake the boys, and I definitely don't want to wake Drew, who'll wonder what I'm doing in the laundry room, his phone in my hand and his clothes in a heap on the floor—in the middle of the night.

I'm not quite calm enough to exit this tiny room when the sound of footsteps pulls me from my dejected pity party.

They're too light to be Drew's.

Too heavy to be Cal's.

"Mom?" It's Alec. "Is that you?"

"Just doing laundry, Alec, go back to bed," I call, praying he buys it and that he didn't hear the way my voice cracked when I said his name.

The door swings open. Alec stands there, rubbing his eyes, his white T-shirt practically illuminating the small space.

"I thought I heard something," he says. "Like, I don't know . . . a bunch of weird noises."

Makes sense—his room is right above us.

From the moment he was born, Alec was a light sleeper. It made those first few years trying, and Drew and I had countless sleepless nights because of it, but we always joked that we didn't need a guard dog because we had Alec.

"Can't sleep. Thought I'd do some laundry," I say with a smile he probably can't see in this darkness. "Go back to bed, sweetheart. You have school in the morning."

He lingers, confused and sleepy, and gives me a half-hearted wave before disappearing.

I exhale.

Had he caught me red-handed going through Drew's phone, I'm not sure I could've explained it away.

I listen for the click of Alec's bedroom door upstairs a minute later, and once the coast is clear, I head back to bed.

Without making a sound, I return Drew's phone to his charger and trek across our soft woolen rug to my side of the bed.

He doesn't wake.

And he'll never know I had it.

But while my sole intention was to get answers, I'm going to bed with more questions than I had before.

With our bills magically paid now, I'm tempted to take a personal day tomorrow . . . my first one in over six months. Earlier Drew mentioned he was planning to go into the office—a rare occurrence these days. I have half a mind to drive past his agency every hour to make sure he's actually there.

I log in to my scheduling software from my phone and send an email to the four women slated to come in tomorrow at 9:00, 11:15, 1:00, and 3:30. When I'm done, I bury myself under the covers to get some rest, uttering a silent prayer that I'll have some real answers, real soon.

CHAPTER 21

AFTON

After work, I use the self-checkout at the Walmart on the edge of town, just off the main highway. The fewer face-to-face interactions I have to have with people in this town, the better.

$478.06 later, I'm walking out with overflowing bags of children's winter gear: boots, hats, snow pants, gloves, scarves—multiple pairs of everything in a myriad of sizes since I don't know what the neighbor kids wear.

I also threw in some kid-friendly food: bananas, sliced apples, microwavable Chef Boyardee, frozen peanut butter and jellies, cheese pizza Lunchables, and a family-sized jug of Goldfish crackers. I'd have purchased more, but my cart was already spilling over.

I'll come back in a few days and do a bigger grocery haul.

For now, this should suffice.

Once home, I lug everything from my trunk to the neighbor's house, knock on the door, and wait. The kids should be in school, but Tina's maroon Dodge Caravan is parked in the driveway.

I knock again, in case she didn't hear me the first time.

With her unusual schedule, she could be sleeping.

I'd hate to wake her up.

I twist the doorknob. My breath catches when the door opens freely. As quietly as I can, I place all the bags inside their screened-in porch then head home. It doesn't matter if they know who it's from as long as they get it.

Once inside my house, I hang up my coat, slip out of my boots, and head upstairs to attempt to get some sleep before my next shift.

My days at the Grantwell Hotel are numbered, and while I felt bad at first for quitting so abruptly, I was informed when I left this morning that I'll start training my replacement tonight, and I was asked if I could stay on at least an extra week if needed.

Those millions aren't going anywhere and I've yet to meet with that attorney, so I agreed.

"Afton?" Gram's voice calls from the bottom of the stairs. Turning, I find her standing with her hand on her hip, wearing the same muumuu as yesterday . . . and the day before.

"Hey, Gram."

"You just now getting home?"

"I stopped at Walmart after I got off. I wanted to get some snow gear for the kids next door."

"Aww. Well, isn't that sweet of you?" Her crinkled face softens. "I was going to tell you, I could've sworn I heard someone walking around in the middle of the night last night."

"Hmm . . . wasn't me."

"Yeah. I know."

"You sure you weren't dreaming?" I examine her. Even in her older age, she's as sharp as a tack 99 percent of the time.

"Positive."

"Upstairs? Downstairs?" I ask next.

"Both."

"Huh." I lean against the handrail, racking my brain trying to figure out who could've gotten into our house in the middle of the night—and why.

"Could've been your mother for all I know." Gram throws her hands in the air before settling them on her hips. "Lord knows she'd be one to riffle around here looking for who knows what."

It's not implausible—but my mother doesn't have a key.

"Couldn't have been her. I distinctly remember locking up before I left for work," I say. "And I double-checked that the back door was secure."

Gram shrugs. "I know what I heard and what it sounded like. Locked my bedroom door and stayed there. If they would've busted in, they'd have been met with your grandpa's old nine iron."

An elderly woman wielding a golf club from fifty years ago probably doesn't stand a chance against a more agile perpetrator with a gun or a knife, but I don't waste my breath.

"Why didn't you call the police?" I realize the stupidity of my question after it leaves my mouth. Gram would never open the door and invite a stranger into her house, even if they were there to help. A firefighter might be the only exception to that rule, and her house would have to be actively burning down. "Or me."

She waves her hand, poo-pooing the idea. "You know I won't bother you at work."

"If it ever happens again, I *want* you to bother me."

"Noted."

I head to my room, swallow two blue pills, and make a note in my phone to remind myself to order some security cameras and whatever other items I can find to secure our windows and doors. I add a second note about picking up pepper spray and any other self-defense gear I can trust Gram to use.

Drew—or whoever's coming by—seems to do their prowling when I'm at work, but it won't be much longer until I'll be home all night, every night.

I can't wait to see the look on his face when I catch him red-handed.

CHAPTER 22

SYDNEY

"Say something, Mom." I sit on the plaid sofa my mother normally reserves for her counseling patients while she sits behind her desk on the other side of the room. It's two o'clock in the afternoon, I've driven past Drew's office six times today, and his car hasn't been there once.

I reach for a tissue from the Kleenex box on the coffee table and dab the damp corners of my eyes.

"I'm still processing this," she says, which is concerning. My mother always knows the right thing to say. "It's all out of left field."

"You're telling me." I wipe my nose.

"What I don't get," she leans back in her leather wingback chair, her lanky arms crossing, "is that even if Afton had some sort of 'dirt' or something on him, how would she have gotten it in the first place? She doesn't talk to anyone but you."

Mom slides her mother-of-pearl glasses down her elegant nose and rests them upside down beside her closed laptop.

"Exactly. What could they have possibly been texting about in the middle of the night?" I ask the million-dollar question. "What was so pressing that it couldn't wait until normal hours? The other week at her birthday dinner, she was acting so strange . . . fidgety, impersonal, asking generic questions. It was her, but it wasn't."

"Hmm." Mom sits up, straightening the lapels of her ivory blazer, her lips jutting forward as she contemplates this. "I will say, Afton's always been loyal to you. And she's never been wild about Drew— romantically or otherwise. I think she tolerates him for you, to be frank. Always has. I also believe the feeling is mutual."

My mother is an astute judge of character. She can read anyone like a book and tends to pick up on little nuances most people overlook. People pay a lot of money to be in this room with her and her unrivaled listening skills, but today I can't help but feel like I'm not being heard.

"Normally I would agree, but—" I say before she cuts me off with a single pointer finger lifted in the air.

"Don't go assuming the worst. You have a limited amount of information and you're seeing this through a narrow lens." She steeples her fingers. "I truly don't believe Afton and Drew are having an affair, if that's what you're getting at."

Until I know more, nothing's off the table.

"Should I talk to her first?" I ask. "Before I talk to him?"

"You should talk to each of them. I don't think the order matters . . . hear them both out and see what's going on, then take it from there. That's all you can do." Mom checks her phone. "My next appointment's going to be here any minute, darling. I'm so sorry. I'm done at seven tonight if you want to talk some more?"

Rising, I collect my things and head for the door.

"Sydney?" Mom calls behind me.

"Mm-hmm?"

"Please be careful . . . around Afton, I mean." She winces as if she hates that she has to say that. "You said she was acting strange, and this is so out of character for her to text your husband in the middle of the night. We know how she can get sometimes—or rather, how she used to get. I'll reach out to her as well. Maybe I can stop by for a visit? I've always been her voice of reason."

"I'd appreciate that."

I drive home in silence, my knuckles translucent against the steering wheel, the window cracked a couple of inches to let in a sobering amount of ice-cold air.

Passing Drew's office along the way, I'm semirelieved when I spot his Explorer in the parking lot.

If only I knew where he spent the first six hours of his day . . .

CHAPTER 23

AFTON

Two visits to Walmart in one day—lucky me.

As soon as I got home earlier, I couldn't sleep. Too much restlessness. Rather than pace the house and let my busy mind get the better of me, I came back to grab more food for the neighbor kids.

I'm pushing a laughably full cart of groceries toward the exit when I spot a familiar face, one I haven't seen in ages.

"John," I call out to my former public defender, John Gregory. "Hey."

It's been years since I saw him last. His once dirty-blond hair has faded to platinum white and his face is covered in more wrinkles than I remember, but I'd recognize that stiff gait anywhere.

He scans the area, searching for the person who called his name among the incessant beeps of the checkout lanes. His eyes are squinted behind his horn-rimmed glasses, but they soften when he spots me.

"Afton, hi." He makes his way to me, a slow smile spreading across his mouth. "What are you doing out and about?"

His gray eyes fall to the mountains of grocery sacks in my cart.

"All that isn't for you, is it?" He asks his question with a chuckle and a gleam in his eye. For someone who made a career out of giving people the benefit of the doubt, he's always been an eternal optimist and a bit of a jokester. I've always wondered if it was a coping mechanism given his line of work or if he was inherently that way, though I imagine it's a little of both.

"Buying some food for the neighbor kids." I open my mouth to elaborate before changing my mind. It'd be easy to tell him how starved the kids look and how the mom is never home and how I had to buy them snow gear earlier, but at the end of the day, I don't know their full story. It'd be impolite to elaborate on this any further.

I've been on the receiving end of those kinds of assumptions more times than a person should. Stooping to that level, however natural it may come to us humans, isn't something I want to do—especially in front of John.

He taught me to be better than that.

"So what's going on with you these days?" I ask.

"Retired at the end of last year," he says with a warmhearted smile. "Which to my wife means I'm her grocery getter, her errand runner, and her personal assistant. And here I thought I'd be bored."

There's no hint of animosity or resentment in his tone, and I love him for that. His wife, Betty, was as kind to me as he was—if not kinder. I lost track of the number of dinners I ate at their home during the case. Most public defenders wouldn't dream of having their clients over to their private home, let alone eating with them at their own dinner table, but John and Betty didn't hesitate to show me the love and compassion I wasn't getting anywhere else.

Betty once called me "a wilted little houseplant that just needed some TLC to bring it back to life."

I used to daydream about being adopted by them, which was ridiculous, but for a while we had this wholesome family life going on in my head where John took me fishing and Betty taught me how to bake strawberry rhubarb pie from scratch and Rick Carson was still alive.

After the trial, I served the home confinement part of my sentence at Gram's. John would check in from time to time, but eventually he moved on and I gave them space because they'd already given me so much. I didn't want to be a burden any longer nor did I want to trick myself into believing I was ever anything more than a charity case to a couple of kindhearted people.

"Could always be worse," I tell him.

He points his finger at me. "Exactly. You get it."

"How is Betty these days?"

"She's fostering dogs now," he says. "She turned our entire breezeway into a makeshift kennel. Had me add some heaters and this special waterproof flooring." He waves his hands like he doesn't want to get into the details. "I don't know. I just did what she said. You looking for a puppy these days? We've got eight of 'em. Born two weeks ago to this stray Betty took in. Had no idea the thing was even pregnant, then again she has a lot of fur. Not sure about the breed, but the vet's going to do one of those DNA tests for us."

"I'd love to, but Gram's allergic," I say.

It's true. We'd have to get some kind of poodle or doodle.

John frowns, studying me. I can't tell if he's in human-lie-detector mode or not. But a puppy is the last thing I need. My life is in flux and it's about to change in ways I haven't fully wrapped my head around. I need more stability before I start taking care of a living, breathing thing.

"What are you up to these days anyway?" he asks. "Still working at the hotel?"

"For now."

"Offer still stands if you want that job at my brother's firm in Kansas City . . ."

"Appreciate it, but Gram would never leave Shelter Rock." I give him an apologetic half pout. John's always looking out for everyone, always wanting better for everyone. He believes everyone is redeemable (with a handful of exceptions, naturally).

I've often wondered if it disappoints him that he spent all that time working on my case and ensuring I didn't lose my freedom, only for me to work an easy night-shift gig, live with my grandmother, and keep to myself.

"I've been seeing someone," I tell him. The words fall out of my mouth without me giving them too much thought, like a knee-jerk reaction. Maybe subconsciously I wanted to distract him from the thoughts I assumed he was thinking.

"Is that so?" His frown turns into a curious half grin.

"His name is Keith," I say. "He owns The Crooked Crowbar."

"And how'd you two meet?"

"I had some time off last summer and decided to go out for a beer because I was bored . . ." I figured people who hang out there didn't have much room to judge someone like me. "Anyway, he was serving drinks and we got to talking and we hit it off."

"That's wonderful. Good for you. Glad to hear that." His face lights up, like he's genuinely happy for me. It sends a burst of warmth to my chest that almost makes me forget how distant Keith was the other day.

I should visit him again soon . . .

Or at least shoot him a text.

He needs to know I'm thinking of him but that I've been busy.

"Well, I suppose I should get going." He lifts the two plastic bags he's carrying. "The missus is making her famous chicken pot pie tonight if you're hungry later."

"Appreciate the offer, but I'll have to take you up on that another time." I've got too much to do right now, too much to think about. "Tell Betty I said hi."

"Will do." With that, he's on his way.

The door greeter lets him go with a nod and a smile that fades into scrutiny the instant she spots me.

"Do you have your receipt, ma'am?" she asks, lumbering my way.

I pull the mile-long paper out of my purse and she all but snatches it from me. She goes through each item, line by line, one by one, making sure everything in my cart is accounted for while ignoring a handful of customers who exit the store without so much as a glance from her direction.

"Have a nice day," she says when she's finished, but there's no sincerity in her voice.

I'm on my way home when Syd calls.

"What's up?" I place my phone on speaker since my archaic Honda lacks Bluetooth capabilities. I make a mental note to upgrade my wheels once my money comes in. Nothing over the top or ostentatious, but something with the kind of everyday luxury features that make life a little easier. A heated steering wheel would be nice. Maybe even a moonroof. A backup camera would come in handy as well. Satellite radio. Navigation, too, for when I'm living in a new city.

"Thought you'd be sleeping," Sydney says. "Was going to leave you a message. Why are you up? Don't you work tonight?"

I don't waste my breath telling her my medications aren't working nor do I tell her I'm not particularly concerned with my lack of sleep now since my days at the hotel are numbered.

"Running a quick errand. What's going on?" I ask.

"Was going to see if we could get together and talk . . ."

I just saw her last week.

Is this about Drew?

Did she figure it out on her own?

"Of course," I say. "Tomorrow? We could get coffee in the morning?"

"I have patients at 8:30 and 10:30. Could you stop in around 9:45 and we can talk then? It won't take long."

Other than trying to talk me into Botox or facials, Syd's never once invited me to her med spa. She's always known it's not my thing. I don't even wear makeup.

"I can make that work," I say.

There's something off about her. A despondency in her tone. Or maybe it's exhaustion.

"Is everything okay?" I ask as I cruise to a stop at a red light. I can feel the man in the car beside me staring me down—his glare heavy and laced with hatred so thick it penetrates the glass and steel that separates us.

A familiar sinking sensation fills my stomach and chest.

I'd do anything to blink and be home already.

After twenty years, I should be used to this by now, but it still gets to me.

The light switches to green, and I return my attention to my best friend.

Exhaling, she finally answers. "No. Everything's not okay."

I check the dash clock. By the time I drop off groceries, I might have an hour before I have to get ready for work. It kills me that I can't go to her and be there for her right now.

"Do you want to meet tonight?" I ask.

"I wish I could . . . let's just plan on tomorrow morning."

"Of course," I say before adding, "Whatever it is, it'll be fine. I promise."

Because I'll make sure of it.

CHAPTER 24

SYDNEY

"You'll never believe what happened this week," I tell Drew over dinner Thursday evening. The chicken on my plate is dry—my own fault. I was spacing out, too busy mentally practicing what I was going to say to my husband instead of listening for the oven timer.

It's a rare evening when it's only the two of us. Alec's working at the grocery store, Cal's having supper at a friend's house, and Quincy took his food to go—opting to eat in his room, in front of the gaming rig he built after stockpiling two years' worth of chore money. Ordinarily I wouldn't allow that, but I needed some alone time with Drew so we can have a desperately needed conversation.

"Oh yeah? And what's that?" My husband's handsome face is painted in flickering candlelight. Once he realized it was just going to be us, he dimmed the lights, lit some dusty pillar candles, and uncorked a bottle of merlot he found in the back of the garage fridge.

I can't recall the last time we went on a proper date—it must have been Valentine's Day last year?

"You going to tell me? I'm on pins and needles over here." Drew flashes his megawatt grin from across the table before reaching for his wineglass.

Is he smiling because he knows?

Is he smiling because he's the one who paid everything off?

I snap out of it before my mind wanders down the same dark and winding path it traversed earlier today. For a solid two hours, I was convinced he was embezzling (from his own company, no less) and that he only paid things off because he felt guilty for cheating on me with Afton.

I *know.*

I know how it sounds.

"So. Um. Apparently someone paid off the minivan for us." I hide my face behind a sip of merlot, gauging his reaction as best I can in the subdued light that surrounds us.

Drew laughs.

"I'm not joking," I say. "I'm being serious. Someone paid off our van."

The amusement in his eyes vanishes. "Who would've done that?"

"I was going to ask you the same thing."

"You're sure this isn't some kind of joke or something?" He scoots in his chair, adjusts his posture, and clears his throat. "Or maybe a mix-up?"

I shake my head. "Nope. Not a joke. Not a mix-up. Not a technical glitch. The bank is mailing the title to us in the next seven to ten business days."

His cheeks puff as he exhales, and he brings his fingers to his temples. If I had any pennies to my name, I'd give them all for his thoughts.

"Not only that," I add, "but whoever paid off our van also paid off all our credit card debt *and* medical bills."

He sniffs. His lips move, as if he wants to say something, but nothing comes out.

"Seventy thousand dollars of debt *gone.*" I snap my fingers. "Just like that."

Drew rakes his hand along his five-o'clock shadow.

"I don't understand," he says.

"That makes two of us." I lean back, distracted by the way the candlelight turns my bloodred merlot into the prettiest shade of scarlet, like an incandescent ruby.

"Was it your mother?" he asks.

I shake my head. "She couldn't have done that and she wouldn't have—she doesn't know a thing about our finances."

And she never will.

She'd be devastated to know that her one child who didn't screw up their life is screwing it up financially in real time. While I'm not in jail like my brother or checking in and out of rehab on a regular basis like my sister, the shame is heavy all the same. The prideful light in her eyes would extinguish, and maybe it would come back someday down the road, but it would never be the same. It'd always be a little less bright—and that would kill me.

"It wouldn't have been my parents," he states the obvious. "Who else . . ." Drew sits straighter. "You told Afton last week that we were struggling, right?"

"She doesn't have that kind of money and even if she did, she wouldn't use it on us," I say. "Don't be ridiculous."

"Are you sure?" He tips his chin, swirling his merlot. "She's been a little off lately. Maybe she's having another psychotic break? I know we're not supposed to use that word, but I don't mean it in an offensive way. She has a history . . ."

My mother implemented a rule twenty years ago that we never use words like "mental" or "insane" or "psycho" or "psychotic" when talking about Afton because those were derogatory terms.

I close my eyes and gather a deep breath.

There are many things we don't talk about.

We don't talk about my father's death. We talk about his life, his legacy, and our memories of him. But not the circumstances surrounding his murder, the trial, or the fallout—family rule.

My mother had us all in counseling for years afterward to deal with the trauma of losing him the way we did.

Max turned to alcohol.

Stacia turned to hard drugs.

I turned to my boyfriend—Drew became my drug of choice, and I suppose he still is.

I meant the vows I took on our wedding day . . . 'til death do us part.

Lately, I'm questioning if he meant them, too.

"Why'd you change the passcode on your phone?" I ask while I have his undivided attention.

He sniffs. "Where'd *that* question come from?"

"The other day, I needed to make a quick call and my phone was in another part of the house. I went to use yours and I couldn't." I'm a terrible liar but the situation is plausible.

"Why didn't you just ask me?"

"You were sleeping. I didn't want to wake you."

He rolls his eyes, giving a slight groan like he doesn't want to elaborate.

"What?" I ask, blinking, all ears. "Tell me."

"I sold my phone on craigslist a few weeks back," he says. "We needed the cash, and I got seven hundred for it. I've been using my old phone."

Reaching into his pocket, he pulls it out, showing me the two cameras on the back. Now that I think of it, his old phone had three camera lenses plus a light.

"Why would you change the passcode, though?" I ask the question he still hasn't fully answered. "It's always been our wedding anniversary."

"Security reasons. I've used that old code for the last fifteen years. I didn't swap out my SIM card or anything when I sold this one, and I gave the kid my old code so he could deactivate the device himself. You know I'm terrible with that stuff."

"Why didn't you ask Alec? Or Quincy? Hell, even Cal could've done that for you."

"And what would I have told them when they asked why I was selling my seminew iPhone?"

He has a point. The boys have no idea how hard it's been to put food on the table lately. The last several grocery store runs were put on credit cards that were already bloated and pushing their limits. I don't want to burden them with that knowledge.

My heart breaks at the thought of Alec handing over his paychecks to chip in or Cal pulling out of basketball to save us money. We've worked hard to instill altruism and compassion into our boys—I never dreamed they might one day need to use it on us.

"So you changed your passcode for . . . *security reasons*." I restate his answer, making sure I understand it. "Were you worried the craigslist kid was going to break into our house and steal your old iPhone?"

"Syd, I love you to death, but you're making this way more complicated than it needs to be." Drew slices into his dry chicken. "The way I see it, you can't be too careful anymore. People can hack into things remotely. I've used those same numbers forever. Since Cal was a baby. You know that. You want my new code?"

Of course I do, but in the vein of this conversation, it makes me feel petty to say yes.

"It's 090800—our *dating* anniversary," he says. "Anyway, can we get back to the seventy grand thing? That's kind of a bigger deal than a stupid passcode, don't you think?"

It is and it isn't.

I still don't know why he was texting Afton in the middle of the night.

"Can they trace the funds or anything?" Drew asks.

"They all said the payments were made using their automated systems. They wouldn't be able to tell us the name on the payee's account or any banking information. It's all encrypted."

He chews, swallows, and points his fork in my direction. "I swear it has to be Afton. I know you don't think she'd do it, but you didn't see that crazy look in her eyes the other day when she was giving me that come-to-Jesus talk."

"What all did she accuse you of anyway? You never elaborated."

"I don't even want to say them out loud because that's how *insane* they are." He shakes his head in disgust. "Sorry. I know we're not supposed to use that word when we're talking about her . . . I just . . . you know what I mean, right? She needs help. Something's going on with her. She's not all there."

What he's saying gels with what I experienced at El Guapo's a couple of weeks back, but if he truly felt she was having a mental health crisis, why is he texting her? Why is he feeding into it? Why didn't he come to me or my mother and let one of us handle it?

"She told me you two have been texting." It's my second lie of the night, but it's necessary. "Why?"

Drew all but throws his fork and knife down; they clang against his plate so hard that I jump.

"So much for a romantic dinner tonight." Rising, he carries his dishes to the kitchen.

I follow.

"Why are you so worked up?" I lean against the counter while he rinses his plate, his shoulders knotted with tension as he moves with quick, abrupt motions.

It normally takes a lot to tick Drew off, and it's concerning that his text messages with Afton are the trigger tonight.

"Lately I feel like you're looking for reasons to be upset with me." He dries his hands on a dish towel, keeping his back to me. "Lately I feel like I can't do anything right around you."

I counter with, "Lately I feel like you're keeping things from me."

My mother would be proud of us, using "I" statements and discussing our feelings. Her only critique would be that we're not making enough eye contact.

"If I had anything to tell you, I would," he says, "but there's nothing to tell."

"You still haven't told me why you've been texting my best friend." Swallowing, I quickly add, "In the middle of the night."

Drew turns to face me, his expression incredulous and his eyes dark but wild.

"I told you, she's worried about you," he says. "And as for why she was texting me in the middle of the night, who the hell knows? She works nights, right? Doesn't she text you pretty late sometimes?"

Never.

"You texted her back, though," I say. "What was so urgent that it couldn't wait until morning?"

"Why are you making something that isn't a thing into a thing?!" He smacks the dish towel against the sink. "Everything I do, either you question me or you don't believe me, when everything I ever do, Sydney, is for *you*."

"I never said I didn't believe you."

"You didn't have to. It was written all over your face."

"There's just a lot going on . . . I'm trying to make it make sense."

Drew slicks his palm against his slackened jawline as if he's putting his guard down, and then he makes his way to me, wrapping his arms around me and pulling me in. Breathing in his familiar scent—the faded laundry starch, what remains of his morning aftershave, the warm musk of his skin—I'm comforted.

But my solace is temporary.

As much as I'd love to accept our good fortune and believe every word coming out of his mouth, there's still one more question I've yet to ask.

"Where were you earlier today?" My tone is more accusatory than I intended, but I don't have the energy to moderate my emotions anymore. I'm exhausted, still as confused as I was before, and all I want is for one damn thing to make sense.

"What are you talking about?"

I remove myself from his embrace, peering up at his expressive, coffee-colored irises with the fringe of lashes so dark it makes him look like he's wearing makeup. I've always loved that feature of his, always wondered if we'd someday have a daughter who would inherit his gorgeous, disarming gaze.

All three of our sons have my eyes—which can only be described as dark denim that's been washed a few too many times—dusty, boring blue.

But I digress.

So much of this life is beyond our control, but I never thought my marriage would be one of them.

"I worked all day," he says. "Why do you ask?"

"I drove by your office . . . you weren't there."

He squints, glancing to the side. "What time?"

"Eight AM . . . nine AM . . . ten . . . eleven, twelve, one . . . I believe your car was there at two." The entire day feels like a surreal blur, and I can't believe I'm admitting to stalking him today like it's no big deal.

"Jesus, Sydney. Really? I thought you had to work today?" Pinching the bridge of his nose, he then waves his hand and adds, "Did you cancel your appointments so you could follow me?"

"I wasn't following you." I don't tell him I was fully prepared to do so if I saw him out and about. Not sure how long I'd have gotten away with it before he'd notice our van tailing him, but I wasn't above trying had the chance arose.

He takes a step back, giving me the kind of bewildered glare you'd give an audacious stranger, not your beloved wife.

I remind myself he's the one in the hot seat, not me.

A moment later, Drew pushes past me, our shoulders brushing, and then he swipes his phone off the charger.

"What are you doing?" I ask.

"Calling your mother." He enters his *new* passcode—090800—then pulls up her contact and places the call on speaker.

I reach over and tap the red button, ending the call in the middle of the first ring.

"Please don't get her involved," I say. "She's already got enough on her plate with work and my sister."

Drew slams his phone down so hard I recoil.

He'll be lucky if the screen isn't shattered.

Grabbing a fistful of thick hair, he blows a breath between taut lips.

"I was calling your mother because someone needs to talk some sense into you," he says. "Not because I want to get her involved in . . . whatever the hell is going on here. I think you've been working too much, not sleeping enough, and now you're having these . . . I don't know . . . delusions, paranoias."

Pointing in his face, I say, "Don't you dare turn any of this around on me."

I will *not* be gaslit in my own home by my own husband.

With that, I leave the room.

The number of major fights Drew and I have had in our marriage I could count on one hand—before tonight.

"Please don't walk away from me," Drew calls out, but he doesn't follow.

I stop at the bottom of the stairs, my back turned toward the kitchen where he remains planted. Early in our marriage, we promised we'd never walk away from each other nor would we go to bed angry. We've yet to break that promise in all these years, but there's a first for everything.

"I need some space," I say, looking back over my shoulder.

A hint of pain registers on his face, followed by a flash of confusion in his eyes.

"I'm meeting with Afton tomorrow," I add, "so if there's anything you'd rather me hear from you, say it now. Otherwise I'm sure she'll tell me everything I need to know. She'll answer all my questions without turning it around on me. I wish I could say the same for you."

"You and I both know she's going through something right now. I wouldn't trust anything coming out of her mouth."

"Why were you really texting her in the middle of the night? What was so urgent? Anyone else texting you would've ignored until morning."

"Seriously?" Drew lets his arms fall, limp and defeated, against his sides. "You think I'm doing something shady behind your back because your best friend—who hates me and who has always hated me—was texting me in the middle of the night, reminding me of what a shitty husband I am."

"Can I see them? The texts?"

He grips a fistful of air.

"If it'll make you feel better," he says. Unlocking his phone, he hands it over.

Despite the fact that this is what I wanted, getting it makes me feel like the loser in this scenario. Nevertheless, I hold my chin high and pull up his most recent texts with Afton.

"These don't make any sense . . ." I scroll through them, noting how Drew only ever replies with question marks or polite requests for her to leave him alone. He's not feeding into her. All the animosity and antagonizing is coming from Afton. "It's like she's accusing you of something without saying what that something even is . . ."

Drew closes his eyes, nodding. "That's what I've been trying to tell you. She's not herself right now. She's not making sense."

I give his phone back.

"I'm going to go for a drive," he says, "to clear my head. I think we could both use a break from *this*."

Drew disappears into the kitchen. I don't move from my place at the bottom of the stairs. A second later, his keys jangle and the garage door opens and shuts on its whiny hinges.

Returning to the dining room, I clear the rest of the dinner dishes, dumping my uneaten food in the trash. All day, I haven't been able to take more than a handful of bites of anything without feeling like I'm going to get sick.

Exhaustion washes over me, settling deep into my marrow.

I wash up for bed and collapse on top of our comforter, throw pillows and all. It doesn't feel right climbing under the covers without Drew, ending the night with the bitter taste of our conversation in my mouth instead of the minty sweetness of his toothpaste.

I close my eyes for just a second . . .

When I wake, the space beside me is still empty and the alarm clock reads 12:08 AM.

There's a missed text from the ER supervisor on my phone, asking if I want to pick up any shifts this weekend, but I don't reply.

I'm more concerned with the whereabouts of my husband.

Tiptoeing downstairs, I hold my breath as I peek into the living room, fully expecting to find Drew passed out under his favorite Kansas City Royals blanket.

But the sofa is empty, nothing but a big, dark blob in a big, dark room.

I make my way to the garage to see if his car is still here.

My stomach plummets when I flick on the light and find his stall vacant.

I trek from room to room to see if he left a note.

He didn't.

And he never texted me.

I don't know what this means . . . and I don't know if I want to know either.

CHAPTER 25

AFTON

"So, the owner has a strict no-phones-at-the-desk policy," I say to my trainee, Caden, Thursday night. He can't be older than twenty-one, maybe twenty-two. It's his first night and as I took him around the hotel, giving him the grand tour, every time I turned around I swear he was sliding his cell phone out of his pocket and sneakily texting someone or checking some social media app. "If you think this is one of those jobs where you can sit around on your phone all night, wasting time, you're wrong."

I keep my tone light, so he doesn't shoot the messenger.

Then again, this won't be my problem before too long.

Still, I want to train him properly.

Pointing to a black camera in the ceiling, I say, "See that? The owner can check those any time she wants. If she sees you're on your phone a lot, you might get written up."

In fifteen years, I've not been written up once. I've only called in sick maybe five times total, and I've never been late for work. It still hasn't hit me that soon I'll walk out those automatic doors forever.

"Yeah, I know," he says. "She's my aunt."

Apparently nepotism is alive and real, even in Shelter Rock.

I'm glad she's starting him at the bottom rung of the ladder, though with his current mindset it's going to be a while before he reaches the top.

"Okay, what's next," I say to myself. I've already shown him every floor, taught him what to do when the second floor ice maker is screeching, and showed him where we keep housekeeping carts and supplies. "Do you know the history of the Grantwell?"

The owner is huge on making sure all staff are educated in that regard, though in my tenure here I've never once had to act as a docent. I imagine the day shift is different, and in case they ever move Caden to days, he'll need to know.

He blinks his watery eyes, yawns, and looks like he could pass out standing up. I remember those early days, thinking I didn't need to sleep before coming in. I was young and convinced I could pull an all-nighter and just sleep the next day, but it always catches up with you.

He'll figure it out with enough time.

"Okay, so the hotel was originally built by a man named George Grantwell II. He moved to Shelter Rock in the late 1800s—1892, I think? Anyway, he opened a garment factory that at one point employed over a thousand people, most of whom were locals. Because this town was so small at the time, there weren't enough houses or living accommodations, so he built this hotel—which used to actually be an apartment building. Hundreds of families lived here for the first few years, while he developed some of the local neighborhoods around town. Grantwell Pass is one of them. Grantwell Cove is another. Then there's Grantwell Commons. Millicent Street is named after his first wife, who died of tuberculosis before this building was even finished. That's her portrait on the wall over there, by the way. Then we have Hortensia Drive, which was named for his second wife, Hortensia Rothschild—of *thee* Rothschilds."

Caden looks as lost as a toddler in a Halloween corn maze.

I'm not even sure he's listening, but at least I'm doing my due diligence and passing on this information.

"Honestly, I'm shocked George Grantwell didn't petition to have Shelter Rock renamed for himself after everything he did for this town," I say. "He built the first hospital, funded the first fire department . . ."

Caden coughs into his elbow.

This must be what it feels like when an adjunct professor lectures a room full of bored, dead-eyed students.

Cynthia used to be an adjunct instructor at the local community college many years ago—which reminds me, I owe her a call. She called to check on me yesterday, and I completely spaced it off.

"Do you know how Shelter Rock got its name?" I ask. Back when I was in high school, our history teacher, Mr. Klinefelter, spent a full week on Shelter Rock's infamous Civil War–era past. I'm pretty sure he retired shortly after we graduated. Maybe he took all that information with him when he left.

Caden doesn't answer my question, so I take it as a no. Regardless, I launch into a whole spiel about the Civil War battle that took place here and how our troops were obscured by the rocky cliffs along the riverbank, which ultimately saved the lives of 184 men, nurses, and medics.

He sniffs, itching his nose.

There's a whitehead on the side of his nostril, ripe and distracting.

"You're not much of a talker, are you?" I ask.

His aunt was smart sticking him on nights because he is not a people person. I'm not much of one either, but I've learned how to fake it when necessary.

He'll get there someday.

"You're going to have to smile when we have guests," I tell him. "You know that, right? You'll need to look alive."

Heading behind the check-in counter, I log back in to the system and pull up the main software.

"Why don't we have you practice checking people in?" I make a dummy reservation under my own name and step aside. I showed him how to do this earlier, but this will tell me whether or not he was paying attention.

Caden plops in front of the computer, taking his time adjusting the chair before reaching for the mouse and clicking around on the screen.

A million seconds later, I'm checked in.

Huh. He *was* paying attention.

Could have fooled me.

"I'll show you how to view the reservation list next." Hunching over him, I take control of the mouse and pull up a different screen.

"Is it true you killed someone?" The Nepo Baby finally breaks his silence.

Standing straight, I clear my throat. "No."

"Why does everyone say that?" he asks. There's a light in his eyes when he swivels to face me. For the first time all night, he's animated and engaged. "Like, what really happened that night?"

I ready one of my canned, go-to responses that I've honed over the years, but then I stop.

He isn't looking at me with hatred or disgust, but almost an innocent curiosity.

He isn't afraid of me—he's genuinely interested.

But I don't let it flatter me. He's probably one of those true crime junkies.

I've never understood those kinds of people. Who wants to be entertained by someone else's horrific tragedy? Cynthia says it's because some people's baseline is "anxious" and watching or listening to content that makes them anxious feels normal to them. Alternately she said that some people enjoy true crime because morbid curiosity is a natural human trait. That and it's a way to protect and educate ourselves about our deepest fears.

Perhaps it's different for people who actually lived these so-called true crime stories.

"Have you listened to that podcast episode *Crime Junkie* did on your case?" Caden asks.

"No." I've never heard of them, and you couldn't pay me enough to listen to what someone else has to say concerning something they know nothing about.

The truth is, no one knows for sure what happened that night.

Not even me.

"Let's stay on task, please," I say. "Here, you take the mouse. Click on that green button on the top that says 'reservations,' then click on 'view upcoming reservations,' then click on 'populate.'"

A list of names fills the screen. Maybe a couple dozen or so. For a hotel in the middle of nowhere with few amenities (not even an indoor pool), it's amazing it gets enough business to keep the doors open. Supposedly there's a state historical society grant the city uses to cover the property taxes, and the building has long since been paid off as the owner inherited it from her grandfather—who'd be Caden's great-grandfather. Judging by the way his eyes glazed over when I was running through Shelter Rock history earlier, it's probably safe to say he doesn't care about any of that.

There's a buzzing noise coming from the drawer containing my purse. I'm tempted to check to see who could possibly be calling me this time of night, but after lecturing this kid on staying off his phone ten minutes ago, it wouldn't be right.

"You want to get that?" he asks.

"Nope." I point to the computer monitor. "Okay, so we're going to print that out so you can see how to print something."

"Let me guess, I go to the drop-down menu and select 'print' . . ." His sarcastic tone is grating, but I let it go. There's no use getting worked up over something as trivial as this.

The printer behind us whirs to life, spitting out two white pages that are warm to the touch and smell of LaserJet ink. Some might find it pointless to print these, but the system goes down from time to time, so I like to have a backup on hand.

"Is it true you used a butcher knife to do it?" he asks.

Oh, my God.

"Like, what was that like? What did it feel like?" he continues his shameless inquisition. "They said you came up from behind and slit the guy's throat."

The prosecutors put a pretty strong case together based on the coroner's report and blood-splatter evidence. The horrible text messages I'd been sending my mother prior to that served as a motive. And me being the only one there, holding the murder weapon when my mother came home, pretty much sealed the deal.

But because I was only seventeen and had a history of blackouts, anger issues, anxiety, depression, and whatever else the child psychologist added to my laundry list of diagnoses, my public defender originally wanted me to plead insanity. In the end, after putting together an extensive self-defense case, we decided the best route for me was to enter an Alford plea—stating I was pleading guilty but maintaining my innocence.

The judge—a fair-haired woman with eyes like polished sapphires—must have felt sorry for me. Or maybe she attended the John Gregory School of Compassion. Either way, she deferred my prison sentence and condemned me to one year at a juvenile detention center followed by one year of home confinement and five years of supervised probation.

As long as I kept out of trouble, paid my fines, completed requirements like abstaining from drugs and alcohol, met with my probation officer regularly, and held down a job for those five years, I'd never have to spend a single day of my adult life behind bars. One misstep and I'd have been sent to prison to carry out my deferred sentence.

I'd never walked a straighter line in my life during that period.

Now, at thirty-seven, I'm free as a bird, though it's never felt that way.

Soon, though . . .

"You should let them interview you sometime," Caden says.

I frown. "Who?"

"The *Crime Junkie* podcast people. They would kill to talk to you—no pun intended."

"Hard pass."

"I'm just saying, if someone accused me of something I didn't do . . . I'd want to share my side of the story."

I've lost count of the number of news and media outlets who begged me for interviews, one offering to pay me fifteen grand for an exclusive sit-down. I was even approached by a publisher once with an enticing book deal. While it was tempting, I wouldn't be able to fill any of those pages or answer any of their questions.

With my blank memory, the best they'd get are blank pages and a blank stare.

I didn't want to waste anyone's time or money nor did I want to kick the hornet's nest by getting folks riled up about the case all over again.

"My aunt thinks you're innocent," he says. "For whatever it's worth."

"I know." She was a friend of John Gregory's, which was how I got this job in the first place. Had he not introduced us, who knows what I'd have been doing all these years.

"She's pretty upset about you quitting, but it worked out for me. My parents have been on my case to get a job all year. Took a year off of college because I didn't know what I wanted to do and now they're making me work."

"Sounds like you have decent parents."

He rolls his eyes.

I don't tell him I'd have given anything for two parents who gave one-fourth of a damn about me.

"How old are you?" I ask.

"Twenty-one, why?"

"Do you know Vanessa DeOliveira?"

Caden slants his head to the side. "Yeah. I do. Graduated with her. Why?"

"What's she like?"

He brushes his messy bangs off his pimple-covered forehead and shrugs.

"I don't know," he says, "she was a cheerleader—no, she was on the dance team. All the guys liked her. Ran with the popular, preppy crowd. I never talked to her. Oh, there was a rumor once . . . that she was hooking up with the PE teacher, Mr. Jorgensen."

"Do you believe that?"

"I mean, everyone was saying it so it had to have been true."

I disagree with his sentiment.

Just because a lot of people say something doesn't make it factual.

"I once saw her coming out of his office by the gym, and her hair was sort of messed up. The blinds on his window were closed." He juts his thin lips out. "Looked pretty sus, but obviously I didn't see anything happen. She always liked older guys, though . . . our freshman year, she lost her virginity to a senior homecoming weekend. Next thing you know, all the freshmen girls are chasing the senior guys. We were chopped liver."

So Vanessa was the typical high school pretty girl who could have any man (or boy) she wanted. The world of Shelter Rock High was her oyster. She reminds me of Sydney, though Sydney had eyes for Drew and Drew only.

I lost track of how many guys tried to steal her from him, but those two were obnoxiously ironclad.

Grabbing the registry we printed a few moments ago, I scan the list of names, holding my breath and praying Vanessa's is absent. Slamming the paper on the counter, I steel my nerves to keep from reacting when I find her halfway down the page. According to this, she's coming in tomorrow night. And unfortunately for me, I'm off then—unless I can get someone to switch me.

If everything falls into place, this could finally be my chance to confront Drew in the act.

It's too bad they weren't coming in tonight. I'm supposed to see Sydney in the morning, and I'd love nothing more than to tell her what I know with cold, hard proof in hand. While my word is my honor, you can't end a marriage based on hearsay.

I know what I saw.

But Sydney needs to see it, too.

CHAPTER 26

SYDNEY

"Hey." Afton knocks on the half-open door to my med spa suite. With two paper coffee cups in hand, she places them on a little side table before hanging up her purse, shrugging out of her jacket, and getting comfortable in one of my guest chairs.

"Hi," I say, shutting the door behind her. "Thanks for coming."

"I brought you a hazelnut latte." She points to the coffee cups, one is labeled HAZELNUT LATTE, the other DECAF. Her eyes are weary, bloodshot. She looks on the outside the way I feel on the inside.

"Thanks for coming. I don't want to keep you long. I know you have to get to bed soon."

Afton waves her hand like it's no big deal.

"So what's up?" Cupping the decaf coffee in her hands, she gives me a sleepy grin that soon fades when she sees I'm not smiling.

"I want to know why you've been texting my husband in the middle of the night." I cross my arms, though I don't mean to come off as defensive or aggressive.

Afton swallows her mouthful of coffee and places the cup aside. Glancing down at her hands, she picks at a hangnail before smoothing her palms along the tops of her thighs.

"I didn't want to say anything . . ." she begins. "At least not until I had more proof."

My heart sinks down to my stomach, which is practically on the cold tile floor at this point.

Proof?

"What?" I lean forward, impatient. "What do you know?"

"I don't know how to say this . . ."

I unclasp my arms and let them fall. "Just say it. Whatever it is, just say it."

For the love of God.

"The other week, I saw Drew." She pauses, her eyes searching mine. "At my hotel."

We don't have the kind of money to waste on a hotel . . .

But I'm listening.

"He walked past me, kept his head down, got on the elevator," she speaks, motioning with her hands as if she's reconstructing the scene from her vivid imagination. "Got off on the fourth floor. I checked the security cameras and saw which room he went into."

The knots in my middle grow tighter, tenser with each word.

"The room was registered to a girl—a woman, I mean. A young woman," Afton continues. Her face shifts into a painful grimace.

"Do you know her name?"

Afton draws in a long, slow breath. "Vanessa DeOliveira."

It doesn't ring a bell.

I've never heard of this person in my life.

One of my patients is a DeOliveira, but she's my mother's age and never had any kids.

"You don't know her?" Afton asks.

I shake my head.

"She never . . . babysat for you or anything?" Afton lifts a brow as she studies me. "She's young. Graduated from high school a few years ago . . . I thought maybe that's how she knew Drew?"

The thought of my husband, my soulmate, my high school sweetheart stepping out on me with a high school babysitter is both humiliating and infuriating. Warmth floods my cheeks at the mere thought of this cliched nontruth getting out.

"What night was it?" I ask.

"It was a Thursday night, technically Friday morning, I guess," she says, eyes wrinkling. "Little over two weeks ago."

I check my phone, scrolling through my calendar. I was working a shift at the hospital on that date.

He was at home, with our boys. Granted, they're old enough to be left home alone, but surely Alec would've heard something or said something, right?

The entire notion of Drew running off in the middle of the night to have sex with some young woman while I'm trying to dig us out of financial ruin is laughable.

Yet it isn't implausible.

"What time did you see him exactly?" I ask.

"Three AM."

That would've been in the middle of my shift, so he wouldn't run the risk of me coming home early and catching him missing in action—if this is, indeed, what's going on.

"Vanessa is a local dental hygienist," Afton says. "I mean, I couldn't find much on her. Just a LinkedIn page. I had a cleaning with her last week, but I didn't have a chance to ask half the questions I wanted to. She's not very personable. Kind of like the lights are on, but no one's home? She's pretty but that's where it ends."

"Ah. He's only using her for sex. What a relief." I shouldn't be sarcastic at a time like this, but I'm not sure what else to be right now.

"I didn't want to tell you any of this until I had more proof . . ."

"Any chance you have the security camera footage?" I ask.

"No. I'm not allowed to . . ." She starts to say something then stops.

"What?" I ask.

"I saw her name on the guest registry for tonight. Vanessa's."

Interesting. I'm supposed to work at the hospital tonight . . .

"Things have been strange lately. With Drew and me. I, uh, actually stayed home from work yesterday so I could drive by his office every hour to see if he was there like he said he'd be. He was gone from eight to two," I say. "When I asked him about it, he didn't give me an answer. We actually had a pretty big blowout. He left last night. Said he needed to clear his head, but he didn't come home until this morning. I thought things were okay, but we haven't said a word to each other." Dampness clouds my vision. I reach for a tissue. "We never fight like this. He's not himself. I'm not me. Nothing makes sense."

Afton's concerned gaze washes over me. She's usually quick with an "it'll be okay" or "everything will work out" line, but today she's quiet.

"What are you doing later?" she asks after a bout of silence.

"I'm going into the hospital around ten. Why?"

"Maybe we could do a stakeout?" she asks. "We could hide in my car, in the hotel parking lot, and see if he shows up?"

It's a brilliantly terrifying idea.

I want to know the truth—I'm not sure I'm prepared for it.

A vision of me hauling after him with claws for nails comes to mind.

Catching him in the act would, no doubt, bring out the worst in me.

My mother always says that inside each of us is a stranger—someone who looks like us and sounds like us but is anything but. She calls it our shadow self. It's where we keep our anger, our shame, our guilt, our darkness.

"I feel like I'm living in a nightmare," I say, "like I'm living in some alternate reality. Do you ever feel that way?"

She shakes her head. "I'm sorry. I wish you weren't going through this."

"Oh—did I tell you? Someone paid off seventy grand of our debt." I slash my hand through the air. "Poof, gone. They called in and used the automated system and we can't figure out who did it or why. Drew swears up, down, and sideways he knows nothing about it, but who else would've had access to those accounts? What else is he doing behind my back?"

Afton chews the inside of her lip, resituating herself on her chair.

"It was me," she says. Her shoulders deflate, as if she's released some invisible weight, and she bites the smile curving on her lips.

"What?"

"I paid your bills. You told me how underwater you were, how you were working two jobs and still struggling to make ends meet," she says. "I wasn't going to say anything. Ever. And you don't have to pay me back. This is my gift to you. I wanted there to be nothing left for you to worry about. You shouldn't have to work yourself to the bone while your husband sits at home in his pajamas."

She's always hated the fact that Drew can work remotely, but most of his job he can do from his laptop. If I could do the same, I'd work at home in my pajamas, too. Though I can see how it looks from Afton's perspective: seeing him so comfortable and unbothered by life's burdens while I'm running a business solo and picking up twelve-hour night shifts at the ER.

It's harshly unbalanced, but other than filing for bankruptcy, cramming our family into a tiny house, and selling everything we own, running myself ragged seemed to be the lesser of those evils.

"Afton, how did you get that money?" I ask.

"I've saved it over the years. I don't have a mortgage or kids or any major expenses . . . the money was sitting there doing nothing. I wanted to do something positive with it."

At the very least, she should have been investing that kind of money—even I know that. Who knows, maybe it would've doubled or tripled by now?

"Th-thank you." I'd love to throw my arms around her and offer her some flowery show of gratitude, but I'm shell-shocked at the moment. "Afton, you do realize we won't be able to pay that back, right?"

Her rosy lips curl into a soft smile. "Like I said, it was a gift. You don't repay gifts."

"I . . . I don't know what to say . . ."

"You don't have to say anything," she says.

I've always hated feeling indebted to anyone. Fierce independence is deep within my marrow. My father was the same way. My mother, too. Asking for help isn't in our DNA or our language.

We give help.

We never need it.

At least, we never needed it until now.

Afton checks the time and rises from her chair, collecting her things.

"I have to bounce," she says, "but if you want to take me up on that stakeout, come to my place around eight thirty. You can park your car in our driveway, and I'll drive us there so that way he won't see your van."

I nod, my throat tight and full of all the things I don't know how to say.

Who knew it was possible to feel grateful and awful at the same time?

CHAPTER 27

AFTON

"Gram?" I call out when I get home. Locking the door behind me, I trot to her bedroom on the main floor and knock on the door. *The Price is Right* isn't playing on the other side. I check my watch. It should be on right now, only it's pure silence. "Just wanted to let you know I'm home . . ."

She worries sick when I don't walk in the door within fifteen minutes of clocking out. The other morning when I ran to Walmart, she gave me a stern talking-to about letting her know things like that. I told her she worries too much, but I agreed to be better about letting her know.

I'm about to head upstairs when a niggling sensation in my middle keeps me planted in place.

"Gram?" I call out again.

One of my biggest fears is coming home and finding her dead. At eighty-two, it's not out of the realm of possibilities. And I'd much rather her pass naturally, in her sleep, warm and comfortable in her favorite muumuu, but it always seemed like something that was still years away.

With my heart inching up my throat, I twist her doorknob and give the creaky wooden door a gentle push.

Holding my breath, I peek inside.

On her nightstand rests her water jug, the roll of toilet paper she uses as tissues, a TV remote, her reading glasses, and a stack of paperbacks.

Her bed is unmade.

And vacant.

Leaving her room, I trot down the hall, stopping at the door to the basement. Gram hates stairs on account of her bad knees, so she never ventures down there. She would if there were a tornado siren going off, but it's early February, hardly tornado season. Regardless, I call down there for her.

"Gram?"

No response.

I head down to look around anyway. Peeking around stacked storage bins, overflowing laundry baskets, and old wooden shelves filled with decades-old canned beans and pickles, Gram is nowhere to be found.

I check the living room on the main level next . . . no sign of Gram anywhere.

The baby blanket she was knitting the other day is folded neatly on top of a basket of yarn, with her favorite knitting needles poking out of one of the white skeins.

"Gram?" I call out, louder this time as my head fills with a dozen ugly scenarios which involve Drew—or whoever's been coming around here lately—harming her to spite me. "Gram, where are you?"

Sprinting upstairs, I check the spare room, the hall bath, and my room, only she's not there either. My heart hammers and every breath is shallower than the one before, but I make it back downstairs, find my phone in the bottom of my purse, and dial Izzie.

Maybe Gram had an emergency and Izzie took her to the hospital?

It'd be hard as hell to convince Gram to go willingly—but if she was unconscious and didn't have a choice, it'd be doable.

"Hi, you've reached Izzie Valdez with Visiting Nurses of Shelter Rock," her voice mail greeting plays, "please leave a message and I'll get back to you as soon as I can."

I'm pacing the kitchen, waiting for the beep, when I spot the two bottles of Gram's medication from last week, both of which are still empty.

I called in refills days ago.

Izzie should've picked them up by now.

What is going on?

I phone the Shelter Rock Hospital main line, request the patient directory, and ask the young man on the other end if Beatrice Murphy has been admitted there. He tells me he doesn't see her on the list, but if she was admitted in the past hour, they might still be entering her into the system.

Hanging up, I shoot Izzie a text, asking her to please call me ASAP.

It's then that I spot Tina's car in the driveway next door.

Maybe she saw something?

Throwing my coat on, I spring for the door and dash over. Breathless, I pound on her front door. By the time she finally comes out, my knuckles are beet red and numb.

"Tina? Hi," I say. "I'm Afton—I live next door. Have you seen my grandma, Bea, by chance? I came home from work and she's not home."

As she moves from the other front door to the one I'm standing at outside her screened-in porch, she hugs an oversized cardigan against her shapeless body. She's younger than I expected; I'd only ever seen her from a distance. And her eyes remind me of my mother's in a way— fierce yet sad all at the same time.

"I'm Afton," I say again, "I live next door. I know we haven't met but—"

"Yeah." The melancholy ferocity that resided on her face a moment ago turns into something darker. Normally I'd walk away and not give it another thought, but this is about Gram. "I know exactly who you are."

"Have you seen my grandmother? She's eighty-two, never leaves the house, and she's gone. I can't find her anywhere."

She takes her time peering over at our avocado-colored house. Lifting her arm against the doorframe, she takes a long, hard look at me.

"Or maybe you saw Izzie today? She drives a red Toyota Prius," I say. "She's Gram's nurse. Comes twice a week."

"I don't make a habit of sticking my nose where it doesn't belong," she says. "So no, I don't know where your grandma is. Can't say that I've seen her or her nurse either. Now, you, on the other hand—I do make a habit of keeping my eye on you. I know what you did. I know what you are. And I don't like you coming around my kids nor do I appreciate you insinuating I don't feed or clothe them."

"I'm sorry . . . you weren't home and they said they were hungry, and they were playing outside in the cold. I wanted to help."

"Because you think I'm a bad mother, is that it?"

"No, of course not," I lie. Shame on me for assuming. "My mom was a single mom and I know how hard it can be."

"How do you know I'm single?" she asks. While I've never seen a second vehicle at her house, I haven't ruled out the chance that maybe there is someone else in the picture, someone who maybe stays home and doesn't work, own a car, or get outside much?

"I'm sorry." I lift my palms in apologetic protest. "I shouldn't have presumed anything about your situation."

Tina moves closer to me, white cloudlike wisps of breath evaporating into the cold morning air with each exhale.

"I love my kids," she says, clutching at her chest.

"I know."

"They have everything they need." She takes a step closer.

I take a step away. "I'm sure they do."

"I mean, who do you think you are? Coming here? Knocking on my door when I'm trying to sleep?" she asks. If this conversation weren't so hostile, I could commiserate with her on the whole working-nights thing—if that's what she does. "I was on my feet all night, worked a double, just so I could come home, go to bed, and be woken up by Little Red Riding Hood looking for her grandma."

"And I'm so sorry about that . . ." The sooner I get away from this woman and out of this conversation, the sooner I can find Gram.

"And all those boots and snow pants . . . look at the size of my house. You think I have room for all that extra crap?"

That was the furthest thing from my mind at the time.

"What sort of mother would I be if I let some psychotic lunatic give my kids food and clothes?" She's fully outside now, her body shivering from the cold, though it doesn't seem to bother her. "We're not your charity case and we don't need your help. You talk to my kids, you give them anything again, and I'm calling the cops."

"Okay. Fair enough," I say, "but just so you know, I was only trying to help."

"By luring my kids into your home? Telling my son if he ever needs anything to go to you? Are you insane?" She laughs, raspy and thick and mean. "Actually, don't answer. I already know. You're crazier than an outhouse fly, everybody knows that."

They say no good deed goes unpunished.

There's nothing more I can say to this woman to make her see the errors of her misjudgment, so I turn to leave.

"Hey," she yells. "I'm not done talking to you."

The sound of her bare feet slapping against cold concrete behind me precedes the hard shove I didn't see coming. It happens so fast—one minute I was walking and the next I'm stumbling forward, tripping over the uneven crack of her walkway. Falling to the ground, I smack the back of my head against an old landscaping brick.

My vision turns blinding white before fading to the palest blue, which I eventually realize is the sky.

"You come over here again, there'll be more of that waiting for you." She wraps her frumpy cardigan around her torso and turns to leave, slamming the screen door to the front porch behind her and making a show of securing the lock.

Everything hurts when I try to sit up.

How a single fall can make all your joints and bones ache and throb all at once is beyond me.

"Hold on, hold on," an unfamiliar voice calls out.

My head thunders when I attempt to lift my neck to see where it's coming from.

A second later, a short, round woman with a white bob, rosy cheeks, and a lavender parka is crouched down beside me. She slides her arm under my elbow.

"I'm going to help you up, okay?" she says. "Looks like you took a little spill there."

I have no idea who she is, but I appreciate her assistance.

"These sidewalks can be so slick this time of year," she says. Clearly she missed the Jerry Springer-esque altercation. "Okay, hold on to me now, I'm going to hoist you up. I'm Ursula by the way, Ursula Finch. I live in that little brick ranch across the street."

I hold on to the thick fabric of her winter coat as she helps me stand. The world around me tilts sideways, causing me to stagger when I attempt to take my first step.

"Whoa, whoa, whoa," she says, grabbing fistfuls of my jacket to support me. "Let's take it easy . . ."

Her warm tawny eyes blanket me with a saccharin sweetness that makes me think of Gram—who's still missing.

I take another step, despite the ground feeling unsteady beneath my feet, and Ursula trots after me.

"Oh, honey, you're bleeding," she says, clucking her tongue. "The back of your head."

Reaching, I trace my fingertips just under my crown, where it throbs the most. There's an instant wetness, thicker than melted snow.

Examining my fingers, I'm met with the same sticky crimson liquid I found myself face-to-face with that fateful night two decades ago.

"I think we ought to get you to a doctor, make sure you don't have a concussion or anything," Ursula says. "You know that woman never salts her walkways, and she really should. I've seen her kids take a spill or two or three."

"I didn't fall." I grimace as I touch my throbbing wound. "Tina pushed me."

"Tina?" Ursula's lashes flutter, as if she's confused. "You mean Cassidy? The woman who lives in that house with her three kids?"

Why did I think her name was Tina?

"Yeah, whatever her name is—she pushed me."

Ursula's eyes rest on mine and she tilts her head to the side just so.

"Oh, honey, you really must have hit your head when you fell and it's got you all confused. I saw the whole thing from my living room window." She points across the street to the brick house with pretty white shutters and the American flag poking out from the front stoop. In the summertime, she plants red begonias and every spring a row of sunny yellow daffodils fill the landscaped sides of her driveway. "You were standing in front of that house for the longest time, looking like you were talking to someone, and then all of a sudden you turned to leave, took one step, and boom."

I appreciate her assistance, but I didn't hit my head *that* hard.

I know what happened.

"I have to find Gram." Every step I take toward our house makes me feel like I'm walking on a moving merry-go-round. I stop and rest when I get to my car, leaning on the trunk to gather my strength.

"Why don't you come home with me?"

Over the years, I always wondered who lived in that cheerful little brick ranch. It always looked so cozy at night, glowing with warm lamplight as the flicker of evening television painted shadows on its gauzy curtains. But working nights, I was never around when the homeowner was outside. I probably couldn't name three-fourths of the people who live on this street, and I've been here longer than most of them.

"I don't want to inconvenience you," I say.

"Don't be ridiculous, I insist," she says. "Why don't you come to my house? I'll get you all cleaned up and then you'll be on your way."

Still dizzy with a side of shell shock, I reluctantly agree to go home with Ursula. While I'd much rather be searching high and low for Gram, there's no denying I'm in no shape to drive.

Two minutes later, I'm seated at her kitchen table. It's a waxy golden oak that makes me think she's probably had it since the nineties, but it looks brand new. Not a nick or scratch anywhere. Her home is warm. Too warm. And it smells like blue Dawn dish soap and lemon Pledge. A crystal dish on the center of the table holds those little strawberry hard candies with the shiny red-and-green wrappers, the same ones Gram makes me buy each month because they're her favorite afternoon treat.

"Sit tight, I'll be right back," she says before returning with a first aid kit. "Believe it or not, a million or so years ago, I was a paramedic."

She pulls out gauze, Band-Aids, little bottles of rubbing alcohol and hydrogen peroxide, as well as various ointments.

"Your pupils aren't dilated, so that's a great sign," she says before examining my hands. She flips them palm-side up. "Looks like the sidewalk got you pretty good." Reaching for the gauze and one of the little bottles, she says, "Fair warning: this might sting a bit."

The burn of the peroxide against my raw palms is nothing compared to the screaming throbs pulsing through the back of my head.

"All right, let's check out your noggin next," she says with a loving, grandmotherly smile. Rising, she moves behind me. Her fingers are light in my hair as she searches for the open wound. "Ah, found it. Hmm. It's not as sizable as I thought it would be. Head wounds tend to bleed more than others, though."

"Do you think I'll need stitches?" I imagine my insurance expires soon, though what's an out-of-price ER visit to a future multimillionaire anyway?

"I don't think so?" she says with a little less confidence than I'd have liked to have heard. "But I'll be able to see it better once we clean it up."

Ursula gets to work behind me, apologizing every few seconds in case what she's doing is painful, but the truth is, I can't feel a thing going on back there—because I'm feeling *everything*.

"There we go," she says when she's finished. "I don't think you'll need stitches, but if that starts bleeding again later, you should probably get it looked at." Pointing at me, she adds, "And please don't drive yourself anywhere, okay? Wait at least twenty-four hours. If you absolutely need to go somewhere, come and get me and I'll take you."

"I appreciate that," I say, "but I have to find my grandma. She hasn't left the house in twenty years and she's not home. I think something might have happened to her?"

The jovial glint in Ursula's eyes fades.

If she lives across the street and saw me fall on the sidewalk, maybe she saw something else?

"What?" I ask. "Was an ambulance at the house earlier? Did you see Gram's nurse at all? Did you see them leave?"

Ursula presses her lips flat and takes the seat beside me. Placing her hand over mine, she says, "Sweetheart, like I said, you seem to be a bit confused . . ."

What the hell is she talking about?

"Your grandmother passed away . . . last month." She pats my hand, as if to comfort me, but I jerk it away.

She's lying.

"I was with her last night," I say. "We had dinner. I've been with her all week . . . you must have her confused with someone else."

"Beatrice Murphy, right?" Ursula asks.

"Yes, but she's not dead."

Lifting a finger, she says, "Be right back."

Waddling over to a kitchen drawer, she pulls out a small, thin newspaper clipping and hands it over.

There's a photo of Gram, maybe taken twenty or so years ago, but it's unmistakably her. Silver curls. Squared-off glasses. Pointy chin. Contagious smile.

"What's this?" I ask before I catch the heading along the top of the clipping that clearly states: Obituaries.

> Beatrice Louisa Conrad Murphy peacefully departed this earth on December 29, 2023. The only surviving child of Lloyd Conrad and Hilly Beecher Conrad, Bea was born at Shelter Rock Memorial Hospital on August 11, 1941. Beatrice attended Shelter Rock High School, where she met the love of her life, Dennis Murphy. Together they had one daughter, Evangeline "Vangie" Murphy Teachout. There was nothing Beatrice loved more than making her house a home and spending time with her beloved granddaughter, Afton, who took care of her until the end.

> At Beatrice's request, there will be no memorial service. Her cremated remains will be interred alongside her husband's at Grantwell Cemetery.

This can't be real.

"Are you all right, dear?" Ursula asks, her voice pillow-soft. She places a hand on my shoulder.

"It doesn't make sense . . . I was *just* with her."

The logical part of me knows the newspaper wouldn't print it if it weren't true, but I also know we had dinner together last night—pot roast with cherry-chip ice cream for dessert. And I watched her knit that baby blanket the other day. She had curlers in her hair. And she was upset with me for not telling her where I was going the morning I went to Walmart after work.

"Time has a tendency of playing tricks on our mind," she says. "Especially when it comes to grief. After I lost my husband, it took a while before it finally felt real. The days sort of blurred together for a while."

Handing the newspaper clipping back to Ursula, I manage a stunned and monotoned, "Thank you for getting me cleaned up, but I have to go now."

"Do you need me to walk you home?" she calls after me, but I'm already at her front door.

A burst of February cold fills my lungs as I make my way across the street, to an empty house now filled with more questions than things.

Once inside, I linger in the entrance.

Everything looks real.

I place my hand along the wall. Its hard plaster presses back.

The house is real.

The wall is real.

Heading to the living room, I sort through her basket of yarn, squeezing the soft skeins between my fingers before tracing my fingertips along a knitting needle. I press its tip against my arm until the sharpness digs into my flesh.

This, too, is real.

Dragging in a lungful of air, I can still smell her lilac perfume and her morning coffee and the gallon of Aqua Net she used to set her curls every day, but maybe those scents are baked into the walls and carpet and rugs and furniture.

After all, this was her home for over sixty years.

Ambling to her bedroom, I stand in the doorway for a bit, taking in the fact that the space still looks like she was here. It's like she could walk in at any moment, grab her remote, slip her glasses over her slender nose, and settle in for some daytime television.

All this time . . .

Was I hallucinating?

Did I imagine hearing her TV playing every morning?

Were those conversations we shared a figment of my imagination?

I take a seat on the edge of her bed as pressure builds behind my eyes followed by the gush of grief-stricken tears. Sobbing, I climb beneath her covers, inhale their familiar soft scent until I can no longer smell any of it, and cry into her pillow.

I never got to tell her how our lives were going to change.

I never got to buy her a new house.

I never got to tell her bye—at least, that I can remember.

The persistent buzz of my phone against the pillowcase pulls me out of a deep, dark sleep. With one eye open, I glance at Gram's old-school alarm clock on her dresser, the one with the bright red numbers.

It's 4:32 PM . . . I've been out for hours.

It takes a moment for my eyes to adjust to the caller ID on my screen.

"Restricted."

I've lost track of how many times this person has called me the past couple of weeks, but enough is enough. I'd block them if I could, but the fact that they're hiding behind a restricted number means that's not an option.

"What?" I practically scream into the phone when I answer. "What do you want?!"

"Uh, yes, hi. Is this Afton?" a woman's voice says from the other end. There's no telltale beep, like with one of those overseas scam operations, nor is there the noisy chatter of a call center in the background.

"Who's this?" I ask.

"This is Brenda Spooner, I'm Dr. Kleiner's nurse," she says.

Sitting up, I massage my temples. My head is still pounding from that little incident outside earlier, but I'm cognizant enough to recognize the name of my longtime psychiatrist.

"We've been trying to get ahold of you for a while," she adds. "You missed your last appointment, and according to our records, some of your refills have run out. It's important that you don't stop those cold turkey . . ."

I shake my head, despite the fact that she can't see me.

"I'm not out of refills." All the bottles in my nightstand drawer have more than enough in them last I checked.

"Anyway, we'd like to see you as soon as possible," she says. "Dr. Kleiner can fit you in . . ."

I tune her out for a moment, though not on purpose.

Gram was always the one who managed my appointments. Even though it wasn't necessary, she felt like it was the least she could do since I did so much for her. She'd always write them down on the calendar in purple ink and make sure to remind me in the days leading up to them.

But that's not what's on my mind—it's my lottery ticket.

If that episode outside with the neighbor never happened, if I've been hanging out with Gram's ghost all this time . . . what *else* have I imagined?

"I'm sorry, can I call you right back? I'm in the middle of something." I end the call without giving her a chance to respond and sprint upstairs, nearly toppling over on the way. My balance is still off-kilter, but I'll crawl the rest of the way if I have to.

The next thing I know, I'm on my hands and knees, shoving the mess under my bed aside and fishing that lockbox out from the pillowcase.

Propping the lid open, I'm met only with a crumpled Qwik Star gas station receipt.

"No," I say, unfolding it and smoothing it with the palm of my hand. "No, no, no, no, no . . ."

Rubbing my eyes, I squeeze them as hard as I can before checking the paper again.

It's still a receipt.

Nothing but a gas station logo where the Missouri Lottery emblem should be.

Slumping with my back against my bed rails, I bury my head in my hands, but I'm too cried out to shed another tear.

That ticket was real—to me.

I saw it. I double- and triple-checked it. It was a winner.

I've never been so sure of anything in my life.

And Gram . . . she was here, talking with me, eating with me, watching the news with me, telling me about the strange person coming around the house while I was gone . . .

Giving my arm a narrow pinch, I yelp in pain, pain that is undeniably real.

Phone in hand, I google "Beatrice Murphy Shelter Rock obituary." Normally when someone dies, their obit is posted on several different places online.

Sure enough, Gram's shows up on no less than seven websites. I click on the one for the local funeral home, read her obituary once again, and scroll down to read a handful of condolences, the first of which is from John Gregory.

> Beatrice was a delightful person that I had the privilege of spending time with many years ago. Our thoughts are with Afton during this heartbreaking time.

I think back to our little exchange at Walmart earlier in the week, specifically the funny way he looked at me when I mentioned I was still living with Gram. Here I thought he was disappointed in me for not making more of myself when he was probably wondering why the hell I was still talking like Gram was alive.

Heading to the hall bath, I splash some frigid water on my face, dry my eyes, and pull my messy hair into a low ponytail. I imagine there's still some dried blood in there and it could use a wash and some deep conditioner, but I can't stay here a minute longer—physically stagnant while my mind is laced with a cocktail of confusing thoughts and emotions.

Grabbing my keys, I drive to Keith's bar.

Seeing him always puts a smile on my face or at least provides a temporary distraction from whatever's going on in my life, and I sure could use one of those right now.

By the time I arrive, I have no recollection of the drive over, and I almost forget to shut my car door after climbing out.

Happy hour has already kicked off, and he's busy behind the bar when I stroll in. I find an empty seat on the end and wait for him to notice me.

Hard at work, Keith mixes a Tom Collins for an older man before pouring a draft Bud Light for the younger gentleman beside him.

Moving to the next patron, he nods as they rattle off their order and he gets to work.

I've always loved watching him in his element.

I've never been much of a drinker. Other than the lack of self-control that comes with being drunk, liquor could negatively interact with a couple of my medications. The first time I came here, I asked him for a mocktail and he laughed before making me a Shirley Temple with extra cherries. I hate maraschino cherries, but I was so taken aback by his kind gesture that I ate them all.

Keith's busy mixing another drink when he finally looks over and spots me.

I smile and wave—no small feat given the events of the day, but I'll muster up all the strength I have to wear a brave face for him. I don't want to sully our meetings with bad moods. I'd hate for him to think I only go to him in times of trouble. I want him to associate me with everything that is good in this world. I want to instantly put a smile on his face the way he puts one on mine.

It takes a good while, but eventually he makes his way to my end of the bar.

"Afton, what are you doing here?" He squints, his mouth agape.

This isn't exactly the warm welcome I was expecting.

He was like this the last time I stopped in, too, but I chalked it up to him having a rough day or maybe being mad that I hadn't been texting or calling him as often as before.

"What kind of question is that?" I chuckle because he has to be joking. "I came here to see you. Duh."

He leans in, hovering over his side of the bar. I angle closer, meeting him halfway.

"You have to stop doing this," he says. "We hooked up once. Last year. And you keep texting and stopping by like we're dating or something."

I sit back, attempting to piece together what he's saying.

I can distinctly recall dates we've had and nights we've shared and midnight conversations that have stretched long until the sun has come up. I know he's ticklish and he hates breakfast because it makes him nauseous to eat so early in the day. I know he's had three speeding tickets in his life. I know his sister's name is Hannah and he moved to Missouri from Vermont for a girl who dumped him the second they got here. I know his favorite song is "Blue Eyes Crying in the Rain," and he can't carry a tune to save his life but he has fun trying.

"Someone overheard you telling someone we were dating . . ." He cringes. "I hope I didn't give you any mixed signals last year, but it's not like that. I'm not dating you. I never was. It was a one-night stand, that's all."

I blink away the threat of tears before they have a chance to fall, and then I scrape my bruised ego off the floor and show myself out of The Crooked Crowbar for the last time.

I don't understand . . .

How do I have all these memories of him, all this knowledge, if he was nothing more than a one-night stand months ago?

Seated behind the wheel of my car, I let the engine idle while an obnoxious pop song plays from my speakers. This time it does nothing to lift my spirits or distract me from the shit show that my life has suddenly become.

Pulling up my texts, I tap on my messages and go through my exchanges with Keith. I know we've texted.

Often.

I remember.

Only there's nothing here but me sending him random messages and him leaving me on "read."

He didn't reply to a single message, not once.

"Oh, my God." I sink back, wishing I could melt into my seat and disappear from this earth along with the false reality I'd been living in.

I had a good life in that false reality.

I'd won the lottery.

I'd quit my dead-end job.

I had a boyfriend.

Gram was still alive.

I drive home, curl up on the sofa, and stare at the ceiling for an infinite amount of minutes, minutes that make it seem like time isn't real. Some would argue time is a human construct, but humans construct a lot of crazy things—how do you know what you can trust? What you can believe? What's genuine and what's not?

The sound of the neighbor kids playing outside next door perks my ears and pulls me from my thoughts, but I don't have the energy to get off the couch and see if they're wearing any of the snow gear I gave them.

Part of me doesn't want to know because what if I imagined that, too?

What if I never ordered them pizza or bought them snow boots?

Reaching for my phone, I call Cynthia, hardly able to press the buttons fast enough. I'd been meaning to call her back for days, but I've been preoccupied. If anyone can make sense of this, if anyone can calm me down, it's her.

"Stay put, I'll pick you up in fifteen," she says after I tell her *everything*. "I'll call Dr. Kleiner on my way, see if she can get you in before they close for the day."

Perched on the sofa, I draw my knees against my chest and hug my legs.

The bones of this old house creak and moan, but there's an unfamiliar sound in the mix . . . a loud, metallic banging, happening in irregular intervals.

Getting up to investigate, I discover the back door is open—the door that is always locked and never used, the door that Gram—or the hallucination of Gram—claimed was open last week. Was it her ghost trying to warn me, keep me safe?

I laugh at how ridiculous it sounds.

My brain is broken—that's the most logical explanation. It's always been broken. It breaks down from time to time. I just need to see my doctor and everything will be fine . . .

I pull the very real, very open door closed and lock both the handle and the dead bolt, checking them over multiple times.

Upstairs, I grab my prescription bottles from my nightstand and throw them in my purse. Dr. Kleiner has everything on file, but I want to know why her nurse said their records show I'm out of refills when the bottles are all mostly full.

Something isn't adding up here, and I need someone of sound mind and judgment to figure it out for me.

I wait by the front door, watching out the sidelight window for Cynthia to arrive. She should be here any minute now—which reminds me, Sydney and I were supposed to do a little stakeout tonight before her shift at the hospital. We were going to hide out in the parking lot for a few hours until she had to leave for work and I had to report for front desk duty. I switched with the Friday night clerk so I could be there when Vanessa and Drew come in. Between our stakeout and my night shift, I was certain we were going to spot them.

As disappointing as it is, there's nothing else I can do. I've no business working or being around other people when I can't distinguish real from fake.

I shoot a text to my boss, calling out for the night and citing a personal emergency. She probably thinks I'm checked out since my time there is coming to an end, but I don't care to elaborate. She's been so good to me over the years. I'd rather have her be frustrated with me than worried sick about my mental state.

Next I text Syd, telling her I'm not feeling well and won't be able to join her tonight. I tell her I'll explain more tomorrow, though I've no doubt Cynthia will fill her in. She doesn't reply, but she's probably with a patient.

If the lottery ticket was a hallucination, and Gram was a hallucination, what's to say Drew sneaking into the hotel to see Vanessa DeOliveira wasn't also a hallucination?

I picture Sydney from this morning, the tears streaming down her face, the defeat in her eyes, the sorrow in her voice. The only thing she loves in this world more than her boys is Drew, and at times, I question if Drew isn't number one.

What if I caused a rift in their marriage for nothing?

Would she be able to forgive me?

Could she trust a single word I say ever again?

Jobless, potentially friendless, dirt poor, and alone—not sure where I go from here.

My breath shallows as I contemplate my new reality, and little by little, the walls close in around me. Shutting my eyes, I cover my ears and hum to myself—a technique a therapist taught me years ago to calm my nerves.

I'd grab one of my blue round pills—the ones for stress and insomnia—as they're predominantly intended for anxiety attacks, but given the fact that they don't seem to be working for me anymore, I don't bother.

When the gentle honk of Cynthia's silver Lexus sounds from my driveway after an undetermined amount of time, I open my eyes.

If there's one thing I know for sure, if there's one thing that can't possibly be a delusion, it's that Cynthia Carson makes everything better, always.

CHAPTER 28

AFTON

October 24, 2003

"Hey, stranger," a woman's voice interrupts my focus.

I glance up from my shopping basket and spot Cynthia standing at the end of the women's hygiene aisle at the grocery store.

"Thought that was you," she says as she walks toward me with a grin that tells me she's happy to see me. "Feeling better?"

I nod. Last week was . . . weird.

I still don't know what caused the episode, but I'm feeling better and back at home.

She glances down into my basket, where I've thrown my jacket over a box of Tampax and a case of maxi pads. I know every woman has a period and everyone has to buy "supplies," but it's still embarrassing. Most people I know have moms who buy these for them. The last three times I've asked my mom, she keeps forgetting.

I don't want to keep shoving crumpled toilet paper in my underwear, so here I am.

"The joys of being a woman, huh?" Cynthia chuckles. "It's a blessing and a curse sometimes."

Lifting my jacket, she takes the pads and tampons and places them in her shopping cart.

"You don't have to do that," I say.

She waves her hand like it's no big deal and gives me a wink, like she gets it.

Cynthia gets everything, always.

Sometimes I think about reincarnation. If it's real, if I get another life someday, I want to come back as Cynthia's child. Then again, reincarnation can't be real because no one in their right mind would want Vangie for a mom and a dead guy for a dad.

"How's your mom?" she asks as we head to the checkout lanes. "Still keeping away from Eddie?"

"I think so. Haven't seen him around." I don't tell her it's because Rick threatened him, at least that's what Mom told me. She didn't get into specifics and I didn't ask.

We get in line at lane number seven.

"Good." Cynthia places her items on the conveyor belt, along with mine. "Those kinds of relationships are toxic and they never end well. I wish your mom knew she deserved better. She's always gone for the emotionally unavailable types, the damaged ones. Something about them excites her, I guess. I told her long ago that the boring nice guys are the way to go. Not that Rick is boring, but you know what I mean. What you see is what you get with him. I spend my life working with complicated people—I don't want to have to come home at the end of the day and live with one, too, you know?"

"Makes sense," I say.

She swipes her card to cover the total—$42.11 for everything. By the looks of her haul, she's making chicken Kiev and balsamic brussels sprouts for dinner tonight.

"Here you are." Cynthia hands me the bag with the hygiene products as we make our way to the parking lot.

"Thanks so much for doing that," I say, fishing in my purse for some cash.

Cynthia shakes her head. "No need. Just let me know next time you need anything like this, okay?"

I could hug her and cry at the same time, but I keep my composure.

"You coming over Friday night?" she asks. "I'm making my famous chili cornbread casserole."

"I'll be there." I wave and head to my car, which is parked at the opposite end of the lot, grateful for Cynthia's kindness tonight but equally grateful to end our conversation.

Last night, while Mom was in the living room watching late-night TV, someone called the house phone. I heard her giggling, giddy and flirting like she always gets when there's a new guy on her radar.

I waited until she fell asleep to check the caller ID, because I wanted to make sure it wasn't Eddie.

Only it wasn't Eddie at all.

It was Rick.

I know what I saw.

And I know I have to do something about it—I just don't know what that is yet.

CHAPTER 29

SYDNEY

"Where'd you run off to last night?" I ask Drew Friday evening. It's the first time we've spoken since our fight. "Woke up and you were . . . gone."

It was a doozy of an argument, but he's never flown the coop like that before. He's never physically left me or needed space or gone radio silent.

Though maybe all those other times, he didn't have an extra nest to fly to. If what Afton is saying is true, he very well could have gone to Vanessa's for the night.

A hundred knots fill my stomach at the thought of him seeking comfort in someone else's arms, complaining about his nagging wife, making plans for a future that doesn't involve me . . .

Drew looks up from his phone, lines spreading across his forehead, as if my question confuses him.

"Didn't Cal tell you?" he asks. "I told him to tell you I was staying at my parents'."

That's what he told Cal to tell me, but that doesn't mean it's what he was actually doing.

"Ah. I see. So now our youngest child *and* your parents are a part of . . . *this*," I say, pointing between us. "Nice."

Drew shoves his phone down, tilts his head back, and groans. "Are we back to that? Are we going to pick up where we left off? Is that what you want? Round two?"

"What I want," I say, arms crossed, "is to know who the hell Vanessa is and why you've been meeting up with her when I'm at work."

My husband is speechless.

Is he taken aback that I'm on to him?

Or is he floored that I would make such an accusation?

"Sounds like you've been talking to Little Miss *One Flew Over the Cuckoo's Nest*," he says.

I roll my eyes at his dig at Afton. "Unnecessary."

"Easy for you to say. She's not making up stories about you, trying to sabotage your marriage."

"You're right," I say. "She's actually trying to help us."

He chuffs. "In what way?"

"That seventy grand? It was Afton. She paid it all with her own money. She felt bad that I was working two jobs. She saw the toll it was taking on me and decided to do something about it."

"Sounds like she'd make one hell of a spouse. Maybe you should leave me for her? We both know she'd love nothing more than having her best friend all to herself."

"Grow up." I walk to the next room. This argument is getting uglier by the minute, and it's not us.

We are not these people.

We don't throw barbs.

We don't hurl unkind accusations.

I hate the way I sound.

I hate the way he sounds.

I don't know what's going on, but neither of us are ourselves and if one of us doesn't walk away now, it's only going to get worse.

Only Drew follows me into the living room.

"You want to call my mom? Ask her if I was there last night?" He offers his phone to me, but I refuse to take it. I will not be calling my mother-in-law, whom I have a loving and functional relationship with. I won't drag her into this.

"Pass." I lift a palm and head for the back door, grabbing my keys and purse and the little bag I packed with my scrubs and nursing sneakers.

A little while ago, Afton texted me to say she wasn't feeling well, that she'd called in sick to work, and that she wouldn't be able to do the stakeout with me. She seemed perfectly fine, if not unusually chipper this morning, but I'm trying not to read into it.

I'll go by myself.

"Where are you going?" Drew asks, once again following me.

"I'm meeting a friend for dinner then going to the hospital," I say. I point to the dry-erase calendar on the wall beside me where all my hospital shifts are written in red marker—though now when I see them, all I think about is Drew and Vanessa. "I trust you'll figure out dinner for the boys?"

His jaw sets. "I was actually planning on grabbing a drink at Spectator's and watching the game. I thought you'd be home until nine."

"Hmm." I shrug into my wool peacoat and tie the belt. "You can still go. Just order a pizza for the kids. I'd hate to keep you from your Friday night plans."

With that, I'm gone. I could have easily guilt-tripped him into staying home, but I want to see what he does with the opportunity I've handed to him on a silver platter.

I'm backing out of the driveway when I notice him standing at the living room window, watching me leave. He doesn't smile or wave like he normally would. He's just staring, thinking.

I'd give a million pennies for those thoughts if I could.

It's a little early yet, so I cruise past Afton's house. Her car is parked in the driveway and the place is pitch black. If she's not feeling well, she's probably sleeping. I consider checking on her but change my mind. I'd hate to wake her up.

I pass Spectator's next.

Drew isn't there yet.

It's anyone's guess if he'll have the balls to go now.

By the time I pull up to the Grantwell Hotel, the place is lit like a Christmas tree, people trekking in and out in their heavy winter jackets and knit hats, some lugging suitcases, some not.

I park behind an overgrown row of evergreen bushes and a catering van from a neighboring business. This is as hidden as it's going to get. If I know Drew and he does show up, he'll likely be so focused on getting inside as quickly as possible that he won't be scanning the parking lot for my van.

Then again, there's a chance I don't know him as well as I thought.

If he notices me, I'll cross that bridge when I get there.

Earlier today, I had a couple of free hours at work, so I attempted to look up Vanessa. Facebook was a bust—she's too young for that platform, I'm guessing. Instagram makes it impossible to find people by their full name, so then I turned to TikTok. I only have an account so I can keep an eye on what the boys post, but I'm pretty sure I found her—a raven-haired petite thing with expressive eyes and mile-long lashes. A blindingly white dimpled smile. Obvious lip filler but it suits her. Most of her videos involved dancing to some trendy sound, shaking her perky ass to the camera while she wears outfits that leave little to the imagination.

There was one video of her with a young man who appeared to be similar in age to her. She was climbing on his lap, kissing him, and teasing him with some prank filter, but it was posted months ago.

Ugh. If *this* is what Drew wants . . . if *this* is all it takes to destroy twenty-plus years of a beautiful relationship, I don't know what I'll do—though I won't have to wonder much longer.

The charming little home-wrecker just pulled in.

CHAPTER 30

AFTON

"Afton, how's your salmon?" Cynthia asks over dinner. It's late and it's been an exhausting evening, but I'm grateful to be here.

"It's perfect," I say.

After Cynthia picked me up earlier, she drove me to Dr. Kleiner's office. An hour later, we walked out with more intel than either one of us planned for . . . it turns out someone has been tampering with my medication. Specifically my somatapine—the medication I've relied on for years to tamp down my anxiety and to help me fall asleep.

No wonder it hadn't been working.

Dr. Kleiner explained that being on the highest dose of a medication like that over an extended period of time and then abruptly stopping it—which is essentially what happened—can often cause hallucinations and other side effects. She says it's a miracle I wasn't going through withdrawal severe enough to land me in the hospital.

She wasn't sure what the little round blue pills were, exactly. She said they could have been store-brand aspirin that someone dyed, or they could've been sugar pills or vitamins. It'd be impossible to know without laboratory testing, but she kept the bottle and said she planned to send it off so we knew for sure I wasn't putting anything nefarious into my body.

Dr. Kleiner also said my hallucinations should begin to subside once I'm back on the real somatapine, which my pharmacy can fill first thing in the morning.

Until things are back on track, Cynthia insisted I stay with her. She doesn't want me alone nor does she want me putting myself in potentially dangerous situations or doing things like emptying out my life savings because I genuinely believed I'd won the lottery . . .

My case isn't extreme enough to warrant an inpatient stay, but even if it were, my insurance ends soon and I don't have the funds to cover it myself.

I was grateful for Cynthia's offer, though, and didn't hesitate to accept it.

The idea of going home to a silent house after the day I've had felt overwhelming.

Terrifying, even.

What if I saw Gram again? Knowing what I know now, I'm not sure how I would process that. I'm just thankful I won't have to find out.

After dinner, I wash the dishes for Cynthia, clean the kitchen until it sparkles, and head upstairs to Syd's old bedroom to retire for the night. Dr. Kleiner was able to give me a sample of a strong sedative to take so I could get some sleep. Closing my eyes and checking out of my life for a good ten to twelve hours would be a godsend. I need a break from all of this.

I swallow one of the pills dry and lie down on Sydney's pillowtop bed with its white floral quilt that her grandma Lola made. Staring at the lifeless ceiling fan with its crystal prism pulls, I mentally place myself in a simpler time—namely before her father was killed and before Drew became the epicenter of Syd's world. Once upon a time, we were a couple of giggly girls playing truth or dare, riding our bikes, and doing the things kids do when they haven't been burdened by adulthood yet. I'd give anything to go back to that, if only for a day.

Rolling to my side, I reach for the silver-framed photo on Sydney's nightstand—a stiffly posed junior prom pic with purple and gold balloons and streamers for the backdrop—school colors, of course. Her palm is flat against his tuxedo lapel while his hand rests lightly on her hip. She looks lovely in her teal sequin gown, a dress I distinctly remember because I had my heart set on it, not knowing she did, too.

In the end, I picked a red satin dress with a small train and told her the teal number looked better on her anyway, because that's what best friends do.

Rolling to my other side, I stare at the bulletin board on her wall, the one covered with an abundance of accolades from high school and college.

Ribbons, awards, newspaper clippings, medals . . .

While I was beyond proud of her growing up, the tiniest part of me always wished we could trade places. I used to daydream about swapping her beautiful pink-and-white room for my beige-and-gray one, having a handsome football player boyfriend (who wasn't Drew) instead of the noncommittal castoffs I always got stuck with, a mom who cooked a nutritious meal every night in place of one who forgot to buy groceries half the time.

Placing the frame back, I turn my focus to the dresser across the room, where a family photo of the Carsons is nestled between bottles of perfume, a lamp, and an ornate golden earring tree. The portrait had to have been taken during our freshman year of high school because Syd still has braces but her hair is as long as it ever was, all the way past the middle of her back. That was the year she donated it to Locks of Love. I wanted badly to do the same, but my hair was never as long, lustrous, and thick as hers. As soon as it got past my shoulders, it would inevitably snap off.

The five Carsons are smiling wide for the camera, standing beneath a shady oak tree in matching denim and white button-downs. I won't give them an A for originality, but they do get an A plus for looking like the quintessential happy, small-town, all-American family.

They truly had it all.

Why Rick chose to step out on Cynthia for my mom is a question we'll never be able to answer, much like what *truly* happened that night in December.

When it comes to that entire situation, Cynthia has always hammered home the concept of acceptance. She says acceptance is acknowledging something happened without obsessing over how or why it happened. In a nutshell, that old saying *It is what it is* is acceptance at its core.

While I like the thought of that, it's different when you were the one accused of a heinous crime.

I don't know that I've ever truly accepted that nor if I can.

I've ignored it.

I've pushed it to the back burner.

I've distracted myself from it fifty ways from Sunday.

But accepting it? I'm not there yet.

Maybe someday.

After a while, my eyelids start to grow heavy and my mouth turns to cotton, which means the sedative Dr. Kleiner gave me is starting to kick in. Climbing out of bed, I trek downstairs with heavy, slow strides to drink a glass of water before it's lights-out. But nothing prepares me for the skeletal figure hoovering leftovers over the kitchen sink.

"Stacia." Thinking fast, I disguise my abrupt shock with a pleasant smile. "Hi."

I haven't seen her in years.

"Oh, hey, Afton." She offers her famously friendly Stacia grin, showing off a set of teeth that hardly resemble the ones I remember. They've lost their brightness, and a little bit of their straightness, but I focus my attention on her eyes. While her gaze is more sunken than it used to be, her hypnotic emerald irises remain the same . . . probably the only feature that's recognizable if I'm being honest.

Her once elegant prima ballerina arms are now covered in tattoos.

Her complexion is sallow and lackluster, speckled with acne scabs along her chin and jaw.

Low-slung jeans hang off her gaunt frame, held up by a leather studded belt cinched to its tightest hole. Her sandy blonde hair has been dyed sunflower yellow, and there are at least three, maybe four inches of dark brown outgrowth.

If you put Stacia and Sydney side by side, you'd never believe they were sisters, let alone related.

"Mom says you're staying with us for a bit," she says. "If you need anything, let me know, okay?"

My heart breaks for Stacia, for the person she used to be, for the pieces of her that still remain, and for the person she never had a chance to be. God love Cynthia for never giving up on her. I'm sure she sees what I see—that the old version of her is still in there somewhere, behind the tattoos, the addictions, and all the other vices she used as coping mechanisms after Rick died.

"Thanks." I take a glass from the cupboard and fill it with water from the fridge. "I will."

"You want to watch a movie downstairs? I was thinking of putting on something funny. Maybe *Dumb and Dumber*? In the mood to laugh tonight. It's been a *week*."

That's putting it lightly . . .

"That sounds amazing, but I've had a long day. Think I'm going to turn in. Another night for sure, though."

"Of course," she says. "Hope you feel better soon."

I don't know what I'd do without these people—and I hope I never live to see that day.

While today was filled with more answers than questions, one question still remains: Who tampered with my somatapine?

And why?

CHAPTER 31

SYDNEY

My hand was on my driver's-side door handle.

I was seconds from confronting Vanessa, all the things I wanted to say already on the tip of my tongue the instant I saw her unloading her powder-blue carry-on-sized suitcase from the back of her little red BMW X3. Her hair was done up in glossy curls, and the cherry on top of her glamorous facade was a full face of impeccably applied makeup. The little black dress she was wearing had her feminine silhouette on full display, cold weather be damned. There was no question she was dressed for the male gaze.

But something stopped me.

I froze.

Like a coward, I did nothing as she walked inside.

She was right in front of me—and I let her go, just like that.

Then I drove away.

She looked so young she reminded me of my boys, which then had me thinking about her as someone's daughter, someone's child. It made me think back to a conversation I'd had years ago with a friend whose husband was having an affair. We were discussing how a woman's first instinct is to go after the other woman, as if she was the sole cause of the indiscretion, as if she stole the man in the middle of it all.

But you can't steal someone who wants to be stolen.

This affair, if that's what's truly going on, falls on Drew, not some naive twenty-two-year-old whose brain is still developing and maturing.

With a little extra time on my hands before I need to report to the hospital, I drive past our house to see if Drew's SUV is still there.

Miraculously it is.

I'm not sure what that means—if he's staying in for the night or if he just hasn't left yet—but I'm too mentally exhausted to give it another thought.

Vanessa's at The Grantwell and he's at home.

I'm hopeful, but still not convinced of anything one way or the other.

Killing more time, I drive to Afton's house to check on her.

Her car is still in the driveway, so I park behind it and head up the front walk.

She doesn't answer when I knock, which means she might still be sleeping, so I don't bother with the doorbell. Digging into my purse, I pull out the spare house key she gave me years ago in case there was ever an emergency with Bea and she couldn't get to her for whatever reason.

Given that she's living all by herself now with no one to check on her, I opt to let myself in.

"Afton?" I call out. "It's Syd. You home?"

The place is as inert as a still life painting. The TV screen in the living room is black. There's a stack of mail on the entryway table. And there's no lingering food or coffee scents in the air to suggest she's been up and moving around in recent hours.

Making my way through the first floor, I peek down the hall and into a bathroom before calling down to the basement, but she doesn't answer.

Passing Bea's old room, I hesitate, my hand on the knob.

Everyone grieves differently, but I remember after my father was killed, I slept on his side of the bed alongside my mom every night for months. It was the only thing that made me feel close to him. Mom told me to take as much time as I needed, promising not to pack away his things until all four of us were ready.

"Afton?" I knock three times on the door. "You in there?"

With no response, I decide to go in.

The room looks exactly the way I remember, with the iron farm-house-style bed frame and Amish quilt, the wooden rocking chair in the corner with the folded blanket on the back, and the forty-inch flat-screen TV anchored on the wall above the dresser.

The space reminds me of the private nursing home suite my own grandmother lived in during her final year. There's a bit of an antiseptic smell lingering in the air, the faintest trace of bleached sheets, little orange bottles of prescription medicine lined up beside crumpled tissues on the nightstand. A lavender paisley muumuu is neatly draped over the foot of the bed, as if Bea left it there the day she passed and never had a chance to wear it again.

Afton told me she'd come home from work one morning last month and found Bea dead in the living room recliner, knitting needles in hand and fresh curlers in her hair. The medical examiner determined her death to be natural. Afton didn't want to talk about it after that, insisting she was going to be okay. Mom dropped off a few meals here and there. Other than that, there was nothing more we could do or say. There was no funeral or memorial—a request Bea had made prior to her passing obviously. A true wallflower type, she never was one for fanfare or attention.

I miss her, though.

My grandparents lived out of state.

Much like my mom was a second mom to Afton growing up, Bea was like a bonus grandmother to me.

I reached out to Afton every day in the weeks following Bea's passing, but she never needed anything, and toward the end I felt like my persistent checking on her was becoming more of an annoyance than anything else, so I stopped.

Closing the bedroom door, I head upstairs to Afton's room.

"Hello, hello? You home?" I call out.

Peeking my head into her open doorframe, I gasp when I see the state of her sleeping quarters. Afton's never been a neat freak, but this space looks like a tornado—or some vandal—went through it. Her nightstand drawer is pulled open, practically dangling, and emptied of whatever contents it contained before. There's a mess of pillowcases and random blankets on the floor, as well as a metal box left open and empty in the center of it all.

Something isn't right.

I call her, listening carefully to my surroundings on the off chance her cell phone is here somewhere.

I get nothing but silence—and her voice mail.

"Hey, it's me. I'm at your house and I'm worried . . . call me." I hang up and head out, locking up behind me.

Maybe she's with Keith?

Maybe her car is here because he picked her up?

While the idea of her ditching me and calling in sick to work to play footsie with some random bartender doesn't exactly sit well with me, perhaps it's one of those Occam's razor things—the simplest explanation is usually the correct one.

Once I'm at the hospital parking lot, I text Afton, asking her to call or message me to let me know where she is and if she's okay. Then I head inside to get dressed in the staff locker room and report for my twelve-hour shift.

Looping my stethoscope around my neck, I check my reflection in the mirror by the door. It's clear I've not been sleeping. My eyes are puffy. My stomach grumbles, reminding me I forgot to eat dinner. I yank my hair out of my ponytail holder and redo it, sleeker, tighter, neater. It's going to be a long night, and staying focused is going to be a challenge, but if we're busy enough, I should be able to survive the next twelve hours.

By the time I get off in the morning, I should have all the answers I need.

CHAPTER 32

AFTON

Dear Afton,

Hope you slept well! I'm running errands at the moment and plan to pick up your prescription at the pharmacy on my way home. Please help yourself to whatever you'd like in the kitchen. I've laid out fresh towels in the hall bath for you.

xo—

Cynthia

I read the note Cynthia left on my nightstand through bleary, sleep-filled eyes. I must've been out hard because I didn't hear her come in. The clock on my phone reads 12:14 PM, which means I slept for fifteen hours straight.

A record.

That sedative was no joke—that or my body was making up for all those sleepless days the last couple of weeks. My bones feel heavy and anchored to the mattress, and despite the bright midday sun shining in through a break in Sydney's curtains, I'm positive if I closed my eyes again, I could sleep another fifteen, maybe sixteen hours.

Unlocking my phone screen, I notice a barrage of missed calls and texts from Sydney. From what I'm gathering she went to my house, let herself in, and freaked out when she realized I wasn't there.

I shoot her a text, letting her know I stayed the night at her mom's and to call me when she gets a chance, and then I head downstairs in search of some cereal, something I can eat without making a mess in Cynthia's pristine white kitchen.

I'm pouring a bowl of plain Cheerios—it was either that or Shredded Wheat—when my boss calls me.

"Making sure you're alive," she says when I answer. "It's not like you to call out, especially when you're in the middle of training someone."

"Yeah, sorry. Yesterday was a little . . . unexpected. I'm feeling better, though," I say, if only because I don't want her to worry nor do I want her to ask any questions. "How did Caden do on his own?"

"He didn't burn the hotel down, so we're off to a strong start."

Leaning against the counter, I drag my fingers through my messy hair and exhale a slight chuckle.

"So, look, I know I turned in my notice a few weeks ago, but I've been having second thoughts," I say.

"Oh yeah? Your other plans fall through?"

If she only knew . . .

"It's complicated." I bite my lip, hoping she lets me leave it at that.

"Listen, I'd love to give you your job back, but the position's already been filled and I don't have it in the budget to have two overnight clerks. If Caden quits or it doesn't work out for whatever reason, though, it's yours."

"I understand."

"Stop in sometime this weekend if you can and finish up your time card. Looks like you've got a couple hundred hours of accumulated PTO, so I'll pay that out with your last check."

It's not much, but it's something.

"Thank you," I say, pressing the phone against my shoulder as I splash milk over my Cheerios.

We hang up and I eat my breakfast alone at the Carson kitchen table, in a house so quiet you could hear a pin drop—a far cry from the bustling, lively place it once was.

If I close my eyes, I can put myself right back there, to those post-sleepover mornings where Cynthia would make pancakes topped with strawberries and powdered sugar and Rick would sing Beach Boys songs at the top of his lungs, dropping into the harmony parts every so often.

Ever the little artist, Stacia would be sketching at the kitchen island or making a mess with her pastels, smudging the colors together and leaving dust everywhere.

Max would always skip breakfast in lieu of playing on his PlayStation in the family room.

The washer and dryer would be humming along in the next room, tumbling towels and jeans that smelled like Heaven on earth, and the kitchen window above the sink would be cracked enough to let in a crisp morning breeze and the sound of robins chirping gleefully as they pick worms from the dewy grass.

Now it's nothing but the smell of bland cereal and the barely audible tick of the wall clock by the fridge.

I think of the younger versions of us, sitting at this exact table, our entire lives ahead of us, blissfully unaware of how sideways things would go in a few short years.

I'm finishing up, rinsing my bowl in the sink when Sydney calls.

"Hey," I answer.

"Oh, my God, Afton. I talked to my mom this morning and she told me what happened yesterday. How are you feeling?"

"Rested," I say. "Sorry I missed the stakeout."

"I saw her. Vanessa. She was dressed to the nines and heading into the hotel. I wanted to run after her, but I couldn't do it. I don't know—I got cold feet or something." She exhales into the phone. "I can't stop thinking about all the stuff I wanted to say to her. That might have been my only chance."

"It's probably for the best."

"You think?"

"I mean . . . there's no way to know if what I saw that night was real or not. A lot of what I've experienced the past few weeks have turned out to be . . . delusions."

Sydney is quiet, and I pray she doesn't hate me for this. Not that she's the hateful type. But I caused a rift in her marriage by texting her husband and then telling her he was cheating.

I thought I was doing the right thing . . .

I thought he *was* cheating.

"But you saw her and you saw her name on the reservation list and she was there last night," Syd says. "That couldn't have been a hallucination because I saw her myself."

She has a point.

"Drew left last night," Sydney says. "I checked our doorbell camera and it showed him backing out of the driveway around ten. He didn't get home until after midnight. Where do you think he went?"

Jesus.

Maybe I wasn't seeing things that night after all?

"Have you brought it up to him yet?" I ask.

"No. And he still hasn't accounted for those six hours when he wasn't at the office when he said he'd be," she says. "The other night, when we had our big fight, he left and didn't come home until the next morning. He claims he stayed at his parents' house, but I don't know? I don't have the heart to call his mom and get her involved in this. She'll ask questions that I won't know how to answer, and she'll never look at me the same after that. As far as she knows, it's another day in paradise over here. I'd hate for her to worry."

"None of that sounds like Drew."

As much as I loathe the man, he's never been outwardly shady. He's always walked a straight line in front of Sydney. Perhaps approaching middle age has emboldened him.

"I know, right?" She's whispering, which means either he's home or she doesn't want her boys to hear an ounce of this conversation. "What should I do? Mentioning it's going to kickstart WWIII all over again."

"Let me do some thinking . . ."

Until my hallucinations subside, Dr. Kleiner has forbidden me from driving, so keeping tabs on Drew might be off the table until then.

Either way, I'll come up with something.

In the end, secrets like this don't stay buried forever.

CHAPTER 33

SYDNEY

"You look stressed. Thought you could use one of these." I hand my husband an uncapped bottle of Michelob ULTRA—an olive branch of sorts. I even placed it in the freezer for five minutes first, ensuring it was ice cold the way he loves it.

The tension running rampant in our home lately is becoming unbearable.

It'll be impossible to have a productive adult conversation if we keep this up.

"Thanks." He glances away from the college basketball game to offer me some semblance of a gracious smile, but the brief warmth of his attention ends as soon as it began. His favorite team is down seven points and there are only two minutes and thirty seconds left in the game. "Oh, come on! He had that. These refs . . ."

The little divot above his jaw pulses as he glares at the television screen.

I settle in beside him on the couch, draping his favorite Kansas City Royals blanket over us both like we usually do when we cuddle watching TV. I'm sure he's wondering what the hell I'm trying to do here, but I have a strategy.

"I hate when we fight," I say when a commercial comes on.

He turns away from the TV, his eyes searching mine, though for what, I can't be sure.

I reach for his hand, interlacing our fingers. He doesn't exactly hold mine back, but he doesn't pull away either. His grip is limp but it's there. Only time will tell if it's because he's bitter over my accusations or if it's simple guilt causing this emotional distance between us.

It's difficult not to imagine this very hand freeing Vanessa DeOliveira's curves from that skintight dress she wore last night, but I force the thought from my mind.

"So the wildest thing happened yesterday," I begin. "Turns out someone was messing with Afton's medication, and she'd been having hallucinations."

Drew mutes the TV despite the game being back on, and he points his attention my way—no easy feat given how much time is left in the game.

His investment in this Afton situation is clearly overriding his love of Michigan Wolverines basketball.

"You might want to pause that." I point to the screen and sure enough, the man who refuses to watch games unless they're live pauses it without hesitation.

In the ten minutes that follow, I tell him everything my mother told me.

"Makes sense," he says. "She'd been saying some pretty crazy things lately."

"Who would've done something like that?" I ask. "Who would steal her anxiety medication?"

"Maybe it was that bartender guy you said she was seeing? What was his name? Ken?"

"Keith," I say.

"Was it a benzo? Aren't those pretty valuable on the streets?"

I'm impressed that he even knows any of that as he's the type who won't even swallow a single Tylenol unless he's on the brink of death or it's doctor's orders.

"They are," I say. "Or so I hear. Someone at work was telling me a while back that those can fetch something like twenty-five dollars a pill."

"Pretty shitty if it was the boyfriend."

"They weren't even dating, though," I say. "It was another one of her delusions. Supposedly it was a one-night stand last summer, so who knows if he's been into her house, and I doubt he knows about the medications she takes. She hooked up with him once, I can't imagine her giving him a full rundown of her psychiatric history."

"So who else would've done it then?"

"That's the million-dollar question."

"Didn't her grandma have a home health aide or something?" he asks.

"These scripts were filled after Bea died. Supposedly the nurse hadn't been there since before."

"So is she still hallucinating or what's going on with that?"

"Once she gets back on her medication, the hallucinations should subside. She's staying with Mom until then. I thought about going over to Afton's place and straightening up a bit. It was a mess when I stopped by last night."

Drew cocks his head. "I thought you were having dinner with a friend last night?"

"I had a little bit of time before I had to go to work, so I went to check on her. She'd texted me earlier saying she wasn't feeling well." I cover my tracks without breaking a sweat. It's terrifying how proficient I'm getting at lying to my husband. It almost becomes easier with each fib. "Anyway, I thought it might be nice for her to come home to a clean house. It's the least I can do since she paid all those bills for us."

"Is that going to be your thing for the rest of your friendship now? She gave you seventy grand so now you're going to feel like you're forever in her debt?"

"Of course not."

"Maybe you should sell the van, give her the proceeds, and get something smaller and cheaper. You said she quit her job, right? And she blew all her savings on our problems. I'm sure she could use that thirty grand or whatever it's worth."

The Kelley Blue Book value is a hair under thirty-one thousand, to be exact. I checked because I had the same idea the other day.

"Our credit is shot after this past year," I say. "No bank in their right mind is going to give us a loan, and if they do, the interest rate will be astronomical."

"I see." His lips form a hard line and he nods. "Then clean her house if it makes you feel better."

Despite the cordial air to our conversation, there's still an edge to his demeanor, a coldness in his words, a distance in his eyes.

And his hand is still limp in mine.

Unmuting and unpausing the game, he shifts his focus to his beloved Wolverines, taking a generous swig of beer, followed by a second, more generous swig.

"Did you ever end up going to Spectator's last night?" I keep a chipper lilt in my voice so as not to come off as accusatory.

"I did for a couple of hours, after the boys went to bed," he says before leaning forward and groaning when the Wolverines turn the ball over to the opposing team. There's a minute left in the game now, and it's not looking good for the Maize and Blue, which means he's going to be in a sour mood the rest of the day regardless of how nonchalant I sound or how much I handle this tension with kid gloves. "You want the receipts to prove it? I saved them in case you asked. They're in my wallet. Go see for yourself."

Wow.

All at once, I'm relieved, insulted, and disappointed that it's come to this.

Maybe I'd have been better off sticking a tracking device on his car and using that to answer all my pressing questions. Never thought I'd be that kind of wife, but maybe it would've saved us some strife.

"Drew," I say.

"Hmm?" He doesn't look away from the game, though I don't hold it against him. The shot clock is running out and the Wolverines managed to get the ball back. Even with a three-point buzzer-beater, they're not coming back from this loss. "It's been bothering me that I still don't know where you were on Thursday. Six hours is a lot of time to be gone from your office."

The Wolverines miss their last shot.

The final buzz sounds.

Drew releases his hand from mine, springs up, and paces the living room, dragging his palm along his slanted jaw.

It's a loss for Michigan and maybe the worst possible time I can bring this question up, but I have to know. It's been killing me and I don't know when we'll be able to sit alone and have a calm and rational conversation again.

Drew points the remote at the TV and the screen goes black.

"I'd tell you," he says, "but I feel like it's just another thing that'll piss you off in a sea of everything else I do that pisses you off lately."

My mind scrambles in twelve different directions.

"I promise I won't get mad." I go to him, holding my eyes on his and softening every muscle in my face.

"I spent Thursday morning in Kansas City." His words make my heart skip a beat, and not in a starry-eyed way. The fact that my husband drove an hour and a half away and came home like it was any other day and then failed to mention it to me is . . . concerning. "I had two job interviews. A couple of national insurance outfits are headquartered there, and they're looking to expand their executive teams. The salaries are double what I make here. Plus an annual bonus. Benefit package is better, too, obviously."

"What about your business?" I ask. "Our life here? The kids' schools? Our friends and family? Everything is here. *Everything.*"

I hear his words and I understand how much more money he'll be bringing in, but my heart is too shrouded in hurt and barbed wire, too busy being insulted at the fact that he left me out of this decision to appreciate it.

"I knew you'd be mad." He taps his empty beer bottle against the side of his thigh, exhaling hard.

"I'm not mad—I'm trying to wrap my head around this. I thought you loved our life here?"

The plan was always to grow old in our hometown, in this house, a couple of high school sweethearts who made it to the end of a picture book rainbow.

"I do," he says. "But I don't love that I can't support my family financially the way I should. I hate that you've been working two jobs, that no matter what I do to grow my agency, the business just isn't there. Unless Shelter Rock magically gets an influx of new residents, I'll never be able to scale up."

He's not wrong.

But still.

To apply for a job, to interview for a job, and to keep all of that from me . . .

What else is he keeping?

"Anyway," he continues, "the position I'm gunning for would let me telecommute three days a week. Thursdays and Fridays I'd have to report to the office, but they'd put me in corporate housing Thursday nights. Fridays are half days so I'd be home before the kids even got out of school. You wouldn't have to take shifts at the ER anymore. We could actually enjoy our weekends again."

As wonderful as he makes it sound, the idea of Drew being in a whole other city an hour and a half away one night every week leaves an unsettled feeling in my core. Until I know if the Vanessa thing was a hallucination or some perfect storm of coincidences, I'm not completely sold on this idyllic picture he's painting.

"When will you know if you got the job?" I ask.

"Soon. Next week or two."

"All right," I say, forcing a smile despite my initial apprehension. One or two weeks should be enough time for me to do more digging and get to the bottom of his alleged affair. "I should head over to Afton's and get started on her house. As far as the job in Kansas City, we'll cross that bridge when we get to it."

If we get to it, that is.

CHAPTER 34

SYDNEY

October 30, 2003

I'm finishing Drew's midterm paper for chemistry when the computer screen flickers.

"No, no, no." I gasp, frantically trying to move the cursor to the save icon before it's too late.

The monitor goes black.

I press and hold the power button on the tower to turn it back on. A million minutes later, it's booting up. I pull up Microsoft Word, searching for the file among hundreds of others—only it's not there.

The entire thing was lost . . .

I'd been working for hours on that thing—now I have to do it all over again?

I fold over, head in my hands, breathing deep through my fingers and trying not to cry.

Drew's entire life he's never been good at anything STEM-related. It took him two times to pass Algebra 101 and he barely scraped by with a D. Lately he's been talking to a basketball scout from Baxterville Tech, and it sounds like they're really interested in him. He just needs to get his GPA up and take all the college prereqs, Chemistry 101 being one of them.

There are a dozen other things I could be doing with my time, especially when I have my own homework to do and we're going to a Halloween party at Tasha Slater's tonight, but the way I see it, I'm investing in our future.

If Drew gets a college degree, there'll be more doors opening for him career-wise. Not to mention, if he gets a full ride, that's one less bill we'll have to worry about when we get married and start our lives together—something we want to do sooner than later.

I've witnessed so many high school sweethearts break up after graduation, or they try and stick it out the first year of college, but it inevitably crashes and burns by Christmas break.

Someone always cheats.

They get one taste of freedom or they catch the eye of someone at a party and it's game over.

That won't happen with us.

I won't let it.

Baxterville Tech has a great nursing program.

Drew's going to study business or IT, I'll study nursing, and after a couple of years, we'll get married so we can live in married student housing.

Afton always teases me for planning out every second of my existence, but I enjoy it.

I live for this.

Planning puts me in control and control makes me happy.

It's that simple.

Besides, I'd rather poke my eyes out with rusty tweezers than leave my life to chance.

"Sydney?" My father calls from the top of the stairs. "Drew just pulled in."

I yell back, "Be right up."

I'll have to deal with the paper thing later. I can't focus on it right now or it'll ruin this night, and I've been looking forward to it all month.

Tugging out of my clothes, I sprint upstairs to my room and change into my costume—he's Fred, I'm Daphne, and Afton is Scooby-Doo. Drew was half kidding when he suggested Afton should join us and go as Scooby, and I for sure thought she'd pass since she hates parties, but she shocked us both when she enthusiastically said she was in.

Adjusting the short purple dress, I fasten the bright green scarf around my neck, slick my hair into a low bun, and pull on a red wig with sideswept bangs, securing it into place with a thick headband. Wiggling into opaque lavender tights next, I shimmy them into place before stepping into purple heels.

Makeup is next—false lashes with cat wing liner and pale pink lipstick reminiscent of the sixties.

I give myself a once-over in the cheval mirror by my bed before heading to meet Drew. Only I stop halfway down the stairs when I see what he's wearing.

Black jeans, a white V-neck T-shirt, and a black leather jacket.

His hair is shiny, slicked back with some kind of product.

He's definitely not Fred.

"What's this?" I ask. "What are you wearing? Where's your costume?"

"Yeah . . . I'm so sorry, Syd. The Fred pants ripped when I was putting them on. The fabric was super thin and they split right down the back. I'm just glad it happened before we got to the party and not after . . ."

"What even are you?"

My costume won't make sense without his.

"Danny Zuko," he says with a mile-wide beam. Reaching into an interior pocket of the jacket, he retrieves a black comb and slicks his already slicked-back hair even more. "From the movie Grease*?"*

"I've never seen it."

His amusement fades. "Oh."

Outside, Afton pulls up, parking by the curb. She climbs out of her Datsun, carrying an oversized Scooby-Doo head, and makes her way up the sidewalk.

This was not the plan.

Sensing my tension, Drew hooks his arm around my waist and pulls me in for a kiss.

I want to kiss him back, but I can't, so his lips are met with flatness.

"It's going to be okay, babe," he says softly into my ear. But his words only make me feel worse. Kind of like when someone tells an angry person to calm down. It's the worst thing you can say at a time like that.

"There'll be more Halloweens," he says. "A lifetime of them. This is just one."

It's not the same.

I'd been looking forward to this for months.

Afton shows herself in, immediately pummeled by my brother and sister who waste no time asking if they can try the Scooby head on. A moment later, my parents are joining in on all the "fun." I wipe away any hint of emotion from my face. I don't want my mom to ask me a million questions later. I'm disappointed. I'm allowed to be disappointed. I don't need to sit down and talk through it. I'll get over it eventually.

"We should probably get going," I say after a bit.

The room turns silent.

Max hands the Scooby head back to Afton.

Drew jangles his car keys.

"Well, you kids have fun," Dad says as he sees us to the door. "Curfew is ten."

"Got it," I call back.

So much for the cute Fred and Daphne pictures we were going to take tonight.

Not to mention people already like to joke about Afton and me being secret lesbians, so this whole costume thing isn't going to help that.

This combined with the chem paper I'm going to have to rewrite tomorrow and I could just break down and cry.

"Wait, let me grab some pics before you guys run off," Mom says. "Stand in front of the fireplace, over there."

We shuffle back to the center of the living room, and I hand her the yellow disposable camera from my bag and we line up in front of the mantel.

Drew wraps his arm around me. I angle my hip, lower my chin, and offer a sultry Daphne-esque smile.

"Drew, I love the costume," Mom gushes as she snaps picture after picture. "I had the biggest crush on Danny Zuko in my younger years."

"You and everyone else," Dad says with a sniff.

"You know, I have an old poodle skirt around here somewhere . . . you could change quick and go as Sandy?"

I think of poor Afton showing up to a high school Halloween party in a hot and heavy Scooby-Doo costume when everyone else is dressed in something sexy or cool.

I can't do that to her.

"It's not a big deal," I say. "We need to go anyway."

Drew squeezes my hand.

"Okay, everyone, smile one last time," Mom says.

Afton crouches down this time, on all fours, like a dog.

This is laughable, and not in a good way.

While I'm smiling on the outside, I couldn't be cringing harder on the inside.

All of the flashes temporarily blind me. I blink until I can see, praying my false lashes don't fall off.

Mom insists on taking two more, just in case. She knows how picky I am with pictures. The slightest bad angle or hint of bad lighting can ruin a great photo and we won't be able to see these until they're sent off and developed.

A few minutes later, the three of us load into Drew's car and head to Tasha's house just outside of town for apple cider, s'mores, and a bonfire. Tonight won't get too crazy since her parents are "supervising," but since the rest of the school was going, I didn't want to miss out.

We're at a stoplight when Drew takes my hand from across the center console, bringing it to his lips.

"You're extra quiet," he says. "I'm sorry about the costume."

"No, it's fine." It isn't but it will be.

"I know you planned it out all perfectly," he says.

"I did."

The light turns green and he gently releases my hand.

"I appreciate all the effort you put into the costumes." He glances in the rearview, nodding toward Afton. "We're going to have fun anyway. Right, Af?"

"Yep," she says, monotoned from the back seat, staring out the tiny triangular window to her right.

I'm not sure why she's tagging along when she doesn't seem excited about any of it.

She's always been a clingy friend, but lately I've been feeling suffocated.

I love her.

She's my oldest, most loyal friend.

But what I wouldn't give for a break from her.

CHAPTER 35

AFTON

The smell of lemons, pine, and lavender fills my nostrils the second I step foot inside my home Saturday night. Clicking on the lamp on the entry table, I can't help but notice the specks of dust that tend to accumulate on the polished cherry console are . . . gone. The rug beneath my feet has been straightened and my shoes are lined up neatly along the wall.

"Hello?" I call out in case my mystery cleaner is here.

Nothing but my own voice echoes back.

In the living room, the throw blankets have been neatly folded and draped over the back of the sofa. The coffee table and side tables are dusted, and the TV remotes are resting in a straight row next to the potted plant. Gram's knitting basket is curiously untouched, though.

I run my hands along the soft pillows of the couch before giving one of them a squeeze to make sure it's real, that I'm not hallucinating this. Dr. Kleiner said if I'm ever not sure if something I'm experiencing is real or not, I should try using my sense of touch.

Visual hallucinations would feel like nothing, she said.

But everything in this immaculately clean room is tangible.

Heading to the dining room next, I find all the clutter cleared and placed in organized stacks on the buffet, and all six of the chairs are pushed in, symmetrically lining up with one another. The curtains on the window are pulled back, showcasing crystal clear panes of glass.

I can't recall the last time I washed the windows . . . working nights and sleeping all day, it was one of those things that never occurred to me to do, and Gram never complained. She preferred the blinds closed and curtains pulled shut anyway—unless it was snowing. She liked the house to be dark during the day, saying it made it cozier. I suspect she just wanted another layer separating her from the outside world.

In the kitchen, the sink has been emptied of the dirty dishes that had been there all week, and the fridge is shiny, as if this person wiped down everything from top to bottom, handles included. A small arrangement of cheerful, multicolored gerbera daisies is centered on the small breakfast nook table and beside it is a handwritten note on the back of a junk mail flier.

Afton—

I hope you don't mind, but I thought it would be nice if when you came home, you walked in to a clean house. I know things have been hard lately, but hopefully this is one less item on your plate as you focus on your recovery.

Anything else you need? I'm your girl.

Love,
Syd
PS—I didn't touch Bea's room. Wasn't sure if I should or not.

Of course.

This is exactly what Syd would do, and years ago, I gave her a key to the house in case there was ever an emergency with Gram.

Heading upstairs, I pass the dining room window with its view of the driveway. Outside, Cynthia waits for me in her idling Lexus. I asked her to bring me by tonight. I needed to grab a few more toiletries and clothes since I've no idea how long I'll be staying with her.

If it were my choice, I'd stay forever.

Earlier today, Stacia and I played UNO and made frozen Hawaiian pizza, and Cynthia baked oatmeal chocolate chip cookies. In a way, I felt transported to the proverbial good old days. If anything, the distraction from everything going on was therapeutic in and of itself.

Once upstairs, I stop when I reach my bedroom. Scanning the space, I note the vacuum tracks in the carpet. The contents on top of my dresser, which are now immaculately organized. My bed is made, fluffed pillows and all. My nightstand drawer is closed, with the little metal lockbox resting perfectly centered on top. Along the far wall are two laundry baskets of clean clothes, the contents folded into neat, proportional stacks.

This must have taken her an entire day.

I locate an extra duffel bag in the back of my closet, fill it with an assortment of toiletries, socks, underwear, pajamas, and a few changes of clothes, and then I return to Cynthia's sedan.

"Syd cleaned my house," I say. "Top to bottom."

Cynthia's mauve lips curl into a knowing smile.

"She wanted to do something nice for you after I told her what was going on," she says as we back out. "Her love language has always been acts of service. Stacia's my quality time kid. Max's love language is words of affirmation. But not my Sydney."

Looking back over the years, I realize Cynthia's right.

Sydney's always been an action-oriented person. Even with her own family, she knew they were struggling so she started working two jobs. If you didn't know her, it'd be easy to brush it off as her being a "workaholic" or "busybody," but that's not her.

If she loves you, she'll move Heaven and earth with her own two bare hands.

And if she doesn't? I hope I never find out.

CHAPTER 36

SYDNEY

Drew got the job.

The one he had his heart set on . . .

The one that would place him in Kansas City every Thursday and Friday indefinitely . . .

"Can you believe it? They want me to start in two weeks, but I told them I'd need longer than that to tie up loose ends at the office," Drew says Monday evening. There's a pep in his step and his words are fast and breathless as he talks a mile a minute. "Brad Crane Insurance is taking over my client roster. We're still negotiating the price, but we're going to come out ahead on that, no question."

I dry my hands on a kitchen towel. "You accepted?"

So much for waiting another week or two.

And so much for crossing that bridge when we get to it—it would seem that my dear sweet husband went on ahead without me, crossing it all by his lonesome self.

"Of course." He frowns as if my question is as frustrating to him as his ballsy decision is to me.

Drew curls his hands around my waist and spins me in the middle of our kitchen like we're a couple of newlyweds. His excitement is infectious, and I can't help but grin right along with him despite the nervous butterflies swarming throughout my middle.

But inside, I'm fuming.

My blood might as well be lava and my smile is so taut it hurts my face.

"This is sudden," I say when he finally lets me go. "I thought they needed more time to decide?"

"Apparently they had their minds made up the second the interview wrapped up. They even canceled the interviews after mine. They had to get some signatures from a few higher-ups before HR could officially make the offer."

There's a light in his eyes that I haven't seen since I don't remember when. It's the same one that resided there the night of our first kiss, over dinner on our first dating anniversary, the same light that beamed from him when he took his varsity basketball team to state and led them to the championship trophy. It's the same light that exuded from him the day he asked me to be his wife, the day we made it official, all the days we welcomed our boys into the world, and a million moments since then.

But it's been a while.

"What's wrong?" His enthusiasm fades as he studies me. "You don't look happy."

"I am," I tell him. "I'm . . . still processing this. Just a little caught off guard here. I thought we were going to make the decision together."

"How could I turn this down? It's going to change our lives for the better. You won't have to work so much anymore. With my bonuses, maybe we could even get Afton paid back sooner than we planned. Syd, this fixes *all* our problems."

Drew is wrong—and he hasn't the slightest clue.

There's still one pesky little loose end, one teensy, tiny little problem . . . and it comes in the form of something I found while cleaning Afton's house last weekend.

CHAPTER 37

AFTON

After one short week of being back on somatapine and living the high life at Cynthia's, Dr. Kleiner has cleared me to return home and given me the green light to resume all normal activities. I run a few errands, stocking up on a few grocery essentials and stopping by The Grantwell to submit my final time card.

Once home, I grab a pen and notebook, sit at the kitchen table, and make a list of all the things I need to do to get my life back on track. It was Cynthia's idea. She says getting things out of your head and onto paper helps clear the mental clutter in your brain.

Flipping to a clean page, I begin:

1. Call John Gregory. Apologize for the confusion the other week, explain what happened, ask him if he can still get me that job in KC.
2. Apply for new jobs in case I can't get the job in KC.
3. Send Cynthia a thank-you card and flowers for her hospitality this week.

4. Check my bank account, go through the pile of bills, make sure everything is current.
5. Find an estate lawyer to sort through Gram's end-of-life affairs.

I wish I could remember if Gram had a will or not. Odds are, if she did, it's ancient. She always said she was going to leave everything she had to me because my mother had never been good at handling money and she'd likely blow it on her boyfriend-of-the-week or God knows what else. Gram always helped her out financially here or there out of obligation, but the love between them had been lost decades ago, and neither one of them made any effort to find it.

As far as I know the house is the only thing of value Gram had.

Pulling up my phone, I type in the website for the county assessor and search up this address. According to these records, the house is assessed at $179,400—not too bad for a house Gram purchased sixty years ago for $15,000.

If I sold this place it would more than make up for the loss of my life savings, and it would definitely help me relocate to Kansas City if that job works out with John's brother.

Aside from Sydney and her family, without Gram to take care of, there's nothing else keeping me here.

I'd be a fool not to start over somewhere fresh now that I have the opportunity.

Placing my phone aside, I head to the kitchen to go through the drawer Gram always called the "paper junk drawer". . . not to be confused with the regular junk drawer. The paper junk drawer was specially reserved for things like instruction manuals, warranty cards, coupons, and the like. I doubt she'd keep something as important as a will in here, but it's not like she had a proper desk or filing cabinet.

I'm fishing through never-ending piles of miscellany when I come across an opened envelope addressed to me.

The return address is vaguely familiar.

Flipping it over, I pull out the contents, and unfold the letter inside.

> Dear Ms. Teachout—
>
> Thank you for booking your appointment with Corcoran Forensic Hypnotherapy Services. We look forward to seeing you on Friday, February 16, at nine AM. Your appointment will last approximately three hours. Please arrive thirty minutes prior to your appointment time and dress in comfortable clothes.
>
> Directions are printed on the back of this letter.
>
> Please call our office should you have any questions or need to reschedule for any reason.
>
> We look forward to seeing you.
>
> The Team at Corcoran Forensic Hypnotherapy Services

I flip the letter over, scanning the directions for the clinic, which is in Overland Park, outside Kansas City. Below that is a photo of Dr. Marcy Corcoran, an auburn-haired grandmother type with an educated air and a disarming expression that makes her appear approachable and intelligent at the same time.

My faded memory sharpens the more I look at her picture. I'd completely forgotten that I booked this last fall. I'd watched some show on Court TV where this woman had amnesia and they brought in a forensic hypnotherapist to help unlock her memory. Interested, I googled it to see if it was a real thing and sure enough it was.

An hour later, I'd found the website for Dr. Marcy Corcoran and spent the rest of the day going down an internet rabbit hole on her extensive and fascinating career. A Stanford-educated psychologist, she specializes in recalling repressed memories and she's famous in her field for pioneering a state-of-the-art technique to do so.

It's all coming back . . .

Including the day I brought this up to Sydney . . .

I told her I was desperate to know what happened that night, that it still haunts me not knowing the truth.

She said she didn't want to know, that going back to that place—mentally—would only dredge up emotions we'd worked so hard to overcome.

"What if you're guilty?" she asked me. "What if you did it? What then? Are you going to make an announcement? Are you going to shout it from the rooftops and let everyone know they were right about you?"

She was trying to make light of a heavy topic at the time, but she had a point.

"And what about everything my mom has done for you?" she asked next. "She's been your biggest advocate since day one. It would devastate her to find out she was wrong, you know that. And I don't even want to think about what that would mean for you and me . . . we've come so far to get to where we are."

"I hear what you're saying, I do. But this is for me," I told her. "For my peace of mind. I want to know. I *need* to know."

"Sounds like your mind's pretty made up," she said.

"It is," I told her.

"Okay," she said. "I don't think you should waste your money on this quack, but I'll go with you if you want. You know, for moral support. I'll sit in the waiting room. Just don't tell me what you find out. I don't want to know. I don't want to know anything, either way."

That was the end of our conversation, and I never brought it up again.

The following day, however, I booked the appointment. The soonest I could get in was in February. At the time, that seemed ages away, so I shoved it from my mind.

Checking the calendar on the side of the fridge, I tear off the January page. Sure enough, my hypnotherapy appointment is written down for February 16 in bold red ink in Gram's handwriting. Circled twice. She was excited for me—I remember now. She thought it was a great idea. It breaks my heart that she won't be here to discuss the findings, but maybe, wherever she is now, she already knows.

I shoot a text to Sydney, telling her my appointment is next week, asking if she still wants to come with me for moral support.

ME: We could make a mini girls' trip of it. Maybe find a cute Airbnb to stay in the night before? After the last few weeks, I think we could both use a little escape.

She replies instantly.

SYDNEY: Anything you need, I'm there.

CHAPTER 38

SYDNEY

"It's nice of you to go with her." Drew watches from our bedroom doorway as I pack my bags. "Especially when I know you're against this. Just promise me you won't let it destroy you like before."

After my father was killed, I became a shell of myself. At times, I couldn't eat and other times I could do nothing except eat to numb my feelings. For months, I kept losing and gaining the same fifteen pounds over and over. Sleep was intermittent at best. I had no choice but to finish my final semester of high school remotely, an exception the school bent over backward to make given the circumstances.

Why Afton insists on digging up the past after twenty years is beyond me, but I promised I'd be by her side for this and I'm keeping my word. She's convinced some hypnotherapist lady is going to unearth these buried secrets, but I don't know how a person can determine if their memories are real or imaginative? Not to mention there are countless studies on the unreliability of memories in general.

On top of that, this lady charges over three grand for three hours of her time.

Last I knew, Afton didn't have that kind of money.

Back in high school, we had a hypnotist at After Prom. I volunteered to go on stage, and all I remember was having to fake it the whole time because everyone else was doing what the guy was telling them to do, but I didn't feel hypnotized. I felt normal. Afterward, a few other people said the same thing . . . most of us were faking it.

"What are you going to do if it turns out she really did it?" Drew asks.

"She knows not to tell me." I fold a striped sweater and place it on top of a pair of jeans. "Honestly, this hypnotist lady is a quack. I'm going for moral support."

I zip my suitcase and grab my duffel bag, making my way downstairs to hug my boys goodbye before heading across town to pick up Afton. We have a ninety-minute drive, and I've loaded up a playlist full of some of our favorite old songs to keep our spirits light during this little voyage into the treacherous past.

I'm backing out of the driveway a few minutes later when Drew dashes outside, holding my duffel bag in the air.

I must have set it down when I was hugging the kids.

"Oh, geez," I say when he carries it to the van. "Thank you."

"Why are you bringing so much stuff for one night, anyway?"

"Do you even have to ask me that?" I wink. He's always teased me for being an overpacker. Why would this trip be an exception?

He places the duffel in behind the driver's seat before leaning in through the window to give me another kiss goodbye.

This time tomorrow, all our troubles will be water under the bridge.

CHAPTER 39

AFTON

"It looks exactly like the pictures. That's a relief," I say when we pull up to the plum-colored Victorian we reserved. The description said it's the home of a former mayor who married some president's daughter. They raised their seven children here at the turn of the nineteenth century before donating their home to the city. Years later, unable to keep up with the maintenance, the city sold it to some private outfit who now leases it out via Airbnb.

"It's charming," Sydney says, resting her sunglasses on the top of her head. "In a creepy sort of way."

"Maybe we should embrace the creep factor and watch a scary movie tonight?" I tease. Sydney hates anything that isn't romantic or funny.

"Not unless you want me to have night terrors." She shifts into park and kills the engine. "I don't think you want to hear me screaming at the top of my lungs in the middle of the night in this big old house."

"True. That would probably give *me* night terrors."

We haul our things inside and give ourselves a quick tour of the historic home. After choosing our rooms—side by side, naturally—we meet back in the kitchen where Syd has already uncorked a bottle of pinot she must have packed for the trip.

Both wine chalices are filled to the top.

She slides one of them my way.

"I probably shouldn't," I say. "I haven't eaten since breakfast, and I don't know if it's going to interact with my meds."

"Oh, come on," she says. "You had a margarita at dinner a few weeks back and you were fine. Besides, I'm a nurse, and I say one drink won't hurt you."

I roll my eyes, feigning annoyance when she and I both know I'm going to give in.

She points to my glass. "I promise I won't let you have another drop beyond this tonight."

"Fine." I take a sip, pretending I hate it when it's probably the most delicious wine I've ever tasted. That said, the number of times I've had proper wine in my life, I could probably count on one hand. I tend to gravitate toward the cheap wines with the screw-off tops because I'm thirty-seven years old and I still can't use a corkscrew to save my life. "What should we order for dinner?"

I pull up my DoorDash app, update my location, and browse the selections.

"I feel like it'd be a crime if we *didn't* get barbeque while we're here," Syd says.

"When in Rome." I tap on one of the best-rated barbeque restaurants and browse the menu, making my selections before handing my phone to her so she can make hers.

We place the order, which is set to arrive in the next hour, and head to the one room in the entire place that has a TV.

"Do you think they have Netflix?" Syd asks, settling into the sofa.

I sit down beside her and grab the remote. "We'll know soon enough."

"Are you nervous for tomorrow?" She takes a sip of wine, examining me from the corner of her eye.

"The opposite, actually. I'm excited."

"That's good."

"Okay, so looks like we do not have Netflix, but we do have basic cable," I flip through the five or six stations before settling on one of the major broadcasting channels airing some detective show I've never heard of before. "Is this okay?"

"It's going to have to be," she says with a laugh.

It's good to see her smile again, and the entire time we've been together today I can't help but feel like we're both gradually getting back to our old selves.

I work on my drink, taking my time since it'll be my one and only for the evening, when halfway into the crime show my temples begin to throb—as if someone has driven an arrow straight through them.

It's an obnoxiously aggressive kind of pain. Ice pick sharp. I'm no stranger to tension headaches, but this is on a whole other level.

"You all right?" Sydney asks when she notices me massaging my head. She places her hand on my shoulder as she frowns.

"Not really . . . my head started pounding a little bit ago. It's weird," I say.

She rises and places her wineglass on a coaster.

"I packed some aspirin. Let me grab it." She's on her way when her phone rings. Stopping, she checks the screen. "It's Alec. I'm going to take this quick then I'll get the meds for you. Hang tight. It'll just take a sec."

She steps out to take the call on the wraparound front porch. I can't say that I blame her. It's unusually warm for the February day we're having. Sunny. Midsixties. The lightest breeze.

I'm hopeful that a little aspirin and some fresh air might kick this headache to the curb here shortly so this night isn't a bust. I'd been looking forward to it all week. The last time Syd and I traveled anywhere together, Alec was a toddler and Quincy was barely crawling. Her life was getting progressively busier by the day, and I felt bad for so much as thinking of dragging her away from the one place she was needed most. I figured when her kids got older, we'd be able to squeeze in more girls' trips—but the older her boys got, the more activities they were in, tying up her schedule more than ever.

The fact that she's here now speaks volumes about her as a friend—and as a person.

I can't imagine doing this alone.

But several minutes go by and Syd's still outside, leisurely pacing the wooden porch, one hand in her back pocket, the other glued to her phone. Judging by her relaxed posture, I'm guessing it's not an emergency, but I don't want to interrupt, so I head to her room to find the aspirin myself.

Her suitcase and duffel bag are laid out on her bed when I get there, the suitcase already butterflied open. I locate her toiletry bag, riffling past a little stick of deodorant and a mini tube of toothpaste before realizing she has everything *but* aspirin in here. I place those items aside and check her makeup bag next.

No dice.

Of course this woman, the Queen of Overpacking, would bring a suitcase *and* a duffel bag for an overnight stay.

Moving for the duffel, I reach inside and find two paperback books, a gray Baxterville Tech sweatshirt, a magnetic phone charger, and a black leather toiletry bag. Unzipping the small case, I feel around for an aspirin bottle, only for my fingers to brush against a little glass tube the size of my thumb. Pulling it out, I examine what appears to be some kind of injectable medication. Squinting to read the microscopic print on the label, it takes me a second to get past the medical jargon and symbols and find the actual name of it.

Liquid somatapine.

Why would Syd have this? Digging back into the bag, I find blue latex gloves, like the kind they use in hospitals, as well as a tourniquet and a 23-gauge needle.

But there's something else in the midnight-black bottom of that little bag that stands out—a folded note written on familiar pale blue stationery with yellow stars. Unfolding it, I instantly recognize my own handwriting, though there's no date at the top. Scanning the first few lines, I quickly realize it's the letter I sent to Sydney shortly after I was released from the juvenile detention center and placed in home confinement.

I'd been lonely and isolated and I missed her so much it hurt.

We hadn't spoken since before the trial and she was ice cold to me then.

I was convinced if I groveled, if I apologized despite my innocence, she would change her mind and stop hating me.

> Sydney—
> I'm so sorry about your dad. I swear I didn't do it, but everyone thinks I did anyway so it's hard not to believe them. It feels like the whole world is against me. I can't describe it that well but it's the worst feeling you can possibly imagine.
> I hate seeing your family in pain. My heart breaks every time I think about you all.
> I love you guys more than my own family.
> Sometimes I think everyone would be better off if I were gone, too.
> If I could trade places with your dad, I would, Sydney. I swear to God. And sometimes I think I should.
> If we never see each other again after this, please know that I never stopped loving you like a sister, and I'm sorry for everything.
> Love always,
> Afton

Why would she bring this letter that reads vaguely like a suicide note?

And the gloves and the syringe and the medicine . . .

The pain in my head hammers harder than before, ricocheting in my skull with pulsing pressure. It didn't start until after I'd drank a couple of ounces of that wine she gave me—wine that was already poured before I set foot in the kitchen.

An internal heaviness washes over my arms, flowing downward through the rest of my body. I lift my foot to take a step, but it's like I'm suddenly wearing concrete shoes. I don't know if I can make it from here to my room like this.

Crawling onto her bed, I lie on my back and try to make sense of all this while the room begins to spin faster by the second.

I think she drugged me.

My best friend drugged me.

And now she's going to kill me.

CHAPTER 40

SYDNEY

"Shit, shit, shit." I come inside from taking Alec's call to find Afton passed out—and very much alive—on my bed. The contents of my black leather toiletry bag are scattered around her.

She saw the note.

She saw the drug.

She saw everything.

Pacing the room, I run my palm over my forehead, trying to think of how best to handle this.

After dosing her wine with a sedative to keep her amiable and uninhibited, I planned to slip into her room after she'd taken her sleeping pill for the night, inject her with a heroic dose of somatapine to make it look like an intentional overdose of her anxiety medication. After that, I was going to place the old letter on the pillow beside her. In the morning, I would call 9-1-1 after "discovering her." From there, I would play the part of the grief-stricken, shell-shocked best friend.

Afton stirs, as if she's trying to open her eyes, but the best she can do is attempt to blink. Grabbing the syringe and everything else, I shove them back into the small bag and zip it shut.

Worst-case scenario, if she wakes enough to mention it, I'll convince her she was hallucinating again. After all, it hasn't been that long since she's been back on her medication.

Holding my breath, I watch her for more signs that the sedative I placed in her wineglass is wearing off, but her momentary restlessness appears to be subsiding.

Last fall, when she told me she wanted to go under hypnosis to try to remember what happened the night my father was killed, I panicked.

I generally don't believe in that sort of thing because the human brain is a complex organ that even the most studious and educated of individuals still don't completely understand. But Afton was so excited, so convinced that she was going to finally get the answers she'd been searching for her entire adult life, that I had no choice but to put on a supportive front.

In my own time, I did some checking into the woman she found online. Dr. Marcy Corcoran seemed as legit as hypnotherapists come, and according to her website, she'd been an integral part in overturning convictions in several high-profile crime cases all over the country.

I knew then and there I couldn't risk it.

If Afton knew what really happened that night, there would be no coming back from it.

The fallout would be devastating, not just for her, but for my entire family.

It wasn't until I was at her house the night Bea died, helping Afton sort through her medications and get to bed, when I had an idea. I knew from my psych rotation back in nursing school that abrupt withdrawal of benzos and certain anxiolytics can cause hallucinations, especially if the patient has been taking them at a higher dose over the long term.

I thought if I could blur the lines between reality and false-reality, it might render her retrieved memories irrelevant or inaccurate.

Secondly, I figured if I cut her off from her anxiety relief and put her in a state of mind where she'd be unable to relax, it might make it more difficult for her to undergo hypnosis at all.

I take a seat next to her, watching her sleep. She always looks so peaceful when she's resting, which I've always found ironic because this life has been so cruel. She's been a victim of circumstance more times in her thirty-seven years than most people are in one lifetime.

It isn't fair.

And it pains me to have to do this, it does.

But it's the only way.

I think of my saint of a mother and everything she has done for all of us, everything she has sacrificed. And then I think of my boys. My sweet, innocent boys who know nothing of any of this and don't deserve to suffer for things that happened long before they existed. Lastly, I think of Drew. The jury is still out on whether or not he's having an affair, but I've been so busy planning this that I've pushed it to the back burner temporarily while I handle this bigger issue.

If my husband has stepped out of our marriage, we can fix it.

It might be ugly, but we can navigate it together.

If Afton makes it to the hypnotherapist tomorrow, if the truth comes out, what happens after that will be completely out of my control.

Checking my watch, I decide it's far too early in the night to inject her. No one takes their own life at six o'clock.

They do it after dark—in the midnight hours when the rest of the world is fast asleep and unable to stop them.

Then again, she's already sedated and there's no way I'll be able to get her to drink another glass of wine if she were to wake up. The plan would be scrapped and she would attend her appointment tomorrow morning as planned.

I snap the latex gloves on, unwrap the syringe, and draw up eight milligrams of the anxiety medication—four times the lethal adult dose.

Once I inject this into her vein, there'll be no surviving it.

I tie the rubber tourniquet tight around her lower bicep and flick the inside of her elbow, searching for the juiciest vein. But before I can finish what I've already started, Afton moans.

Her lashes flutter, like she's trying to wake up again, but her body is working against her.

Klorhazadol will do that.

That stuff is no joke.

As much strife as Stacia causes our family sometimes, her drug dealer came in clutch at the last minute. I used to keep his number on hand to keep tabs on her. Imagine his shock when I asked him to find me klorhazadol and liquid somatapine.

Nevertheless, he said it wasn't his job to judge or ask questions, and within a week, the man delivered.

Afton moans once again, her head moving ever so slightly.

"Shh," I say. "You should rest. Found you passed out in here. Looks like you were searching for the aspirin? I've set it here on the nightstand along with some water. Anyway, you can take my room for the night and I'll take yours. No biggie."

I play dumb, hoping she'll relax and pass out again. The truth is there was never any aspirin . . . I was going to give her another sedative.

"S . . . Syd," she manages to say, licking her lips as a pained wince forms on her face.

Brushing a wisp of hair off her forehead, I soothe her the way I would soothe one of my own children.

I'm doing this for them. For their future. For their lives.

Afton's already sacrificed so much for me: her reputation, the best years of her life, her own hopes and dreams, her life savings . . . if she could fully understand what was at stake here, I know deep down she'd be okay with this.

She would want us to be happy, to be fully free and untethered from that tragic night that has haunted each of us in our own ways for almost two decades.

Afton's been a true friend—a better friend than I deserved, and I'm going to miss her.

But I'm not going to miss worrying and obsessing over the truth coming out. There are times it keeps me up at night, sick with unease, wondering what would happen and how bad the fallout would be.

The thought of my boys watching me getting cuffed and hauled off to prison for the rest of my life sends a dampness to my eyes that I quickly swipe away.

Now is not the time to get emotional.

If anything, this is cause for celebration.

It's all going to be over. Finally.

CHAPTER 41

AFTON

The bed shifts. While I can't see Sydney, I can feel her, sense her moving things, shuffling, pacing. She sits on the bed. She gets up. The mattress depresses again and her signature amber perfume fills my lungs.

I groan through lips that are too heavy to move, too uncoordinated to work together.

"Shhh," she says. "Get some rest. I found you passed out in here. Looks like you were searching for the aspirin? I set it on your nightstand along with some water. Anyway, you can take my room for the night and I'll take yours."

She's lying.

She's playing dumb.

Using all the strength I have, I mutter her name, or some semblance of it.

"S . . . Syd." The sounds are weighty in my mouth and my tongue is all but paralyzed.

I don't understand . . .

Why would she want to kill me? Her own mother championed my innocence from day one and Syd claims she forgave me years ago, that she knew it couldn't have been me. She's stood by me for twenty years—and for what?

"Syd . . . Sydney," I say as she ties something painfully tight around my upper arm. I attempt to swallow, but my throat feels like sandpaper. I need water. And I need to get out of this bed and away from this woman.

She flicks my veins. "Close your eyes. It'll all be over soon."

I don't want to die.

Maybe I did twenty years ago, but I was a kid. I was confused. I thought it was what everyone wanted. I thought my death would bring a strange kind of happiness or an inkling of justice to the remaining Carsons—or at least dampen some of the pain they were experiencing. Then I thought of all the locals and internet strangers who hated me with a frightening amount of intensity, people who would cheer and celebrate my death.

But when Sydney wrote back and told me not to do it, that she would work on forgiving me, all the hope I'd lost was suddenly found.

Mustering every last ounce of strength I have, I force my eyes open in time to see her drawing the medicine into the syringe.

"Please," I whisper, "no . . ."

Placing it on the nightstand, she scoots closer to me and rests her hand over mine.

"I didn't want it to come to this," she says, looking me deep in the eyes. "And you should know, I don't take any of this lightly. You've been like a sister to me from the beginning, and I'll always remember you that way. But things are complicated, more than you could possibly understand."

Reaching for the syringe, she holds it upside down, gives it a tap, and presses on the bottom until the tiniest bead of clear liquid forms at the tip.

"I wish you would've listened to me with this whole hypnotherapist thing," she continues. "We wouldn't be here, doing this. I'm not trying to say it's your fault, but in a way, it sort of is. There was no talking you out of this."

"Why?" I ask.

A thick tear slides down the side of my face, but I'm unable to swipe it away. It drips down my ear before landing in my hair.

Sydney plucks a tissue from a nearby container and dries my tear—a cruel yet tender move.

"Don't cry, okay?" she says. "No tears. Don't make this sad. We had a good run. We had a lot of fun times together. And you're going to see Gram soon. Focus on that."

This has to be a delusion.

A hallucination.

A nightmare.

I refuse to believe this is real.

"Please . . . don't . . . do this." My words are staggered yet slurred as more tears drag down the sides of my face, pooling in my hair. "I . . . won't . . . go . . ."

She chuckles. "It's a little late for that. You should've taken my advice the first time I gave it to you."

"I'll . . . do . . . anything," I say.

"You're making this harder than it needs to be—for both of us." The tiniest hint of bittersweetness resides in her tone, though I refuse to believe it's authentic. Anyone with an ounce of compassion in their heart would never do this to an innocent person. "I don't know if I'll ever be able to forgive myself for this, if it makes you feel better. This whole thing—it's bigger than you. It's bigger than me, it's bigger than all of us."

Oh, my God.

It was her.

It was Sydney who tampered with my medication.

She wanted to sabotage my sanity, ruin my chance of recovering any buried memories.

Sydney must be the only one who knows what happened that night—and she has to keep it that way.

She begins to say something else when the doorbell chimes.

"Ah, that must be dinner," she says. "Be right back."

In her haste to leave, she sets the syringe on the dresser across the room. I wouldn't be able to grab it if I tried. I still can't move my arms or legs. The best I can do is wiggle my fingers. Running them along the comforter beneath me, I find a loose thread and give it a pull until it snaps.

I felt that.

This is real.

This isn't delirium or a figment of a drug-induced mind or my broken brain.

My eyelids grow heavy once again before falling shut. Exhaustion washes over me in waves, drowning out the glimmering final remains of my consciousness.

CHAPTER 42

SYDNEY

"Mom?" I stand at the front door of our Airbnb, wondering if *I'm* the one hallucinating for a change. "What are you doing here?"

I was expecting burnt ends and shredded pork, and the only reason I wanted to fetch it immediately was because if, by chance, there's any suspicion of foul play after Afton's "suicide," I wanted to make every aspect of our evening together seem as casual and logical as possible. Someone ordering DoorDash and not retrieving it until after it'd been sitting on the porch getting cold would be a red flag to any investigator.

There can be no holes in my story, nothing that would make so much as an armchair detective scratch their chin.

I'd already practiced what I was going to say if and when they question me.

We were two childhood best friends having a much-needed girls' night at an Airbnb . . .

I'd tell them the truth—that Afton was scheduled to meet with a hypnotherapist in the morning and she'd asked me to come with her for support.

I'd tell them despite Afton's extensive psychiatric history we've always soldiered through life together.

I'd tell them after we settled in, we split a bottle of wine, then Afton claimed she had a horrible headache and wanted to lie down.

I'd tell them I chalked it up to her being nervous about her upcoming appointment and that I left her alone to get a good night's rest . . . never knowing she had done the unthinkable behind that closed door.

Had there been food waiting here for me instead of my mother, I'd be injecting the medication right now and Afton's body would begin the process of shutting down. I already had my eye on the plump vein in the crux of her elbow, one that would get the drug coursing through her system as efficiently as possible so her death would be quick and painless.

I'm not a monster.

But apparently my mother thinks I am.

Eyeing the doorbell camera, I change my tone from accusatory to pleasantly surprised.

"Mom, oh, my gosh! You came to surprise us! Come on in." I stand back and she steps into the house, giving me side-eye all the while because she knows me better than this.

"Where is she?"

"Are you going to answer my question?" I ask. "What are you doing here?"

"Not until you answer mine."

She places her jacket and purse on one of the ugly plaid chairs before peering around the makeshift family room. I imagine when this house was first built, this space would've served as a scullery or maybe it was a study or parlor. I'm sure the people who built this house and put so much love and thought into every corner of it would be shocked if they knew it would one day be the scene of an unthinkable tragedy.

Mom's gaze lands on the two wineglasses.

"Did you *drug* her?" She strides toward me, peering down her straight nose and maintaining an unsettling amount of composure.

"You should have stayed home."

More than likely Drew or one of the boys let this slip, though it couldn't have been Alec. He would have mentioned it to me on the phone a little while ago.

"What on earth are you thinking?" she asks, eyes winced so tight her crow's-feet are in full display—the crow's-feet she refuses to do anything about because she believes growing old is a privilege. Not that I disagree. But she doesn't have to be all high and mighty about it like she gets sometimes. "Show me where she is—and she better be breathing."

I'd intentionally neglected to tell my mother about our girls' trip and Afton's hypnotherapy appointment because no one knows me better than her. Not even Drew.

Mom knows my heart.

She knows the truth.

And based on the unflinching, determined chill in her demeanor, she's here to save me from myself.

"Afton?" She calls out into the depths of the never-ending yet compartmentalized Victorian. "Afton, sweetheart, where are you? It's Cynthia. Call out to me, please."

This place is practically the size of a Walmart and she's trotting around it like a lunatic, searching high and low, opening creaky bathroom doors and closets, dashing down dim hallways with their flickering aged brass sconces and creepy William Morris wallpaper.

This is a terrible place to take your last breath, in my opinion, but I wanted Afton to choose where we stayed since it would be her last night on earth.

It was the least I could do.

"Oh, my God," my mother cries after opening the door to my room. It bangs against the wall and bounces back. "Afton . . ."

"She's not dead," I tell her while she flits around, checking her pulse and gently smacking her cheeks to get her to rouse awake. "At least not yet."

"What did you give her?" My mother turns to me with wild eyes. The familiar searing heat of jealousy burns through me. A person shouldn't have to compete with their best friend for their mother's tenderness, and I've had to do it my *entire* life.

In a weird, codependent sort of way, my mother and Afton have always needed each other. Afton needed a reliable mother figure. Mom needed someone she could "rescue." That someone has since been replaced by Stacia for the most part, but that soft spot Mom has for Afton has never fully gone away.

Now it would seem it's back with a vengeance.

"Just a harmless little sedative." I wave my hand like it's nothing, and it's true. It'll wear off soon enough. Four to six hours, tops. Had I been able to give her the full dose, it'd be a different story. "You got here just in time."

I point to the syringe resting on its side where I left it.

No sense in hiding something that's already in plain sight.

I leave my mother alone with Afton because I can't take another minute of her frantic fussing over her precious non-daughter, and I return to the other room to finish my wine.

Hopefully by the time Mom comes out, she'll be calm enough to have a rational conversation about what we're going to do with a situation that has officially become *both* of our problems.

Again.

CHAPTER 43

AFTON

I wake with a start, choking on my breath as I sit up straight in what should have been my final resting place.

How am I still alive?

Wait . . . *am* I alive?

Pressing two fingers into the side of my neck, I note the warmth of my pulsing flesh, and I count the tiny beats.

One, two, three, four, five, six . . . all the way to *forty-two* before I'm finally convinced this is real.

None of this feels real as bits and pieces of last night flood my thoughts, each one more disturbing than the one before, kicking my heart into overdrive as the air around me turns paper thin.

Scanning my surroundings, I'm shocked when I spot my suitcase in the corner instead of Syd's. Her things are gone . . . the syringe, the duffel bag, the vial of medicine. It's as if it were never here to begin with—but I *know* I didn't imagine it.

Reality sinks into my bones with razor-sharp teeth: my best friend tried to kill me—and it wasn't a hallucination.

Nothing about this makes sense.

My entire life, I've done nothing but stand by Sydney's side through everything—not to mention I paid off all of her bills. It's been almost two decades since that horrible night and I've had no reason to believe she was still harboring any kind of resentment about it.

Why would she want me dead?

A jolt of adrenaline floods through me with the somber realization that the Sydney I thought I knew is nothing more than a stranger capable of the unthinkable.

I climb out of bed with shaky legs that now feel like they're made of gelatin instead of solid concrete, but at least they work.

Holding my breath, I poke my head out of the doorway and listen for any signs that I'm not alone. I'm not about to go searching for my would-be killer in this antique palace of a place with its intricate layout and myriad bedrooms and parlors and countless potential hiding places.

All I hear, though, is the sound of my hammering heartbeats whooshing in my ears.

A moment later, the grandfather clock in the hall dongs ten times. Given all the daylight flooding this house, it has to be ten AM, not PM.

My appointment with Dr. Marcy was an hour ago.

With soundless footsteps, I leave the room, carefully making my way through the main floor. In the kitchen, I discover our wineglasses from last night are rinsed clean and placed back on the rack, as if they'd never been used. The trash can is empty—not a single food container or empty bottle of pinot in sight.

The entire home is immaculate, unspoiled by any of the things I remember from last night.

It's as if we were never here—or at least, as if Sydney were never here.

I don't waste another second exploring. Hauling my suitcase outside, I lock the door behind me and hit the sidewalk with a breakneck pace.

Sydney's minivan is absent from the driveway, of course.

She left me here.

For all I know, she left me here to die.

Alone.

Dragging my suitcase behind me, I jog along the broken squares of sidewalk, the wheels of my bag whirring behind me as they attempt to keep up.

Five blocks later, I spot a busy gas station on the other side of a major intersection.

For the first time in my life, I want to be seen.

Correction—*need* to be seen.

I need to be surrounded by as many people as humanly possible because most people aren't going to kill someone with dozens of witnesses in broad daylight.

Odds are Sydney's long gone by now, maybe already home with her family, acting like nothing happened because even if she told them everything, who would believe her?

And who would *want* to believe she's capable of such an unspeakable thing?

Certainly not Drew.

Especially not Cynthia.

My chest is tight, aching, and my eyes burn, though they refuse to shed a single tear.

I imagine I'm in shock, but I don't have time to wallow in my emotions.

Not here, not yet.

With my heart whooshing in my ears, I catch my breath beside the propane tank case at a bustling QuikTrip before calling 9-1-1.

And then I wait, my back against the brick facade of the gas station, terrified but grateful to be alive.

CHAPTER 44

SYDNEY

"You doing okay, hon?" Drew takes a break from his computer the next morning to check on me.

I came home late last night and told him a curated take on everything that happened—we settled in, had a little wine, she started saying things that didn't make sense, getting angry and belligerent. I was worried she was having some kind of interaction with the alcohol and her medication. She swung at me. I locked myself in a room and called my mother, who immediately came to help calm Afton down, only Afton lashed out at her as well. In the end, we both felt leaving was the safest option for all involved. "God, that's terrible what happened. You could've been killed."

I press my head against his shoulder as he wraps his arm around me.

He took the day off to spend it with me after seeing how distraught I was last night. That combined with me tossing and turning all night, and he's worried about me.

"I know she's your best friend," Drew says, "and I've never told you who to be friends with. But I think it's time you pull the plug on this. She needs help. Serious help. More help than you or your mom can give her."

I nod, forcing a sniffle since I've not shed a single tear yet.

It's got to be the adrenaline coursing through my system. I'm still too pumped up from everything that happened. Going off a few hours of sleep probably isn't helping either.

Regardless, Drew doesn't notice.

He's never been a details guy when it comes to emotions.

He tenses up at the first sign of tears and finds every excuse not to actually look at someone when they're having an emotional breakdown. Maybe it's a good thing we had all boys. I don't think Drew could've handled even one daughter. That and any daughter of mine would have likely been a handful.

I'd be kidding myself if I expected anything different.

"Someone's calling you." Drew hands me my phone, which is vibrating on the coffee table. "Do you recognize that number?"

"No." It's a Kansas City area code, but that's all I know.

When Mom and I cleaned up and left last night, Afton was still sound asleep. Mom made sure to flush the liquid medication down the toilet along with the vial. I'm not sure what she did with the actual needle and syringe, but it's better that I don't know.

"You going to answer it?" he asks.

Clearing my throat, I grab the phone and press the green circle.

"Hello? Sydney Westfeldt speaking," I say.

"Sydney, hi, this is Officer Clayburn with Overland Park PD," he begins. My heart catches in my throat, but I'm ready for this. With a little coaching from my mother, I prepared for this very conversation the entire drive home yesterday. "I'm here at the station with Afton Teachout."

"Oh, goodness. Yes," I say in an exhale. "Is she okay? Is she safe?"

He hesitates. "She's safe, ma'am."

"Thank God." I splay my hand over my chest. The officer can't see me but Drew is watching me like a hawk.

"Any way you could drive back this afternoon and help me clarify exactly what took place last night?"

His vague wording is concerning.

I don't know how much Afton saw or how much she remembers—sedatives can often cause a form of amnesia.

"We're just trying to piece everything together," he says. "Would really appreciate if you could help us with that."

He's neutral, and I don't know if that's a good or bad thing.

What I do know, however, is that I can't say no.

"I'm about an hour and a half away," I say, "but give me two hours and I'll be there."

"Appreciate that, Mrs. Westfeldt," he says. "Just ask for me when you stop in at the precinct."

I end the call and turn to Drew. "They have Afton at the station. They want to interview me about what happened."

"When?"

"Now."

Drew rises, like he's ready to go literally right now. "I'm coming with you. I don't want you alone around her."

"It's fine. Nothing's going to happen. She's not going to rip my face off at a police station."

"I don't care, I'm still going. You're not doing this by yourself." The determination in his eyes and the overprotection in his words send a fullness to my heart, one that's been running on fumes as of late.

Vanessa or no Vanessa, Drew still loves me.

He still cares about me.

He's dropping everything to be there for me in my time of need, and that counts for something.

"I'm going to get cleaned up," I say. "Let's plan to be on the road in the next twenty minutes."

Twenty-two minutes later, we're en route to Overland Park.

"Let's get this over with," I say when I buckle in.

Drew angles his head, scratching his temple. "Get it over with?"

Shit. Poor choice of words.

A victim probably wouldn't treat this like an annoying task on their overflowing to-do list, but that's what it is—to me.

"I just mean, I already explained what happened to Mom and you. I just don't feel like revisiting it. But it's okay. I need to do this. Maybe this'll be the key to finally getting her the help she needs."

The idea of Afton spending the rest of her life in an institution breaks my heart, but as we make our way down our familiar little street and eventually to the highway, the sun beats down through the window on the passenger door and floods me with warmth and light.

In the end, this is a good thing.

She'll have someone to take care of her the rest of her life, she'll be around other people who are somewhat similar to her so she can make new friends, and she'll never have to work again. In the grand scheme of things, it's more like a medically supervised forced retirement than prison. Without Gram to worry about, she'll move on. She'll adapt. She'll be fine.

We're halfway to the city when Mom calls. Since we're in my van, it comes over the Bluetooth. I'm about to press ignore when Drew reaches for the screen first and answers it.

"Hi, Mom." I color my words with a hint of despondency.

"Hadn't heard from you yet today," she says. "Everything all right?"

"Yeah, I'm just in the van with Drew," I say, enunciating that crystal clear. "We're going back to Overland Park. I got a call from a police officer. They have Afton and they want to ask me some questions."

It's silent for a few beats.

"Oh my," Mom says. "I hope she's okay."

Of course she does.

"I'm sure she's fine. Probably a little confused. But I'm hoping I can clear things up and we can move on from all of this."

Drew reaches across the car and takes my hand, holding it tight in his and giving me a reassuring squeeze.

"Well, keep me posted," Mom says.

"Will do." I end the call.

"You're pressing charges, right?" Drew asks.

"Charges? For what?"

"Attempted murder?"

I laugh. "She didn't attempt to murder me—she was just acting crazy, throwing things, shoving furniture. She was having some sort of meltdown. She's not a killer."

He's quiet, and I realize the weight of my words.

Of everyone who was affected by my father's death, Drew took it the hardest as he admired my father almost more than his own. And while my family was questioning Afton's guilt, Drew disagreed magnanimously. He said Afton was always jealous of me, that I had the life she wanted, the life she felt she deserved, and that in killing my father, she could expose the affair between my dad and her mom and demolish our picture-perfect family.

It makes sense, I'll admit.

But it's not what really happened.

It's not even close.

CHAPTER 45

AFTON

"Is it true you're on a multitude of psychiatric medications?" Officer Clayburn asks.

I've been at the police station several hours now, with nothing to drink but burnt coffee and no other sustenance besides vending machine junk food—strawberry wafer cookies, crunchy Cheetos, a crumbly honey oat granola bar.

I need a shower.

I need water.

I need to go home.

From what I understand, they called Sydney and she's here.

My would-be murderer is somewhere in this same building.

Who knows, maybe we're even sharing a wall right now? The thought makes me shudder, and combined with the crap in my stomach, I could almost throw up.

Pulling the scratchy blanket they gave me around my sides for comfort, I swallow the lump in my throat. I'm not surprised she's spinning it this way—that I'm "crazy" or that my version of events is unreliable.

I stare at my lifeless phone. Last I checked the battery was at 6 percent, so I'm leaving it be. I asked for a charger earlier, but he must have forgotten.

"I am, but—" I answer him.

"Is it true you were recently suffering from delusions, paranoias, and hallucinations?" he asks, glancing at the yellow legal pad in front of him. His handwriting is awful and impossible to read, but apparently he took a lot of notes because the page is littered with chicken scratch.

"Yes," I say. "But that has nothing to do with what happened last night. She was going to kill me. She drugged me and she had this needle."

My story sounds as ridiculous the fifth time around as it did the first time I told it.

I imagine Sydney sitting in the interrogation room beside me, wide eyed, innocent, prim and proper, using nurse jargon or intellectual phrases she has picked up from her mom over the years.

I'm sure she looks and sounds credible—meanwhile, I'm still in last night's clothes, I haven't brushed my hair or teeth, and he found me at a gas station with a suitcase, claiming someone just tried to kill me.

I don't blame him for not believing me, but it's frustrating just the same.

"We sent one of our officers to the Airbnb you stayed at," he says. "They didn't find proof of anything that you described. There was no drug paraphernalia of any sort. All we have is some video doorbell footage of you two coming, Sydney's mother arriving, and then a DoorDasher—"

"Right. I told you, when I woke up everything had been cleaned . . . wait. Did you say Sydney's *mom* arrived?"

"Yes, ma'am," he says. "Mrs. Westfeldt says she called her mother because she thought she could get you to calm down."

I don't remember seeing Cynthia.

Then again, I was passed out.

"Did you bring Cynthia in? Is she here, too?" I ask because I have some questions for her myself.

I *know* what I saw last night—the syringe, the medicine, the tourniquet.

I remember how heavy my body felt, how sleepy I suddenly became.

I distinctly recall all the things Sydney was saying about making this harder on both of us, how she's sorry . . .

I clearly wasn't a threat to her, so why would Cynthia need to be there?

The junk food I inhaled an hour ago rumbles in my stomach, rising up the back of my throat.

All Cynthia has ever done is take care of me—why would she be there the night her daughter tried to murder me?

"Oh, we also checked the dumpster in the alley behind the house and there were leftover food containers from Bubba's BBQ as well as an empty bottle of pinot noir. That corroborates Sydney's part of the story that you two ordered takeout and had wine. But we couldn't find any syringes, medication, or evidence of an altercation."

"Wait, why did she clean up before she left?" I ask. "If she was truly scared for her safety, why take the time to wash wineglasses and walk all the way outside to throw the trash away in the dumpster? Why not just get the hell out of there?"

The officer taps his pen against the legal pad, like I've stumped him.

"That's a great question, Miss Teachout," he says, "but unfortunately where we are with this right now is that she has the option of pressing charges—"

"Pressing charges for *what*?" My jaw hangs.

"Verbal threats are a form of assault," he says. "Given you had the means and the motivation to hurt her and you made threats stating you planned to do so, Mrs. Westfeldt was offered the opportunity to press charges . . . but she declined. She's requesting a restraining order instead. However, the court isn't going to give her one—not without a report on file and not without proof. Text messages, emails, phone calls, video recordings. That sort of thing. She can't get a restraining order based on verbal accounts alone."

Restraining order or not, I have no plans of ever talking to that woman again.

"We talked it over and she said her mother is making some calls today—apparently she has some connections and knows your doctor personally. I understand you're a longtime family friend of theirs, and while they're deeply upset by what happened, they've decided the best thing to do is to get you some professional help. In the meantime, I suggest you stay far away from Mrs. Westfeldt and her family. Go about your days as if there *is* a restraining order in place. It'll prevent anything like this from ever happening again."

I slide against my chair, unsure if I should laugh, cry, or show everyone just how "crazy" I really am. This is absurd. *I* am the victim here—not Sydney.

Gathering a deep breath, I sit up, reach for my dying phone, and ask if I'm free to leave.

"You are," the officer says. "Do you have a way to get home?"

Sydney drove yesterday, so no.

I'm stranded.

I have no money to rent a car.

A taxi ride would be outrageous.

And I don't even want to know what an Uber would cost from here to Shelter Rock.

It's not like I can call Gram. Even if she were still alive, her driver's license expired a lifetime ago.

"If you need transportation, we can arrange something for you," he says, sensing my hesitancy.

"I would appreciate that. Thank you."

Shelter Rock is the last place I want to be right now, but where else am I going to go?

CHAPTER 46

SYDNEY

"Did you tell them everything the way we practiced it?" Mom asks from the other side of her desk. As soon as we got back from meeting with the police in Overland Park, I dropped Drew off at home and came to her office to catch her between patients.

"I did," I say.

"And everything went well?" She raps her fingers against the top of her desk. One, two, three, four, one, two, three, four . . .

I nod.

"You didn't press charges, correct?" she asks.

One of the first things she advised me on was to not press charges or make this into something big. For starters, she says it would be morally wrong given the true nature of the situation. Secondly, she said it would only make this a long, drawn-out, potentially expensive and time-consuming situation, and that's the last thing anyone needs. Lastly, if it backfired on me, there would be no coming back from it.

"What if she goes to that hypnotherapist? What if she remembers what really happened?" I ask. "All of *this* was to prevent *that*, and it would have had you stayed home."

Mom leans forward, folding her hands on top of her desk. "You are a very intelligent and capable woman, Sydney, but I don't think you were thinking clearly in this case."

I learned yesterday that it was Drew who accidentally let the cat out of the bag about our girls' trip. Mom had stopped by with a batch of fresh oatmeal chocolate chip cookies for the boys and immediately inquired about where I was. After a bit of small talk, she told them she had some errands to run, kissed her grandsons goodbye, and was on her way.

"If everything you're telling me is accurate, I expect all of this to blow over sooner than later," she says. "I plan to check on Afton when I can, but I strongly advise you to steer clear of her like your life depends on it. It's for the best."

"That's what I wanted to do twenty years ago, but you were the one who forced me to accept her back into my life again."

Mom's lips form a hard line. "I think we can all agree it was the best thing to do given those particular circumstances."

Even if I hated it, I understood Mom's reasons.

"If she never would've found that hypnotherapist, none of this would've happened," I say.

"Well she did and *it* did and there's nothing we can do about it now." Mom rises, straightening her suit jacket. "My next patient should be here any minute." She strides to the front of her desk, perches on its polished walnut edge, and looks me dead in the eyes. "I want you to go home, be with your family, appreciate that you still have them around, that your life is still intact, and then I want you to never breathe a word of any of this ever again. Do you understand?"

I swallow and nod.

The instant I walk out of her clinic, I leave everything in the past.

Everything.

CHAPTER 47

AFTON

I'm loading groceries in the back of my car when something in my periphery snags my attention—a Chrysler Town & Country with a blonde behind the steering wheel. She slides her sunglasses down her nose, places them on the top of her dash and gets out, swinging her oversized mom-bag over one shoulder.

Sydney.

It's been a month since she tried to kill me . . . a month of lying in bed every night asking questions I'll never have answers to, replaying conversations and moments six ways from Sunday in a vain attempt to make sense of something nonsensical.

I've stayed home as much as possible—aside from errands and one measly job interview, but everywhere I go, I look over my shoulder, worried I'm going to run into her one of these times—not because I'm afraid of her, but because I'm afraid of what I might do or say when I see her.

I put the last of my groceries in my trunk and slam it shut so hard my palms sting.

Sydney grabs a cart from the cart corral, pushing it over uneven patches of blacktop, its wobbly wheels bringing us closer together with every step she takes.

Because of where she parked, she's going to have to walk past me to get inside.

If she hasn't noticed me yet, she will soon.

That cop in Overland Park told me to carry on as if a restraining order is in place, but all I've thought about for the past several weeks is all the things I want to say to her.

Paralyzed behind my car, I steal a glimpse her way.

My hands ball into fists that I shove into my pockets so I don't lunge at her and claw out her eyeballs. Not that I would. But I'd be lying if I said I hadn't thought about it a time or two these last several weeks.

The idea of her moving on with her picture-perfect life like nothing happened is what gets me the most.

How can you be best friends with someone your entire life, try to take her life, then carry on like it's any other day?

Still frozen, I mentally will myself to get in the car, to drive away, to not engage or make this worse. Then again, I might not ever have a chance to ask her the one question that has haunted my nightmares since that fateful night: Why?

Angling my body toward her, I slide my hands from my pockets and rest them on my hips, taking a more authoritative stance in an attempt to get her to notice me—or to at least pretend she isn't ignoring me if that's what she's doing.

Sure enough, Sydney stops cold, glancing around in search of an alternate route, but unless she abandons her cart and squeezes through parked cars, zigzagging around like a weirdo, there are no other options.

My heart inches up the back of my bile-burned throat.

Heat flashes through me.

I could throw up, cry, and punch her all at the same time.

Meanwhile, the muscles in my body are so tight they could snap.

By the time she's close enough that her amber perfume invades my airspace, I've lost my cool.

"Why?" I ask. *"Why?"*

Sydney jolts her head, as if she's taken aback, as if she'd planned to walk on by like I was see-through despite obviously noticing me a moment earlier.

"Why did you do what you did?" I ask before deciding I owe her no favors by sugarcoating my words. "Why did you try to *kill* me, Sydney?"

Abandoning my fears, I step toward her, effectively blocking her path to the store.

She's not leaving until I get my answer.

"We shouldn't be talking." Sydney clings to the handle of her cart so hard her knuckles turn the color of snow and her gaze averts.

She's afraid of me yet disregards me at the same time.

I search her face for signs of guilt, remorse, conflicting emotions—only there's nothing.

"That's not what I asked. I asked why you tried to kill me." I grip the end of her cart, planting my feet in place as the metal digs into my palms.

"I'm not having this conversation."

"Why not?" It takes all the self-restraint I have not to shove the cart into her, scream in her face, and cause a massive scene because I'd love nothing more than to do that right now.

Sydney sniffs, turning her head away and adjusting her hold on the red handle of her shopping cart. There's a damp sweat shadow where her palms were before.

"You were my best friend. I would've taken a bullet for you, no questions asked . . . and you tried to kill me." My voice is trembling worse than my hands. "For *what*?"

She still refuses to answer.

"Did I do something?" I ask. "Is this because I thought Drew was having an affair?"

Her eyes flick to mine, but only for a second.

After I learned my medications had been tampered with and I spent the week at Cynthia's, I never brought up Drew's affair to Sydney again. It went without saying that both of us assumed it was just another hallucination, like everything else at that time. After a month of racking my brain trying to figure out what I could have possibly said or done to make her hate me, that was the only thing that stood out.

Maybe she thought I was trying to ruin her marriage and she was still angry about it?

Sydney's marriage is the one thing she treasures more than anything in this world.

Her family is everything to her—and I almost dismantled it.

"Move before I call the authorities," she says, her gaze once again meandering anywhere but in my direction. Her tone is harder than before, but it doesn't faze me.

"Call the police if it makes you feel better. There's no restraining order, and I'm in a public place. I have just as much of a right to be here as you do."

An older woman and her husband walk past, staring both of us down.

A young mother hauling a heavy-looking car seat in one arm passes next, giving us a once-over before picking up her pace.

The tension radiating from our exchange is so palpable, even strangers can sense it.

I release my hold on her cart, but I stay put.

"There's nothing I can say that's going to make any of this better," Sydney says, the tenor of her voice giving annoyance more than anything else. "There's nothing I can say that's going to give us back the friendship we lost—and let's admit it, we lost it long before any of this. We were both just . . . playing parts."

"I never felt that way. I was never playing a part."

"Well, I was." Her eyes drop to the ground as her words slice through the center of my chest like a rusted blade that'll no doubt leave an ugly scar.

"It was always real to me." My voice breaks, and I hate that she gets to see how much she hurt me. But more than that, I hate her—and I've never hated anyone in my life. "You're pathetic."

I spit my words at her and fight back the pressure building behind my eyes as a cocktail of betrayal, humiliation, and confusion blankets over me. I refuse to cry over her, in front of her, or because of her.

Not now.

Not ever again.

"I'm sorry." Her eyes are dead and her apology is nothing but a couple of lifeless words; a handful of assembled letters that mean nothing spoken from her lips. She's probably just saying them in a half-assed attempt to end this conversation.

"Sorry for being a horrible person or for trying to murder me? Going to need some clarity on that apology." I fold my arms. This discussion is far from over. "How can you hug your children with the same hands you used to tie a tourniquet around my arm? How can you kiss your husband with the same lips that spoke words of comfort as you filled that syringe in front of me? How can you look in the mirror every day knowing what you're capable of?"

It's in this moment that I realize I couldn't possibly have murdered her father twenty years ago—because I actually have a conscience.

Sydney clucks her tongue and switches her purse to her other arm and repositions her cart. "I've said all I can say. Please leave and please never contact me, talk to me, or so much as look in my direction again. It's in both of our best interests."

Abandoning her grocery mission, Sydney shoves her cart into the nearest corral, returns to her van—the one I paid off—and speeds away like the coward she is.

Like the coward she'll always be.

I hope she spends the rest of her life looking over her shoulder, knowing it's only a matter of time before her bad karma catches up with her.

While I still don't have my answers, I've finally confronted Sydney and rattled her notoriously unshakable facade.

I'll take that as a win.

For now.

CHAPTER 48

SYDNEY

They say every villain is the hero of their own story.

"You'll never believe what Mr. Cunningham said in chorus class today," Cal says with a freckle-faced giggle at the dinner table. It's been a while since we ate supper at a normal time, all together, at the same table.

"What did he say?" Drew asks.

"He said why is it so hard to open a piano?" Cal is almost bursting at the seams, waiting to deliver his punch line. "Because the keys are on the *inside*!"

Drew and I chuckle, and I shoot looks at the older boys, making sure they don't razz their kid brother over his dad joke, but much to my delight, they're laughing, too.

"That's lame but it's clever," Quincy says.

"Pretty sure he's been using that one since I was in your grade," Alec adds. "Tell him he needs some new material."

"Quincy, how's the chicken?" I change the subject. "You want seconds?"

His plate is empty, practically licked clean, and Alec's plate is looking similar.

"Perfect," he says, talking with his mouth full. I let it slide this time because all five of us are together and enjoying each other's company and bonding over a delicious meal that I actually enjoyed cooking because I wasn't trying to run off to my second job.

This is how it should be.

None of this would be possible had the truth come out about my father's death.

Drew reaches across the table to hold my hand. Ever since starting his new job in Kansas City, he's acting more and more like his old self. He's happier than ever, too. He wasn't wrong when he said we've weathered storms before and we'd do it again.

The last few months have been heavy and draining, even hopeless at times. But I'd do it all over again if it meant making moments like this possible.

My mother always says you have to take the good with the bad in life. She says the bad makes us stronger and makes us appreciate the good.

She's not been wrong yet.

Between bites of chicken and roasted vegetables, I scan the room, imagining Drew with a head of silvery hair and our boys older, more mature, educated, with families of their own.

For the first time in forever, it's like I can finally exhale.

I try not to think about Afton if I can help it—not because I'm happy about what I did. I'm not a heartless monster. I'm just a wife and a mother and a daughter doing what needed to be done, and Afton was a casualty of that.

If I were her, I'd focus on the fact that I'm still alive and kicking, that I have a second chance, that I'm now free to cut the cords that kept me tethered to Shelter Rock. Judging by our little altercation at the grocery store the other day, I'd say she's still very much rooted in what happened. While it pained me to pretend I didn't care, I do hope one day she can move on, spread her wings, fly far away from the town that has never done her any favors, and never look back—for her sake and for ours.

Me? I regret nothing.

I did it all for my guys—and I'd do it all a million times over if I had to.

That's the thing about me: if I love you, I'll move Heaven and earth with my bare hands to show you how much you mean to me.

I did it for my mom all those years ago.

For Drew.

And I did it again for my family.

"Alec, seconds?" I ask, forking chicken breast from the dish on the trivet.

He gives me a thumbs-up while he chews his last bite.

For a single fleeting moment, my eyes lock with Drew's from across the table, like we're having a silent conversation in a language only the two of us can understand. He smiles a smile only for me, and I feel his love for me in the depths of my soul: infinite, infallible, indestructible.

It's always been us.

And it's always going to be us.

As long as Drew is by my side, everything else is gravy.

CHAPTER 49

AFTON

Four months later

"Afton, hello, it's so lovely to meet you." Dr. Marcy Corcoran's speaking voice is as soothing as I hoped it would be. Pillow-soft and delicate, it puts me instantly at ease. She leads me back to her office, a large space with ample sunlight diffused by creamy white shades. It smells of lavender, and somewhere there's a white noise machine. "I'm so sorry you had a medical emergency last time. I know you waited a while to get in, so I appreciate your patience."

She motions for me to take a seat on a leather sofa, and she grabs a manila folder before meeting me in that corner of the room.

Pale pink glasses hang from a chain around her neck. She slides them over her nose before gently clearing her throat.

"So, I've reviewed your case file and everything you sent in," she says. "I have a list of your questions as well as my own. Did you watch the videos my assistant sent to prepare you for today?"

"I did."

"Perfect." Her thin lips spread into a warm smile that fills my soul with sunlight. Just being around her makes me want to close my eyes and sleep soundly for a hundred years. "Now, do you need to use the restroom or do you have any questions before we begin?"

I shake my head. "I'm ready."

"Wonderful." Motioning to the basket beside the leather sofa, she says, "Please help yourself to one of the blankets. They're all clean, some warmer than others. I tend to tell people to pick something that won't be too hot or too cold. We want you comfortable enough that you won't notice anything except the sound of my voice and the thoughts in your head."

I select a pink muslin throw.

"Perfect," she says. "Lie back, get yourself situated, and close your eyes . . ."

CHAPTER 50

SYDNEY

December 23, 2003

"Drive around with her for a bit until she sobers up. She can't go home like that," I tell Drew. "Her mom will literally kill her."

It's not true. Vangie couldn't care less about Afton, but Drew doesn't know that.

I just need to buy some time.

It's the first day of winter break, and while my mother has been out doing last-minute Christmas shopping with my brother and sister and my dad has been out doing God knows what, the three of us have been hanging out in my basement, watching movies and drinking blue raspberry Jones Soda spiked with the Grey Goose I found in the back of my mom's closet. I figured whatever we drink, I can easily top off with water. It's clear enough that she won't notice, and if her vodka and sodas taste off, she'll probably blame it on the water.

"If she pukes in my car, you're cleaning it," Drew says as Afton props herself up against him.

While playing bartender, I made sure that Drew's drinks were weak—I can't have him getting a DUI and losing his spot on the varsity basketball team—while also ensuring Afton's were as strong as possible.

My sodas were virgin—much like my drunk-ass friend who hasn't stopped trying to flirt with my boyfriend since her second Jones and vodka.

I lost track of how many times I cringed watching her play-fight with Drew or wrestle over the remote. While he never flirted back, there was no denying they both liked the attention. For someone who claimed he tried to kiss her a few months back, she sure isn't acting like it bothers her anymore.

"She's not going to puke," I say. "Are you, Afton?"

She giggles, swaying and brushing her hand against my boyfriend's arm like it's the coolest thing she's ever touched in her life. She squeezes his bicep, trying (and failing) to wrap her small hand around it.

This is the first time I've seen her drunk, and she's been annoyingly touchy-feely, particularly where Drew is concerned.

Regardless, I've bided my time, watching the clock and topping off Afton's drinks when she wasn't paying attention, praying any minute she'd be asking to go home because she felt sick.

That's the thing with her—as much as she likes to pretend she lives at my house, the second she doesn't feel well, she turns into a sulky baby who wants to go home and sleep in her own bed.

Afton's been extra clingy lately, though that's normal for her this time of year.

I blame my mother. She's always finding ways to make Afton feel like she's one of us. Never mind that she already has three kids. For whatever reason, Afton is like one of those sad-eyed homeless dogs in those humane society ads in the newspaper, and my mom is essentially sponsoring her.

But as much as my mother frustrates the hell out of me (all moms do), I love her more than anyone else on this planet.

I only wish I could say the same for my dad.

Everyone thinks he's some hometown hero.

Whenever we go out to eat, people come up to our table and talk to him like he's a local celebrity. We've had our tab paid more times than I can count, and he never acts annoyed when random kids come up wanting to have their picture taken with him. He lives for that shit.

While he's lapping up all that attention, his wife and kids become chopped liver. The glow in his eyes always fades the minute the fanfare is over and he's back to being Rick Carson, Regular Dad, instead of Rick Carson, Shelter Rock High Head Varsity Football Coach.

The way some of these people act around him, you'd think he found the cure for cancer or saved a school bus from going off a cliff. But this town is psychotically obsessed with football for whatever reason. I've never understood it and I don't think I ever will.

Even when Drew plays, I go to socialize.

I never watch the games.

Too much starting and stopping for me.

My mind is always wandering or watching people around me rather than the long, slow, never-ending game. My favorite part of those nights is waiting outside the locker room for a freshly showered and changed Drew. We usually get into his car, drive to McDonald's so he can eat back all the calories he just burned off (and then some) in the form of two Big Macs and a Coke, and then we cruise around town listening to music and making out at red lights.

Anyway, all this love and adoration has gone to my father's head because last year, I caught him cheating on my mom.

I was driving home from Drew's house late one Saturday night when I saw Dad coming out of some random person's house after he told us he'd be at his assistant coach's place for the night, reviewing game tapes.

I slowed down long enough to see a middle-aged woman in a pink satin robe wave to him from behind the glass front door—and then she blew him a kiss.

He pretended to catch it before blowing one back.

I slammed on my brakes, questioning if that had really just happened.

He must have noticed because he whipped around and spotted me immediately.

When I confronted him in the middle of the street, he broke down into tears, but all I could see was a pathetic coward of a grown man.

I had zero sympathy for him, and I didn't want to hear another one of his lame attempts at justifying his disgusting actions.

I cut him off when he started talking about how he felt "abandoned" by my mother emotionally and "in ways you wouldn't understand," which I'm pretty sure translated to whatever the hell they do or don't do in their bedroom.

Anyway, I didn't appreciate his gaslighting me or speaking to me like I was some kid who didn't understand love. Nor did I appreciate it when I found out he had moved on to Vangie of all people—my mother's lifelong best friend. I suspect it started the night Vangie came over after her boyfriend laid his hands on her. My father took her to the police station after that, like some knight in shining armor.

I can only imagine how much that had to have thrilled Vangie.

She always wanted what she couldn't have, and for the longest time, I saw the way she looked at my dad—like she was undressing him in her head. She'd get giddy any time he paid her a compliment or made small talk. I'm sure my mother was aware—she's exceptionally keen-eyed when it comes to things like that—but she never expected anything to come of it.

It didn't take long for me to figure out his routine with Vangie.

Friday nights were "tape nights" or "play nights," where he and some other coaches would get together at someone's house and go over plays and footage and strategies.

But it was all a lie—a cover.

Friday nights were his nights with Vangie, which conveniently coincided with the fact that Afton always stayed the night at our place on Fridays.

Afton mentioned earlier that her mom was getting off work around eight tonight, and I'm not 100 percent sure, but I imagine Dad probably heads over there to wait for her, knowing Afton's gone.

"Hey, a little help over here?" Drew motions for me to help him get Afton up the basement stairs. It takes a bit of effort and a frustrating amount of time to get from the bottom to the top, but we manage. "You're going to have to help me get her to the car."

"Obviously," I say.

"You guys make a great team, you know that?" Afton says with a dopey grin on her face. Her eyes are slanted and the stench of sugary soda wafts from her warm breath and floods the air around us. "You're gonna be the best parents someday."

Once we get her outside a million years later, I buckle her into the passenger seat of Drew's Firebird. She wastes no time messing with the radio and pressing all the buttons. Drew's jaw flexes. He hates when I do that, so I imagine letting her have full access to his stereo system is chapping his hide.

"If you feel like you're going to throw up, tell Drew," I say to Afton, cupping her chin and angling her face to me so I have her full attention. "He'll pull over right away."

Drew looks annoyed with this little assignment, but I smooth over his annoyance with a blown kiss and some batted lashes, whispering that I'll make it up to him later.

"I appreciate you taking her home," I say when I make my way to the driver's side.

"I don't know why you can't come with us."

"I have to pick up the basement before my mom gets home," I say. Which is true, but it'll take all of five minutes to fluff some pillows and fold some blankets and put the remote control back on the coffee table. "I have to hide the Grey Goose, too."

He unstiffens, like he understands, and then he starts his car.

"Remember, wait an hour and then drop her off at home," I remind him.

It's not yet seven o'clock when they leave. If everything works out the way it should, Afton will get home around the same time as her mom, and she'll see my father waiting for her mother. Knowing Afton's explosive temper, it won't be pretty.

And she'll tell my mother, no doubt—which would take a load off my back because she needs to know and I didn't want to have to be the one to do that.

Afton's convinced my mother is the second coming of Mary Magdalene, and let's be honest, she pretty much is. I wouldn't be going to all this trouble if she was nothing but another Vangie Teachout.

Once they leave, I sprint downstairs, straighten up the basement, refill the bottle of vodka with water and place it back in Mom's hiding spot, and then I hop in my car and head to Afton's street.

Patience has never been my virtue.

I want to see if he's there, not hear about it the next day.

Parking halfway down the block, I spot his waxed Impala immediately, the immaculate black paint reflecting off the starry sky above. Hands tight on my steering wheel, I try to talk myself out of barging in there and confronting him myself.

Why he's there this early is beyond me.

Maybe Vangie's getting off before eight tonight?

Or maybe he likes to hang out in her house for some insane reason?

Never mind that their house reminds me of a stoner college kid's cheap apartment. Blankets for curtains. Questionable odors lingering in the air. Carpet that looks like it hasn't been shampooed since Reagan was president.

If she comes home early and they leave before Drew drops Afton off, this entire day will have been for nothing.

Reaching into my purse, I fish around for a disposable camera. I always keep one on hand because you never know when you're going to find a good photo op. Pulling out the yellow cardboard Kodak, I charge the flash—only to realize when I'm done that the counter shows zero photos remaining.

I toss it on the passenger floorboard and slump against the cool glass of my driver's-side window. My breath paints little foggy patches on the inside that I wipe away with my finger as I stare at Vangie and Afton's depressing, dimly lit house.

But all my simmering and stewing comes to a rolling boil not too long after.

I can't take this anymore.

I can't sit here another minute doing nothing while my Father of the Year hangs out inside another woman's house.

Climbing out, I slam the door and charge up the sidewalk, fists clenched, ready to give him a piece of my mind.

"Hey, babe. That you?" He calls out when he hears the back door open and shut.

I don't answer.

He'll know who it is soon enough.

Following his voice and the sound of ESPN SportsCenter to the living room, I find him lounging on the lumpy, faded couch, his arm resting along the back and the remote in his hand like he lives here.

The audacity of this man.

"Wow," I say. "You really are a giant piece of shit."

My father whips his head around, scrambling when he sees me. "What are you doing here?"

"I came here to ask you that same question."

"Does your mother know you're out? I thought you had friends over?" How cute of him to bring my mother into this.

Fortunately for me, I'm not the one who needs to worry about falling out of her good graces.

"No, she doesn't. Should we both call her and let her know where we are?" I ask, blinking. "I'm sure she'd love to know."

"Sydney." He places a hand out, his lips pressing into a hard line like he's fixing to give me some speech intended to calm me down and downplay his actions at the same time. "I know this is a lot for you—"

"You can't talk your way out of this one, Rick." I use his first name knowing it's one of the biggest forms of disrespect in his eyes. His star quarterback last year called him Rick as a joke, and he made the poor kid run laps around the field until he was puking his guts out in the grass. "Honestly, I don't care what your lame excuse is this time. Save it for Mom. Oh, wait. Mom would see through your bullshit. Sucks to be you, huh?"

"Sydney Elizabeth, I will not have you speaking to me that way," he says. "I know you're angry, but it doesn't give you the right to be disrespectful. You don't have to agree with my actions, but you don't get to barge in here and pull this little stunt. Who do you think you are?"

The man is as red as a maraschino cherry—not unlike when a ref makes a bad call in the final minute of a close football game. It brings me an immeasurable amount of joy and amusement knowing I've succeeded in setting him off to this extent. He can be a firecracker of a man, and I've struck the match that's going to light his fuse.

"We're going to have a conversation, you and me," he says, his voice stern and his finger pointing my way. "Not here. Not tonight. But tomorrow. I've been too easy on you lately, I've given you too much rein, and it's getting out of hand."

"I'm not a horse." I laugh, which only makes him redder.

"Ever since you got your car and your cell phone and your boyfriend, you think you know everything about everything," he says. "Tomorrow, all that changes."

I scoff, crossing my arms. He can take my car keys and my phone, but he can't take Drew. He can't forbid me from seeing him at school every day or sneaking out on dates when I'm supposed to be at a friend's house.

"Have fun explaining why to Mom," I say. "The real reason why, not the one you're going to make up."

"First thing tomorrow, I want your keys and your phone," he says. "The day after Christmas, you're breaking things off with Drew."

"Yeah, no. I'm not doing that." I plant myself firmly in the dingy, shaggy, gray-green carpet of Vangie's living room and cock my chin up. My *father is a larger man, six foot four with a linebacker's build, but he doesn't intimidate me. He may be physically strong, but he's weak on the inside.*

All cheaters are.

"*If you don't end it with Drew, he's off the basketball team.*"

"*You can't do that.*" *I roll my eyes. Nice try, idiot.*

"*Actually I can. And I will. The only reason he's on right now is because of me. His GPA is below the minimum requirement for the athletic department. I pulled in a personal favor from Coach Hunsaker because Drew is one of our top players and Baxterville Tech's been scouting him since he was a freshman. We both know it's the only chance in hell he's got at a full-ride scholarship.*"

As much as I wish my father were wrong, he isn't.

Drew's parents can't afford to put him through college and he's not the best student, but he's one hell of an athlete.

He needs this break.

Our future is riding on this.

"*You can make demands and stomp your feet and threaten me all you want,*" *my father continues,* "*but I'm the one with the power here. I'm the parent and you're the child. I will not have some seventeen-year-old know-it-all telling me how to live my life. So here's how it's going to go, and listen closely because I'm not going to repeat it again—tomorrow you hand over your phone and your car keys and the day after Christmas, you're breaking up with Drew. You do those things and you keep your mouth shut around your mom and Drew stays on the team. One misstep? He's off. Understand?*"

Tears flood my eyes. "*You're a monster.*"

Anyone willing to ruin an innocent person's future all so they can cheat on their wife is a disgusting excuse for a human.

"*I'm embarrassed for you,*" *I say, my lower lip quivering. My skin is hot and I can hardly see and my throat is so tight it hurts to talk, but I keep going.* "*This is pathetic. You should hear yourself, threatening a harmless* person who has nothing to do with any of this all so you can screw around on your wife. I hope you're proud of yourself."

The saddest part is Drew loves my dad as much as he loves his own.

He'd be gutted if he knew he was nothing but a pawn in my father's sick little game.

"If you want to call my bluff, be my guest." He sits back down into the sagging sofa, a smug expression on his pathetic face. Reaching for the remote, he settles in, resting his arm along the back of the couch like it was before. "For now, I think you ought to go home, give it some thought, and decide if you want to do the right thing for Drew."

I stand before him. Unmoving. Speechless. My thoughts retreating into the darker crevices of my mind like never before.

"Go on now, go home." He waves his hand, like he's shooing me toward the door, like I'm nothing more than a pesky gnat ruining his picnic.

That's the moment when everything turns an angry shade of crimson and all I see is red.

With tears streaming down my face, I storm to the kitchen, ready to bolt out the back door. Only something catches the corner of my eye—a glinting butcher knife resting on the side of the sink.

Without thinking twice, I reach for it, catching my reflection in its mirrorlike surface. My eyes are bloodshot, rimmed with damp mascara, but it's as if I'm looking at someone else.

A stranger.

My father's threats play on a loop in my head, intermixing with the ESPN blaring from the living room—a subtle reminder that sports are my father's first and greatest love . . . not my mother, not his family, certainly not his firstborn child.

He doesn't deserve us.

And he doesn't get to steal the only happiness I have when all I've ever done is be the best daughter he could ask for.

I'm standing behind him now, staring at the back of his head and the way his arm is still casually draped along Vangie's sofa.

I don't remember the walk from the kitchen to the living room but here I am, my sweaty palm gripping the handle of a butcher knife that has the power to solve all of my problems.

With my heart ricocheting so hard in my chest that it physically hurts, I lodge the blade deep into the side of his neck.

It glides in like a hot knife into butter, with little resistance.

Who'd have thought it would be so fast?

So easy?

I stumble back as he reaches for the wound. Blood gushes out, blanketing his hands and staining his clothes in a sea of red as his breath becomes wet gurgles and finally, inaudible gasps.

In this moment, the man before me isn't my father.

He's a dying creature who deserves no sympathy.

I wait until the life in his eyes extinguishes, until it appears like he's staring at something a million miles away.

As soon as he's gone, my breath steadies. The sea of red disappears from my vision, replaced with an unexpected tidal wave of calm.

Before I leave, I use my sweatshirt to wipe the fingerprints off the knife that's still wedged in his jugular.

With Mom, Max, and Stacia still out Christmas shopping and Drew still driving Afton around town, no one will know I even left. I take refuge in that fact—until I pull into the driveway and climb out of my car just in time to spot my mother, Stacia, and Max pulling in early.

Glancing down, I realize I'm covered in blood splatter as well as the smudges of blood I wiped off the knife before I left.

From behind the wheel of her van, my mother's mouth is agape. I watch her turn around and say something to my siblings before flinging off her seat belt and trotting up the driveway to ask me what happened.

I don't know how to tell her that Dad was cheating on her with Vangie—and that I killed him. So instead, I fall into a heap on the frozen concrete, sobbing into my bloodied sleeve.

"Go inside, take that off," she says, unusually calm. "Whatever this is, whatever happened, we're going to fix it. I just need you to be honest with me. Can you do that?"

I dry my tears on a clean section of sweatshirt and nod.

I don't know how she's going to fix this—only that she's the one person who can.

CHAPTER 51

AFTON

Everything makes sense now.

I drive home from my hypnotherapy session in a dreamy, surreal daze, playing my recalled memories on a loop in my head the entire eighty miles, memorizing every vivid detail again and again, like I'm studying for a test. When I get home, I'll write it all down. I'll keep it somewhere safe. This information and these details will never be lost again, not if I can help it.

The disgustingly sweet vodka and blue raspberry sodas . . .

Flirting with Drew because the alcohol suddenly made him less insufferable and everything ten times funnier than it was.

I remember Drew driving me around for what felt like an eternity but was maybe forty-five minutes at most. He played Pink Floyd the entire time, and I gave him shit for listening to such weird music. I remember him pulling over twice so I could vomit. An elderly lady walking her French bulldog noticed me the second time. She called me a menace before turning on her heel and heading in the opposite direction, giving the leash a hard couple of tugs when her dog was too invested in what we were doing to notice she'd turned around.

By the end of that ordeal, Drew pulled up to the curb outside my house to drop me off, not so much as bothering to shift his Firebird into park.

The car was pretty much rolling before the passenger door was shut.

At the time, I figured he was afraid I might throw up in his car next time and he was tired of babysitting me. I didn't blame him. But it was in that exact moment that a silver Toyota Celica cruised by, exactly like the one Sydney drives.

The driver looked an awful lot like Sydney, too, though their hair was shoved under a baseball cap and their chin was tucked low.

I brushed it off at the time because Sydney was supposed to be at home, cleaning up, and if she saw me, she would have waved or at least acknowledged me, not driven off with her head down.

At least . . . that's what was going through my head at the time.

The next thing I remember, I'm stumbling up the front door, busting into the house and nearly tripping over the rug in the entry that never seemed to stay put. It was all bunched up, almost like someone else had tripped over it before me and never put it back the right way. I took a moment to straighten it before organizing a handful of shoes lying scattered around.

It was when I passed by the living room that I saw Rick on the couch—and all the blood.

Everything about me froze. Time stood still as I took in the bizarre scene.

The unnatural position of his head.

The slump of his body.

The butcher knife sticking out of the side of his neck.

It was something straight out of a horror movie.

Rushing to his side, I pulled the knife out. Then I shook him, yelling at him to wake up before beating on his chest. I would've done CPR, but there was so much blood and it was everywhere. I shook him again, but it was clear he was past gone.

After all of that, I found myself standing in front of him, the bloody knife gripped tight in my hand while my mom screamed at me, demanding to know what I'd done.

Knowing all this now, knowing that I saw Sydney on my street when Drew was dropping me off, knowing how "easy" it was for her to "forgive" me for the heinous crime I was charged with—combined with the fact that she tried to kill me four months ago so I couldn't meet with Dr. Corcoran—answers the million-dollar question.

It was Sydney.

It was her the whole time.

She killed her father.

Not me.

Proving this will be damn near impossible. All the evidence is long since gone. Doorbell cameras and intelligent security systems weren't a thing back then, at least definitely not in my neighborhood.

All I have are my recovered memories.

You can't convict someone on those alone.

Four months ago, I woke up alive in that Airbnb, walked to the nearest gas station to call the police, and waited patiently—all for some middle-aged man with a badge to insinuate that I was homeless, paranoid, and telling some nonsensical story about a crazy woman who tried to kill me by putting a needle in my arm.

He took down my name and number and drove me to the station.

I was under the impression he was going to help me file a report.

Imagine my surprise when two hours later, Sydney arrives, Drew in tow, to give her side of the story. Only it was pure fabrication and went something along the lines of "we were having a girls' night and I 'went crazy' and started threatening her and since I have a history of hallucinating, she felt her life was in danger so she went home."

It didn't take a rocket scientist to figure out which story made the most sense to a seasoned cop who'd likely heard it all.

In the end, there was no evidence, no marks on my body, no syringe, not an atom-sized molecule of proof that Sydney had done any of those things I witnessed.

I imagine she gave that same story to Drew and he ate up every word of it, because let's face it, he's never been the brightest bulb and he's always been convinced that Sydney shits rainbows and is God's personal gift to him.

It doesn't hit me until this very moment just how diabolically manipulative Sydney is—not just to me, but to her mother, to her siblings, to her in-laws, to Drew. She's a skilled actress. A con woman. She's got everyone fooled, and I was the biggest fool of them all for the longest time.

Not anymore.

It's one of those things that once you know it, you can never unknow it.

Not to mention, it's instant closure.

I no longer miss her presence in my life nor am I mourning the loss of a lifelong "friendship."

Since meeting with Dr. Corcoran, I've only seen Sydney around town twice—once at the Qwik Star, gassing up her paid-off minivan. The second time, she was leaving a nail salon, her blonde hair shinier and longer than ever—like she'd recently gotten extensions and high-lights. Her legs looked leaner, too—maybe she'd taken up running or Pilates? Then there were her lips. Even from across the parking lot, I could tell they were more inflated than usual.

I didn't recognize her, not right away.

Sometimes I wonder if she woke up one morning and decided she wanted to look in the mirror and see anyone but her despicable self, so she changed everything she could on the outside.

There isn't enough makeup, cosmeceuticals, or cosmetic surgeries in the world that can fix the ugliness that resides permanently on her insides.

I hope every once in a while she passes her reflection and gets caught off guard when she sees her father's bright blue eyes looking back at her.

I hope someday she randomly comes across something that reminds her of me and it puts a hitch in her breath.

I hope she's cheering in the stands of her son's basketball game when she suddenly finds her thoughts wandering down a dark path and the unbearable weight of her past steals the smile from her face.

I hope she drives down Wainwright Street, glances at the avocado-green house, and knows deep down that as long as she lives, she'll never have a friend as true as me again.

I hope she spends the rest of her natural life looking over her shoulder, wondering if one of these days, the past will finally catch up to her and steal her joy like a thief in the night.

I believe it will . . .

I believe it will.

EPILOGUE

AFTON

Two months later

"You want to get dinner with us after work? We're thinking of trying that new burger place up the street?" My coworker Jillian raps on my desk as she stops by. "A lot of people don't know this unless they're from here, but on Thursdays in Kansas City—*Missouri* not *Kansas*—any calorie that comes in burger form magically doesn't count."

"Yes!" I say. "Yes" has become my new favorite word. I'm saying yes to things I never thought I'd say yes to, and it's been changing my life for the better in ways I never could've imagined.

"Awesome, meet us by the elevator in five," she says before trouncing off, her chic strawberry blonde ponytail swaying with each step of her patent leather wedges.

Not only has Jillian become a work friend, but she's also become a friend "in real life." She's hilarious. And considerate. And compassionate. She cries when she laughs, and she has a plethora of entertaining dating horror stories. On top of it all, she's the most inclusive person I've ever met, one of those "the more the merrier" kind of people.

No one gets left out on her watch.

I hate to think of how many friendships I missed out on over the years, all because I made Sydney the epicenter of my social life.

Live and learn.

All I can do now is make up for lost time.

Gram's house wasn't on the market twenty-four hours when I received a full-price cash offer, no contingencies, and a thirty-day close. We probably priced it too low, but I was anxious to get out of Shelter Rock once and for all—the sooner the better.

The day I signed the paperwork, I wasted no time also accepting that job at John Gregory's brother's law firm in Kansas City. The next day, I found the cutest little apartment downtown, walking distance from the firm, and I've been enjoying my quiet little city life, feathering my nest with houseplants and new furniture, trying new restaurants in the area, and making an effort to put myself out there. Next weekend, Jillian and I are going cat shopping, which isn't really a thing, but Jillian says there's this coffee shop filled with rescue cats and all of them are adoptable and she thinks I should get one.

I've never had a pet of any kind before, but I haven't ruled it out.

It's been an intense couple of months filled with experiences I never dreamed would happen to me after everything. I've also been in therapy, working on acceptance—which would ironically make Cynthia proud if we were still in communication.

Shortly after the Airbnb situation with Sydney, she ceased all communications with me without any rhyme or reason.

Part of me thinks she believed Sydney's version of events and, naturally, took her daughter's side.

The other part of me knows her better than that.

Her sixth sense when it comes to picking up on other people's lies, nuances, and behavior patterns is uncanny.

Chances are Cynthia knew all about her daughter's actions from the start, that she helped cover up tracks and tie up loose ends, that she couldn't risk the truth getting out just as much as Sydney couldn't because she'd become an accomplice in covering up her own husband's murder.

Cynthia's push for forgiveness, compassion, and grace all those years ago makes more sense now that I know what Sydney is capable of and now that I'm certain it wasn't me who killed Rick.

Syd and her mom were always impossibly close. It didn't matter how much Cynthia included me in their family or treated me like one of her own: I would never hold a candle next to her firstborn daughter.

I left Shelter Rock in the rearview the day Gram's house closed and the last of my things were loaded up in the moving van.

Onward and upward—that's been my motto in therapy. The steps might be jagged and uneven at times. There are moments I still get triggered. There are nights when my dreams reek of the past. But for the first time, there's light in my life after living for so long in the dark, and that's all that matters.

An hour later, I'm halfway through devouring the juiciest wagyu cheddar burger I've ever tasted when in struts a familiar brunette with glossy waves, a skintight dress, and a tiny little designer bag hanging from her shoulder. Sliding her sunglasses down her nose, she whips around and motions for someone behind her to hurry up.

"Oh, my God." I put my half-eaten burger aside when I see none other than Drew Westfeldt strutting in behind her in a suit that looks like it costs more than the rent on my downtown apartment.

What's he doing in Kansas City?

With *Vanessa*?

"Do you know them?" Jillian nudges me when she notices me noticing them.

"Unfortunately, yes." With everything that has happened this year, I'd shoved the Drew-and-Vanessa thing to the back burner, convinced it was another hallucination like everything else that took place around that time. "They're from Shelter Rock."

"They look happy," she says with an indifferent shrug. "Whoever they are."

She isn't wrong.

Grinning like a lovestruck idiot, Drew looks at ease with her in a way that he never did with Sydney.

Drew lifts his left hand to his temple, finger-combing his thick, chocolate waves as Vanessa loops her arm into his elbow and drags him to the hostess stand like a hangry toddler.

He laughs, as if her tugging amuses him, as if she's this young, fun, shiny toy that makes him feel alive again because it has yet to lose its luster. But what stands out the most in this entire exchange . . . is the fact that he's still wearing his wedding band.

This may not be the justice I was hoping Sydney would get, but for now? I'll take it.

ACKNOWLEDGMENTS

A million thanks to my editor, Jessica Tribble Wells, and my developmental editor, Charlotte Herscher, for all of the back-and-forth brainstorming emails, brilliant-as-always feedback, and unstinting enthusiasm throughout the editing process. A million additional thanks to the incredible behind-the-scenes team at Thomas and Mercer and APub, including but certainly not limited to: Gracie, Sarah, Alex, Stef, Kyra, and Hattie, as well as the Brilliance Audio and marketing teams.

To my agent, Jill Marsal, thank you for your encouragement and invaluable insights.

To my husband and children: all the gratitude—especially during deadline weeks when the kitchen becomes a barren wasteland and cereal is on the dinner menu one too many times.

To all the readers, reviewers, bloggers, Bookstagrammers, and BookTokers who share my stories with their friends, family, fellow booklovers, and followers—I cannot thank you enough. Your support means everything and allows me to continue writing these crazy-fun books.

Lastly, thank you to my hometown of Newton, Iowa, for providing the inspiration for an isolated Midwestern hamlet where everyone knows everyone else's business (or some version of it) while also being obsessed with their high school football team.

ABOUT THE AUTHOR

Photo © 2017 Jill Austin Photography

Minka Kent is the *Washington Post* and *Wall Street Journal* bestselling author of *The Watcher Girl, When I Was You, The Stillwater Girls, The Thinnest Air, The Perfect Roommate, The Memory Watcher, Unmissing,* and *Gone Again*. Her work has been featured in *People* magazine and the *New York Post* as well as optioned for film and TV. Minka also writes contemporary romance as *Wall Street Journal* and #1 Amazon Charts bestselling author Winter Renshaw. She is a graduate of Iowa State University and resides in Iowa with her husband and three children. For more information, visit www.minkakent.com.